SOMEONE LIKE YOU

Khalil chuckled. "I've never met anyone like you."

She warmed at his compliment. No one had ever told her that. Parker had always put her down. And her paintings. Blythe smirked. As if he had any room to talk.

In one easy motion, his arm went around her waist. Blythe found herself enclosed in the arms she'd longed for for what seemed like forever. It was as if she'd come home.

Savoring the feel of his body against hers, Blythe inhaled his cologne. She felt as though she couldn't get close enough to Khalil.

Lowering his head, Khalil brushed his lips over hers ever so lightly. "I've been wanting to do this for a while." Reclaiming her mouth, he crushed her to him.

Her kiss shook him to his very soul. It surprised him how delicate and vulnerable she really was. Blythe kissed him with a depth that had both of them swimming in a pool of sexual heat.

BOOK YOUR PLACE ON OUR WEBSITE AND MAKE THE ARABESQUE ROMANCE CONNECTION!

We've created a customized website just for our very special Arabesque readers, where you can get the inside scoop on everything that's going on with Arabesque romance novels.

When you come online, you'll have the exciting opportunity to:

- View covers of upcoming books

- Learn about our future publishing schedule (listed by publication month and author)

- Find out when your favorite authors will be visiting a city near you

- Search for and order backlist books

- Check out author bios and background information

- Send e-mail to your favorite authors

- Join us in weekly chats with authors, readers and other guests

- Get writing guidelines

- AND MUCH MORE!

Visit our website at
http://www.arabesquebooks.com

SOMEONE LIKE YOU

Jacquelin Thomas

ARABESQUE

BOOKS

BET Publications, LLC
www.msbet.com
www.arabesquebooks.com

ARABESQUE BOOKS are published by

BET Publications, LLC
c/o BET BOOKS
One BET Plaza
1900 W Place NE
Washington, D.C. 20018-1211

BET Books is a trademark of Black Entertainment Television, Inc. ARABESQUE, the ARABESQUE logo and the BET BOOKS logo are trademarks and registered trademarks.

First Printing: November, 1999

10 9 8 7 6 5 4 3 2 1
Printed in the United States of America

This book is dedicated to

Tamara Ashton-Monet Thornton

The newest member of my family
Welcome Little Princess!

Wilma Wilkerson
&
Alda Pool

You are two of the most wonderful and supportive women
in Houston, Texas. I have been blessed abundantly in getting
to know you both.

Special Thanks

To my husband and my children
It is your unity that allows me to write without distraction. I love you all.

To my parents: Roger Thornton and Marion Nelson Thornton
Without you both, my life would have no meaning, no purpose. Thank you.

To my Grandmother: Wilsie Nelson
You instilled in me a belief that all things are possible if you have faith. It is a lesson I've learned well and one that I hope to pass on to my children.

To my great aunt: Waver Lee Atkinson
Although you are gone, you will never be forgotten, for your spirit, as well as the collective spirits of my ancestors long departed, flows through me.

To my extended family: Lee, Birdell, Sheila, Anthony and Renae Thomas
Thank you for all that you have given me in the past and for all that you continue to give.

To my friend and sister writer: Carmen Green
You have shown me the mighty sword one can wield with self-determination. Thank you for sharing not only yourself, but your thoughts and your research books relating to Kwanzaa. It has been quite an educational treat for me and my family.

To the rest of my family and all of the very special people in my life whose names are not mentioned here
It's your love, faith, support and friendship that keeps me going. Although your name may not appear in this book, it is forever inscribed on my heart.

Chapter 1

"I've been waiting for forty minutes to see Mr. Sanford. Would you please tell him that I don't have all day," Blythe sniped impatiently. Without waiting for a response, she swung the strap of her leather Coach bag on her shoulders and stormed back to the seat she'd vacated moments earlier.

The receptionist awarded her with an insolent look before picking up the phone. Swiveling around, she spoke in a low whisper.

Rolling her eyes, Blythe prayed for patience—a virtue she didn't possess. How dare this man keep her waiting. Her thoughts dissipated when the receptionist hung up. "Well?" she prompted.

Wearing a look of undisguised amusement, the young woman announced, "Mr. Sanford said that you're free to make an appointment if you're in a hurry."

"What is your name?" Blythe inquired.

"Caryn."

"Well, Caryn, you can tell—no, never mind . . ." Blythe stood up. "I'll tell him myself." In determined strides, she stormed past the stunned receptionist and down the long hallway of the *Heritage Reporter*'s offices. Khalil Sanford was not going to ignore her, Blythe decided. Especially after he set out to deliberately start a smear campaign against Bloodstone's.

Finding the office she was looking for, she opened the door without knocking and marched in. She stopped cold at the sight of Khalil Sanford. Blythe had not been prepared for such a handsome man. His black, wavy hair was cropped close to his head. The coarseness of Khalil's neatly trimmed mustache and beard contrasted nicely with his smooth sienna complexion.

Immediately recalling her reason for being there, Blythe began, "Mr. Sanford, I will not be kept waiting like this—"

"*Miss Bloodstone,*" he interrupted and gestured toward a couple of men she hadn't noticed until now. "As you can see, I'm currently in a meeting. Would you kindly let us finish up? If you can't wait—then feel free to make an appointment for another time."

His caustic tone made her flush in embarrassment. Blythe backed out of the office without another word, but not without being humiliatingly conscious of his intense scrutiny. In all of her thirty-four years, Blythe didn't think she was ever more embarrassed.

Shoulders slumped, she headed back to the lobby and sat down. Catching sight of Caryn's smug expression, Blythe stared at her until the woman had the good sense to turn away.

Checking her watch, Blythe realized that she had been sitting there for well over an hour. She believed Khalil was purposely keeping her waiting, but she would not give him satisfaction by leaving. She was determined to see him today. Opening her Coach attache case, she pulled out a pad of legal paper and proceeded to jot down a few notes.

A few minutes later, Caryn announced, "Mr. Sanford will see you now."

Putting her pad back into her attache, Blythe stood up gracefully. "Thank you," she muttered as she made her way down the hall once more.

"You're welcome, Miss Bloodstone," Caryn called out, but Blythe was already halfway to Khalil's office. She walked in looking around the room. They were alone.

When he didn't even bother to acknowledge her presence,

Blythe longed to strangle the handsome, dark-eyed man for the way he was treating her. Instead, she sat quietly, observing him. His profile spoke of power and ageless strength. She determined that Khalil was a force to be reckoned with. Underneath a vest made of multicolored kente cloth, he wore a mustard yellow shirt. The colors flattered his complexion but Blythe found they weren't to her liking. She preferred a more conservative look.

Finally Khalil graced her with a glance. "How can I help you, Miss Bloodstone?"

Irritated, Blythe held her tongue. Saying what truly came to mind would not help her purpose.

"Did you hear me?" He prompted.

Blythe lifted her bronze cool gaze to meet his. "I believe you know why I'm here, Mr. Sanford." Opening her attache case, she pulled out the latest issue of the *Heritage Reporter*. "Surely you remember all of the lies your paper has been spreading about Bloodstone's Department Store."

Leaning back in his chair, Khalil replied calmly, "They're not lies. My reporter experienced it firsthand. It's a fact that Bloodstone's Department Store treats its black customers like criminals."

"That's not true. In case you haven't noticed, the Bloodstone family *is* a part of the black race. Why would we alienate our own people?"

Khalil seemed to choose his words carefully. "The way I see it, when Bloodstone's moved out of Baldwin Hills and into Beverly Hills, they seemed to have forgotten how they got there. Black dollars put you there."

Her lips twisted into a cynical smile. "Is that the problem, Mr. Sanford? Is the black community upset because we moved to Beverly Hills? Perhaps we should have considered locating it right here in South Central."

"The problem is not the address, Miss Bloodstone. It's the way the people are treated in your store."

"We treat all of our customers the same—"

"What is it that you do?" Khalil asked suddenly.

Her incredulity was quiet and intense. "Excuse me?"

"What is your position at Bloodstone's?"

"I'm the Director of Merchandising and Sales Promotion. Why?"

"So you don't actually know what's going on downstairs then?"

"I wouldn't say that." Inclining her head, Blythe asked, "Have you ever shopped at Bloodstone's?"

"I used to," was his reply. "I don't anymore."

"What happened?"

"I didn't like being followed around the store by your security."

Under his mocking gaze, Blythe's eyes deepened in hue as she considered his comment. She needed time to form a sensible response. "Maybe you were acting suspicious—"

"*Or* maybe it was because I'm a black man." Khalil sat up then and leaned forward, his elbows on his desk. "Look, Miss Bloodstone. Our black brothers and sisters should support each other. We encourage and preach supporting our black businesses, but when you're treated bad by your own people . . ."

"We don't treat blacks bad," she snapped. Choosing her words carefully, Blythe attempted to make her point. "We are always giving donations. Bloodstone's gave clothing and household goods to families after the riots. We donate to the United Negro College Fund. We've even established yearly scholarships for promising young students. And not just black students. Anyone can apply. *All* of our customers are important to us."

"It doesn't negate the fact that your store security appears to only watch black customers. Your sales staff will only help white customers or people they determine to be affluent."

"Mr. Sanford, what you're saying is simply not true. Our security team is one of the best. They know whom to watch. Do you know what happens when a store is besieged by shoplifters? We have to raise our prices," she explained. "Mr. Sanford, we do what we must to discourage theft . . . and keep our prices down. I'm sure you don't know much about customer service and—"

"I understand more than you think," Khalil interrupted.

"Bloodstone's Department Store has made a name for itself by catering to the socially elite and the newly rich. Together they comprise about what? Three percent of the population?" When she nodded, he continued. "About thirty-five percent are impulsive buyers, frequently overpaying because labels are important to them. Then you have another twenty percent whose paycheck goes mostly to improving their personal appearance—"

"I get the point, Mr. Sanford. None of that really matters right now, does it? The reason I'm here is because we would like you to print a retraction of some sort." Blythe shifted in her chair and crossed her legs. "Surely you must know, preconceived opinions are crucial to a store's success. Attitudes are shaped from a wide variety of sources. Such as your newspaper. And attitudes can rarely be changed."

"I won't do it," Khalil cut in. "My paper prints the truth—no matter how ugly it is."

Blythe cut him in two with her eyes. Pulling out her trump card, she said, "I would really hate to have to sue you for slander." She glanced around his office in a disdainful manner. "I doubt if your small newspaper could survive."

Khalil simply shrugged. Her threat of a lawsuit didn't seem to faze him at all.

"Do what you must. I'm not printing a retraction. That article exposes Bloodstone's for what it truly is."

Her eyes narrowed. "And what is that, Mr. Sanford?"

"It is a company who's turned its back on the black community."

Appalled by his suggestion, Blythe rose to her feet. "I will not sit here and listen to—"

"You are free to leave," Khalil cut in. "And in the future, please make an appointment." Without another word, he turned to face his computer monitor once more.

Blythe opened her mouth in shock. She couldn't believe he had the nerve to just . . . just dismiss her like that. Who in hell did he think he was? Flashing him one last furious glance, she grabbed her attache case and stormed out of his office.

She muttered curses all the way to her car. Khalil Sanford hadn't heard the last of her. Fumbling around in her purse for her keys, Blythe dropped her briefcase. She groaned in protest when one of the legal pads fell out. Bending down, she picked it up and sat it on the trunk of her car. Frustrated, Blythe resumed her search for her car keys. She sighed her relief in finding them.

Settled into her car and waiting to exit the parking lot, Blythe spied two young men, one white and one black, coming toward her Mercedes. Knit caps pulled down low on their heads and dressed in oversized pants and sweatshirts, they gave the questionable appearance of being unsavory. She covertly glanced around to assure herself that the doors were locked. Her hands tightened on the wheel, fear knotting inside her.

Blythe froze as one of them knocked on her window. Grinning, he gestured for her to roll down her window. Icy fear twisted around her heart, she floored the gas pedal, causing the car to surge forward into the speeding traffic.

Amidst blaring horns and screeching tires, Blythe managed to control her car as panic lodged in her throat. She drove as fast as she could, needing to escape the preconceived horrors of South Central.

Blythe was calmer by the time she strolled into Bloodstone's Department Store. Her mother, Nadine, met her on the first floor.

"What on earth took you so long?" she asked accusingly. As an afterthought, Nadine added, "I was worried about you."

Blythe contained her surprise. *Her mother concerned about her?* That was hard to even imagine, she thought bitterly. Nadine Winthrop Bloodstone thought of no one but herself. Not even Blythe's wheelchair-bound father warranted her mother's concern.

"Well, Blythe. Are you going to tell me what happened? Is that horrid little newspaper going to print a retraction or not?"

Massaging her temple, she stated flatly, "They're not, Mother."

"What?" Nadine screeched.

Blythe glanced around. Several of the employees were watching them. Lowering her voice to a whisper, she asked, "Can we please discuss this in my office?"

Nadine wrinkled her nose in distaste. "I don't want to go into your office. It's too small and I feel stifled."

Blythe resisted the urge to roll her eyes heavenward. "Then we'll go to your office. It really doesn't matter, Mother."

Standing in the elevator, Nadine admired herself in the mirror. Apparently satisfied with her appearance, she turned to face her daughter. "Well if Mr. Sanford wants to play hardball, we'll just call your brother and have him file a lawsuit. In just three weeks, Thanksgiving will be here. The day after is the biggest day of the shopping season. We most certainly can't have negative articles printed about us and talks of boycotting the store. It just won't do."

Blythe sighed inwardly. "I don't know if there's anything Justin can do. Khalil Sanford is not easily intimidated. He believes that his paper printed the truth."

Nadine glared at her daughter. "Well, he would think that, dear. After all it's his paper. I know his kind. He's just another black man who's angry about the events of the past or else he's trying to blame us for being successful and for moving out of Baldwin Hills. He's one of those people who call people like us Uncle Toms. He's using this so-called newspaper to rouse racial disharmony."

Blythe was surprised by Nadine's statement. "Mother, I think you've got it all wrong. The man I met today didn't strike me as angry or radical. He really believes that the article he printed is the truth."

A soft gasp escaped Nadine. "It's obvious that you haven't a clue. Going to South Central must have traumatized you somehow. Or you've been brainwashed."

"Have you ever been over there, Mother?"

"Heavens no. And I have no intention of ever doing so. You've watched the news—it's a bad area."

"Yet you certainly had no qualms about sending me." Without waiting for a response, Blythe turned away and stepped off the glass-enclosed elevator as soon as the doors sprang open.

Nadine followed her. "That's not the point, dear. What we need to concentrate on is straightening that man out—not your constant insecurity."

Blythe dropped her lashes quickly to hide the hurt. Quiet, she followed her mother down a long hallway.

When they neared Nadine's office, they found Harwood Bloodstone, a tall, portly man in his mid seventies, standing in the middle of the room.

Seeing him caused Blythe's mood to brighten. "Grandfather, it's good to see you." She could tell from her mother's expression that her reaction was the opposite.

Holding out his hands, he said, "Blythe, honey. Come here and give me a hug."

Crossing the floor in quick, feminine strides, Blythe embraced her grandfather. "What are you doing here?"

"I figured I'd better come in for a little visit. Thanksgiving is in a couple of weeks and I want to personally hand out the gift certificates."

Blythe glanced uneasily at her mother.

Nadine seemed a bit nervous herself. Twisting her hands, she said, "Harwood, we discussed this a month ago. I thought we agreed that we weren't handing out certificates this year."

Her grandfather glowered at Nadine. "This store has been giving out gift certificates for over thirty years. The tradition is to continue. Each employee will receive a twenty-five dollar gift certificate for Thanksgiving and one for Christmas. Is that understood, Nadine?" His tone brooked no argument.

Blythe felt perverse pleasure in watching her mother squirm. Her grandfather seemed to be the only one capable of handling her high-strung mother.

"Of course, Harwood. If that's what you want. I just think—"

He cut her off. "In this matter, I don't care what you think, Nadine. You may be the general manager, but this is still *my* store. And don't you forget it."

Her grandfather's voice could still crack like a whip. His

tone made Nadine pause and say, "I'll bear that in mind." She made her way to her desk and sat down stiffly. She pretended to be absorbed in what was written in her appointment book.

"Blythe, darling, I want to talk to you," Harwood stated. "Come with me to my office."

With one last glance at her mother, Blythe followed her grandfather down the hall.

Khalil leaned back into his chair smiling as he recalled his meeting with Blythe Bloodstone. She'd been ready to rip his head off by the time she left his office. If looks could kill . . .

His phone buzzed and Khalil picked it up. Intuitively knowing that it was his sister, he said, "Yes, Kuiana."

"What did you do to that poor woman? She was practically spitting nails when she flew by me."

"Miss Bloodstone will get over it."

"I take it she's not pleased with the article in the paper, then?"

"No, she's not. She even threatened to take legal action if we didn't print a retraction."

"Really?"

Khalil laughed. "She's a feisty one. You should have seen her earlier when she charged into my office. The people from Jefferson Baptist were here."

Kuiana joined in her brother's laughter. "I wasn't here but I heard about it. I'm sorry I missed it."

"Well, next time she comes—you can deal with her."

"No, thanks. Well, big brother, just wanted to let you know that I'm back. I've got a deadline, so I'll be in my office with a do not disturb sign hanging on the knob."

Khalil laughed. "Tell that to Caryn."

He hung up and swiveled around in his chair to stare out of the window. Blythe Bloodstone. He'd seen pictures of her in various news publications over the years. She hadn't changed much, except for cutting off her hair. The short hairstyle suited her much better, he thought. She wasn't at all what he considered pretty—instead, he thought she was rather plain looking.

Her smooth copper skin glowed with golden undertones. Her face was well-structured but her expression morose. She had a nice figure though. Her expensive suit had done nothing to disguise that fact. Blythe had nice hips and long, shapely legs.

Although he found her manner haughty, Khalil had to admit he admired her gutsy attitude. And the way she stormed into his office, ready to do battle. He was sure he hadn't seen the last of Blythe Bloodstone. She was one determined lady. But no matter what she threatened, he would not print a retraction.

He shook his head in disgust as he thought of Bloodstone's Department Store. From the high-end merchandise to the hiring of a predominantly white staff since their move to Beverly Hills, the store had a completely different smell to it and Khalil didn't like the stench.

Looking through a file of old photos, he found one of the Bloodstone family. Both Blythe's brother and sister were fair-skinned like their mother, Nadine. Blythe, being the darkest of the three siblings, had inherited the copper skin tone of her father and grandfather.

Searching his memory, he vaguely recalled reading some-where that Harwood Bloodstone's father, John, had been the grandson of a sharecropper. They were from some small town in North Carolina. After receiving a tidy sum of money from the sale of a large parcel of land, John Bloodstone packed up his family and moved to California.

He and his wife opened up a small dress shop back in the early 1960s in Baldwin Hills. By 1980, the store had grown from a cozy boutique to a department store, thanks partly to the overwhelming support of the black community.

Regardless of what Blythe said, it was obvious that the Blood-stones had forgotten where they'd come from.

Khalil worked steadily until lunchtime. Needing a break, he then decided to head downtown to Alameda street. Spotting his father, he waved and pulled into a parking space.

James Sanford walked over to the car. "I didn't know you were coming down here, Son."

Getting out of the car, Khalil activated the alarm. "I wanted to get out of the office." Being careful to stay out of the way of construction workers, and stepping over pieces of lumber and nails, he asked, "How are things going?"

"See for yourself." James led his son over to the empty building being renovated. He handed Khalil a hard hat to wear. "We're going to be ready by Spring."

"If this is successful, just think, Dad. We might have a solution to the homelessness problem."

"I found a couple of other buildings that we might be able to convert. Thank God, the grant money's here and we've got a lot of supporters."

Khalil nodded. "I've been thinking over Kuiana's suggestion. Maybe we should charge the tenants something once they start working. That way they are able to establish credit and it should ease them back into the world of paying bills."

James agreed. "Bring it up at the board meeting tonight."

"I will." Khalil strolled into one of the apartments, his father following him. He stood in the middle of the room looking around. "I'm not sure about this color . . . it looks dull. I think we need something with more of a gloss to it."

"Deluxe Paints donated the paint."

"I know and I appreciate their help. I don't think we'll insult them if we offer to pay for an upgraded product. Maybe they could give us a discount or something."

"I'll talk to Leo and see what I can work out." James strolled over to one of the huge windows. Looking out he said, "Broadway Computers donated two brand new computers for the training center." He turned to face his son. "Now we only have to buy two more."

"That's wonderful. We're going to buy them from Broadway, of course."

"Of course," James agreed.

Khalil and his father left the apartment and headed downstairs. As they walked through the classrooms, Khalil's chest swelled with pride. This apartment building would be able to house fifty families, and he hoped would be the first of many more. What he wanted most was to find a way to help those less fortunate.

Chapter 2

Blythe followed her grandfather into his corner office on the fifth floor. "It's so good to see you up and about. I think it'll do you good to get out more." She sighed. "I really wish Father would consider leaving the house every once in a while."

Turning an indulgent eye on her, Harwood smiled. Striding behind his desk, he said. "I'm inclined to agree with you, little darling. However, we can't push him."

Harwood Bloodstone had suffered a stroke a year ago. The only telltale sign left was the slight slur when he spoke. Blythe noticed her grandfather moved at a much slower pace these days.

Closing the door behind her, Blythe stood with her hands folded across her chest. "Okay, Grandfather. What's going on? I know there's a reason you're here." She paused before dropping down in one of the plush visitor chairs. "You read that article in the *Heritage Reporter,* didn't you?"

His gaze bored through her. "Well . . . is there any truth to it?"

Blythe shook her head. "Grandfather, I really don't think so."

"But you have no way of knowing?"

"I've never seen it—"

"You know, Blythe, I always thought you were more . . . ah . . . sensitive about certain things. More so than your mother." Harwood settled his large frame deep into his chair.

She was hurt by his gentle rebuke. "Grandfather, it's only been four months since I moved back here. I've been busy trying to settle in."

Harwood nodded his understanding. "Blythe, honey. I gave you this job because I believed in you. You've worked in this store from the time you were sixteen until you up and decided to move to France with that artist fellow." He pointed at her. "I know how much this store means to you. Now your sister Moira, she refused to have anything to do with the store. Except shop."

Blythe rolled her eyes at the mention of her sister's name. Moira was a computer analyst and Nadine's favorite. "What do you want me to do, Grandfather?"

"I want you to spend more time on the sales floor and less time in your office or running errands for that self-centered mother of yours."

Blythe smiled. "You don't like my mother much, do you?"

"Nadine was my son's choice for a wife. Not mine." He waved his hand in disgust. "Look at your father now."

"In Mother's defense, I have to say that she's dedicated her whole life to making this store what it is. The Couture Salon was her idea and so was getting the Personal Shoppers. She's done a lot for this store."

Harwood nodded. "You're right, but she's getting a little too big for her britches now." He spoke in harshness and derision. "Nadine wants me to retire and just hand over the reins to her. Well, I'll tell you this much. I'm not going to do it."

"What are you going to do?"

"I'm going to make sure she's earned the right to run this company. I didn't know how much the store meant to your father until I made Nadine general manager."

"It's not your fault what happened."

"I'm not so sure, darling."

"He and Mother had been arguing. Father had been drinking that night . . ."

"I don't want to talk about your parents anymore." He tilted his brow, looking at her, concerned. "How are you doing, honey? I know it was hard to come back, but you did the right thing. You didn't need to be over in Paris alone. You should be with family somewhere nearby."

"I'm fine."

Harwood's eyebrows flickered a little and he snorted. "Now, I know you don't think I'm buying that hogwash."

"Really, Grandfather, I'm okay. Getting along with Mother is quite another story," she said in terse terms.

"I told you that you're welcome to stay with me. Or you can get a place of your own. I don't know how you can live with all those danged flowers on everything. And pink. Lots of pink! I don't cotton to living in a bottle of Pepto-Bismol."

Blythe giggled behind her hand. Her grandfather was hilarious at times. "I know what you mean, but I just don't want to leave Father alone with her."

"I'm real sorry about Parker and the way—"

Cutting off the rest of Harwood's statement, Blythe stated, "I don't want to talk about it. It really doesn't matter anymore." Rising to her feet, she said, "I'm going to spend the rest of the day on the sales floor."

"That's a fine idea, honey."

Pausing at the door, Blythe asked, "Will you be around long enough to have lunch with me? It's my treat."

"Of course, Blythe. I'll be right here."

After spending a couple of hours in both the women's and the junior's departments, Blythe met Harwood in his office. Together they traveled by elevator to the sixth floor.

"Cafeteria or private dining room?" she asked her grandfather.

"Cafeteria," he responded. "I'm hankering for some of Lucy's meat loaf."

Inside the cafeteria, Blythe and Harwood stood in line with the others. After making their selections, they carried their trays to a corner table. Sitting in the chair he held out for her, she asked, "Are you going to be in town for Thanksgiving?"

Harwood shook his head. "No. I'm going back to North Carolina. Martha Belle invited me to spend the holidays with her and the rest of the family."

Blythe smiled at the mention of her great aunt's name. "How is Aunt Martha doing?"

"She's doing fine." He chuckled. "Still getting on Leroy's nerves. He threatens to divorce her every day." Picking up his fork, Harwood stuck a piece of meat loaf into his mouth. "Mmmm, Lucy sure has a knack for making meat loaf. Think I'll have her make up one for me to take home."

"Aunt Martha and Uncle Leroy are constantly at odds with each other, it seems."

"If Daddy John hadn't made me promise on his deathbed to take care of my sister, I probably would've hung Martha Belle a long time ago. She can make a whipped pup turn vicious."

Blythe broke into laughter. "Well, please give them my love." Picking up her glass of iced tea, she sipped it slowly.

"I sure will. What are your plans for the holiday?"

Placing her glass back on the table, she then daintily wiped her mouth on the corner of her napkin before she spoke. "A quiet dinner at home with Father. That's about it."

"Where will the rest of the clan be? Going to some fancy restaurant I bet."

"Then you'd lose your bet. They're going to Barbados."

"Barbados!" Harwood spit the word out as if he had a bad taste in his mouth. "For Thanksgiving?"

Blythe nodded. "Mother's taking Justin and Moira."

He was bristling. "I could strangle that skinny witch! When I get downstairs, I fully intend to give that wretched mother of yours a piece of my mind."

Placing her hand over his, Blythe sought to calm him down. "Grandfather, it's fine. I'd rather spend Thanksgiving alone with my father. Mother and I don't get along and I don't want him to feel like he's caught in the middle. And then there's

Moira and Justin. I want to enjoy the day—not spend it fighting back and forth. It would only upset Father.''

Throwing his napkin on the table, Harwood stated, "I'm going to have my say."

Blythe held up a hand in defense. "Oh, I know that. Once you're on a roll, there's certainly no stopping you."

"I could wring that scrawny neck of hers. That's my son she's treating like ..." Harwood shook his head. "I won't stand for it. Not with Adam in the condition he's in."

Finishing her food, Blythe listened quietly as her grandfather railed on and on. He was fighting mad and she had to admit that she couldn't blame him. This was just one of many of her mother's selfish antics.

Back downstairs, Blythe ran into Nadine outside of her office. Mentally preparing for battle, she gathered up all her strength to keep her nerves in check.

"Are you just getting back from lunch?"

"Yes, Mother." She seethed underneath, but kept an outwardly composed demeanor. "Why?"

"Please don't take that tone with me, young lady."

Rubbing her temple, Blythe brushed past her mother. She stopped and turned around. "Grandfather's looking for you, by the way. He's probably in his office right now."

A shadow of annoyance crossed her face. "What on earth does he want now?"

Blythe shrugged. "I haven't a clue. However, I'm sure you don't want to keep him waiting. He seemed awfully upset over something."

For just a moment, Nadine was not as assured. "Well, I'll talk to you later. Let me see what this bossy old man wants."

A small part of Blythe felt guilty for sending her mother into a war zone, but then again ... Blythe placed her hand over her mouth and giggled.

Kuiana knocked lightly on her brother's door. "How much longer will you be here?"

Khalil looked up from his computer monitor. "For a little

while." He leaned back into his chair. "You going by the house to see Mom and Dad?"

"I was thinking about it. What about you?" She dropped down into a chair facing her brother's desk.

Stretching, Khalil nodded. "I'm considering stopping by there. I called over there earlier. Mom was cooking red beans and rice for dinner."

Kuiana licked her lips. "Mmmmm, I think maybe I'll have dinner there, too. I love red beans and rice. Besides I'm not in the mood to go home and cook."

Khalil laughed. "I know what you mean. Feel like hanging out a little while longer?"

"Sure." She leaned closer. "What's up? You need help with something?"

"No. I was just thinking—if you wait for me to finish up, I'll follow you over to Mom and Dad's. We can go to tonight's board meeting from there."

Kuiana's stomach growled loudly. Putting her hand to her mouth, she giggled. "I think you'd better hurry."

"Did you take a lunch break?" Khalil asked, his concern growing. "I don't want you getting sick." Kuiana was a diabetic.

"I had half a sandwich and some chips."

"You know that you need to eat healthier."

Holding up her hand, Kuiana stopped Khalil. "I'm fine, big brother. And I'm too tired to hear a lecture on my eating habits. Save it for another time." Shifting her position in the chair, she eyed him. "What you need to worry about is getting out and finding yourself a girlfriend. When was the last time you had sex?"

Khalil arched an eyebrow. "That is none of your business."

She laughed. "I can't believe you are such a prude."

"I'm not. I just don't think I should discuss my sex life with my little sister. I don't go around asking you about yours."

"That's because you couldn't handle knowing the real deal."

Laughing, Khalil nodded. "You're probably right." He pushed away from his desk. "Come on, I'm going to call it a night.'' Rising to his feet, Khalil grabbed his keys. "Let's go have dinner with Mom and Dad.''

Blythe unlocked her office and stepped inside. She'd spent the afternoon in the men's department. Deciding that the article in the *Heritage Reporter* had been wrong, she made her way upstairs. It was time to go home.

"Blythe, where have you been? I've been all over the store looking for you.''

She plastered on a fake smile before turning around to face her sister. "Moira, I really can't imagine why you'd be looking for me.''

"I thought we'd have dinner, silly.''

Blythe was suspicious. "I see. What is it that you want?''

Moira looked hurt. "I just thought we'd spend some time together.'' She swung her long, wavy hair over her shoulders. "We haven't since you've been home, you know.''

Blythe folded her arms across her chest, her lips pursed in annoyance. "Moira . . .''

"Please, Blythe,'' she pleaded. "I don't want to fight. We're sisters and we should start acting like it. All I want to do is spend some quality time with you. We can do some catching up.''

"You're right,'' Blythe murmured as she examined her unpainted nails. She felt a thread of guilt over her treatment of Moira.

Except for the slight difference in their stature and the color of their skin, the two women were remarkably similar in appearance.

"So then we'll have dinner together?'' Moira persisted.

Blythe nodded. "I guess so.'' She stopped, asking, "Mother won't be joining us, will she?''

"I was going to ask her to—''

She shook her head no. "If you do, Moira, then I won't be going. I've had enough of Mother dear for today.''

Her sister seemed shocked by her declaration. "Blythe, that's not a very nice thing to say.''

She lifted her chin in defiance. "Maybe not, but it's the way I feel."

"Did you two have another fight?"

Blythe stared at Moira, astounded. "What do you think?"

"Stupid question, I know." Moira looped her hand through Blythe's. "Come on, I'll drive. You can pick up your car afterwards."

Moira drove to Prego, located on Camden Drive, north of Wilshire. The Italian restaurant featured Blythe's favorite, homemade pasta and grilled seafood. Because Moira had called ahead, they were seated immediately.

Over a glass of wine, Moira studied her before asking, "So, Blythe, are you thrilled to be back home?"

"It's okay. I haven't really done much of anything outside of work and spending time with Father." She paused long enough to give the waiter her order. "Besides, the store keeps me pretty busy."

While they waited for their food to arrive, Moira continued to make small talk. "How do you like the house? Mother had it completely decorated by Armando. He's the interior designer on staff at the store."

"I've met him," Blythe stated. "The house looks nice, but then Mother really wouldn't have it any other way." Blythe picked up her glass and slowly sipped her Chablis. Putting the glass back down, she added, "She simply has to have the very best."

Moira's eyes clouded over but she remained quiet.

They sat in uncomfortable silence. When it became unbearable, Moira spoke up in her sing-song voice. "Oh, I know what I had to tell you. Guess who's dying to take you out?"

"Who?" Blythe pushed her wineglass away so that the waiter could place her food before her.

"Percy Wilcox."

Blythe's eyebrows flittered upward. "Really?" She hadn't thought of Percy in years.

"Yes, aren't you excited? You used to be so crazy about him. I told him you were coming back home and he wants you to call him. Isn't that great?"

Blythe played with her food. "That was a long time ago," she replied curtly. "A very long time ago. As for calling Percy ... I don't think so. I'm not interested in being dogged right now. I've had more than my share."

"Well, aren't you being just a tiny bit negative." Moira's eyes sparkled as she continued. "I don't think you have to worry about that with Percy. He talks about you all the time. I think you two should at least have dinner together. What harm can come of it?"

"I don't know. I'll have to think about it."

"You're not still in love with that no-good Parker, are you? Look at the way he dumped you shortly after you moved to Paris. Now he's married and—"

"Let's change the subject, Moira," Blythe interjected. "I don't want to talk about Parker." Although three years had passed since their breakup, the heartache was still there. Parker had been the love of her life. She'd had a couple of bad relationships after that and they'd all left her with a bitter taste in her mouth. She leaned back in her chair, tapping her fingernails on the table. "So, tell me, who are you going out with these days?"

"I'm still with William."

"Really? I thought he was old news." Blythe reached for her wine. Sipping slowly, she eyed her sister. Something was missing. Moira didn't have the magical glow of a woman in love.

"I know he and I broke up right before you left, but every now and then we would see each other. Then last year, things kind of heated up again. He's asked me to marry him."

Blythe blinked twice. "What did you say?"

"I said yes. What did you think I'd say? I'm thirty-two years old. I figure I'd better do it now because I want children and I'm not exactly getting any younger."

Shaking her head, Blythe replied, "Don't remind me. I'm two years older than you." Leaning closer, she asked, "Do you love him? You *are* getting married because you love William, right?"

Moira countered by asking, "What other reason would there be?"

"Well, you could be marrying him because Mother wants you to," Blythe suggested.

Moira was becoming flustered. "Blythe, why are you asking me this?"

"Because I know you, Moira, and you don't look like a woman in love. I didn't even know you were still seeing the man."

"Well, it's not like you and I have been in constant communication with each other."

Blythe ignored the defensive tone in her sister's voice. "Moira, please don't marry William if you don't love him. It's not fair to either of you."

"I know. The truth is that I love him—maybe not in a wild, passionate way, but he comes from a good family and . . ."

"And he's rich," Blythe threw in.

"Yes, he happens to be rich," Moira agreed. "But he is also a very sweet and generous man. He's very good to me."

"But mostly he's rich." Blythe refused to believe her sister was even considering marriage to this man.

"I'm not going to make this about money," Moira replied.

Blythe wasn't going to be put off. "Well then, let's make this about age. He's fifteen years older than you. And what about children? Does he want more children?"

Moira shrugged. "I don't know. We've never really discussed it."

She wanted to take her sister and shake her. Moira wasn't thinking clearly. "Well, don't you think you should?"

"Why? I'm going to stop taking the pill as soon as we get married. If I get pregnant—"

"William may not be very happy about it. He's already raised four children. He may not want to do it again."

"How can you be so negative?"

"I'm not trying to be negative, but you've got to admit that it's a possibility, Moira."

"William should know that I would want children. Surely once I'm pregnant he'll have to accept it."

"I hope that you know what you're doing."

Moira dove into her linguini. "Don't worry. I can handle William."

Blythe was not convinced.

After dinner, Moira returned her safely to her car, and Blythe drove home. She found her father sitting in the living room reading. She broke into a smile and raced across the room. "How are you feeling, handsome?"

Adam looked up at his daughter. "Same as always. Can't move a muscle from the waist down. How about you? You look like you've had some day."

"It was okay." She bent over and kissed his cheek. Lowering her voice to a whisper, she asked, "Where's Mother?"

"Upstairs somewhere," was his reply. "She arrived about an hour ago."

Blythe sank down in a high-backed chair, crossing her legs. "Would you like for me to sit with you for a while?"

Shaking his head, Adam said, "No, you don't have to do that. I'm sure you've got better things to do than keep an old man like me company."

"I'll always have time for you." She softly stroked the back of her father's hand.

Together, they discussed their day until Winston, Adam's nurse and companion, entered the room.

"Blythe, how are you this evening?"

"Hello, Winston. I'm just fine. Would you like me to help you with my father?"

Standing with his hands on the back of Adam's wheelchair, Winston replied, "I can handle it from here. I've got his bath ready and his medication."

Blythe rose to her feet. "Well good night then. Father, I'll see you in the morning." She leaned over to kiss his cheek. "Remember, we've got a date for breakfast."

"I'll be there. Sleep well, darling."

"You, too." She watched Winston and her father leave for his downstairs bedroom before heading up to her own.

Nadine met her at the top of the stairs. "Are you just getting in?"

"No, Mother. I was downstairs with my father."

"He's still up?"

Her voice sounded hopeful, surprising Blythe. "He was. Winston's taking him for his bath."

"Oh. Well, I guess I'll speak with him in the morning then." Nadine headed toward her room.

"I guess," Blythe muttered.

Stopping, her mother turned around, asking, "Is there a problem?"

"No." Opening the door to her room, Blythe entered. Just as she was about to close it, her mother burst through.

Slapping her palm down on the antique dressing table, Nadine stated, "Blythe, I'm your mother and I demand respect."

"You've always told me that one has to earn respect—it's not freely given."

Wiping her hands, her mother sat down on the edge of her bed. "It's not my fault your father is in that chair, Blythe."

"He had the accident after fighting with you, Mother. After you threw him out of the house. He'll never be able to walk again and you still haven't forgiven him."

"You don't know what you're talking about."

"Yes, I do. Father told me everything. He loves you."

Nadine's bottom lip trembled in her anger. "How dare he discuss our problems with you?"

"Don't be mad at him, Mother," Blythe pleaded. "He needs to talk to someone. You certainly don't talk to him."

Nadine rose to her feet. "Blythe, this conversation is over. I don't owe you any explanations. This is between your father and me."

Reaching out to touch her mother, Blythe had a sudden change of heart and pulled her hand back. "Mother, I'm not trying to interfere. Really, I'm not."

"I know you love your father, but you don't have to be his protector."

"I wish you still loved him." Blythe headed to the door, opening it. "Good night, Mother."

Nadine paused at the door. "Don't forget we're attending the party at the Grayson Mansion on Saturday evening."

"I'd rather not go," Blythe replied quietly. "Moira will be there with you. I don't need to go."

"Everyone knows that you're back in town. We should attend as a family."

"Grandfather's not going. Neither is Father."

"We've donated a large sum to Gloria's AIDS Foundation. We should be there." Nadine waited for Blythe to respond, but when she didn't she shook her head in resignation. She left the room.

Blythe didn't see the tears that welled in Nadine's eyes as she stiffly strolled past, nor did she hear her mother's soft reply, "I do love your father, but he broke my heart."

Chapter 3

Glittering crystal chandeliers hung from the high ceiling of the forty-two-room mansion in Holmby Hills, owned by aging actress Gloria Grayson.

Studying her surroundings, Blythe decided the house was a fine example of Spanish-Moorish style architecture. A lover of art, she most admired the murals and the Tunisian tile that decorated the interior.

"It is you." A tall, slender woman walked gracefully toward her. "I told Helen that it was you."

Blythe had recognized the woman immediately and had tried to escape unnoticed. Resigned, she turned around. "Hello Kelly."

Lavishly adorned in a forest green gown, the woman wore her hair in long graceful curls over her shoulders. Ostentatiously, she planted a kiss on each of Blythe's cheeks. "It's so good to see that you've come to your senses and returned home." Perusing her from head to foot, Kelly said, "You look wonderful."

"So do you."

"So tell me, how long are you planning to stay home this time?"

Blythe gazed at the red-haired, green-eyed woman a moment before responding. "I'm not really sure, Kelly. For a while, I guess." As if it's any of your business, she silently mused.

Tossing her long hair prettily across her shoulders, Kelly's mouth twisted into a frown. "You were always on the move. I don't think I could just pick up and leave like that."

Kelly and Moira were best friends. Had been since high school. For the life of her, Blythe couldn't understand how her sister could stand being around such a shallow woman. "Why not? Afraid you'll miss your parents' money?"

Kelly's green eyes gazed into Blythe's. "Well, that's certainly part of it. But I'm really happy here. I've never had the desire to live like a nomad. I don't see how you can do it."

"It's simple really. If I decide I want to move, I just do it. I guess I'm impulsive that way."

"But don't you miss your family?"

Blythe accepted a stuffed shrimp offered by a passing waiter. "Not really. I would usually get a little homesick around the holidays, but that's it."

"Did you come home just because of your father's accident? Or was there another reason? I remember Moira mentioning that you were supposed to get married." She glanced down at Blythe's left hand. "Whatever happened with that?"

She simply shrugged. Kelly was digging, but she wasn't about to explain her actions.

Realizing that she wasn't going to find out anything, Kelly sighed in resignation and said, "I thought Moira would be here by now."

"I wish she were," Blythe commented dryly. She was tired of listening to Kelly's mindless chatter. "Why don't you go in that direction looking for her and I'll circle around the other way. One of us is bound to run into her." Silently she added, I hope you find her first. Then maybe you'll leave me alone.

"Sounds like a good idea." Whirling her expensive gown around, Kelly navigated through the masses, nodding and waving like a beauty contestant. Blythe smiled. Her description was dead-on. Kelly was a professional beauty contestant. Watching her leave, she breathed a deep sigh of relief.

"That wasn't very nice," a bass voice whispered in her ear.

Blythe turned around quickly. Her breath caught in her throat as she discreetly assessed the man standing inches away from her. Underneath a black, single-breasted tuxedo, Khalil wore a bow tie and scarf with an African motif. His slender build tantalized her. Her curiosity, as well as her vanity, was aroused. Masking her true feelings behind an air of gaiety, she said, "Mr. Sanford."

Khalil grinned devilishly. "How are you this evening, Miss Bloodstone?"

Feeling wretchedly uncomfortable about her attraction to him, Blythe's stomach felt like one huge twisted knot and her body felt as if it would break into a cold sweat. Nonetheless, she formed a soft, sultry smile. "I'd feel better if you would agree to print a retraction in your paper about the store."

He shook his head. "I can't do that."

Blythe took a deep breath to control her frustration, her mouth a painful grimace. "Mr. Sanford—" She didn't want to be attracted to this man. All Blythe wanted was to convince him to change his mind.

"Please call me Khalil." He offered her a glass of champagne.

Accepting the flute, she stated, "I don't think we have anything further to discuss, Mr. Sanford. Have a good evening." Blythe started to walk away. Closing her eyes, she mentally counted to ten when she realized Khalil was not going to leave her alone.

The orchestra started up, playing a lilting melody.

Easing up beside her, he said, "I'm sorry to hear that. I was hoping we could get past all of this. Actually, I was hoping we could perhaps have one dance."

Blythe shook her head. How she longed to have this night over. "Fraid not."

Khalil leaned over and whispered, "I'll even let you lead. You strike me as a take-charge kind of person. What do you think?"

"I don't think that's the least bit funny."

Standing in her path, Khalil grabbed her gently by the elbow to keep her from storming off. "I didn't come over here to upset you. I apologize if I have."

Standing so close to him, she was awestruck by his look of sincerity. Blythe relaxed. "You didn't. Not really," she admitted. "I didn't want to be here in the first place."

His hand still on her elbow, Khalil asked, "Why is that?"

Glancing over at her mother, Blythe stated, "I'd rather not say." It was something she could not explain. How could she tell him that she longed for her mother to wrap her arms around her and hold her tight, but that it was futile? Nadine would never show such a display of emotion toward her.

His eyes raked over her. "How about some fresh air?" Khalil suggested. "We could take a walk."

Blythe drew her attention from her mother and regarded him pensively for a moment. "Now why would we do that? I was under the impression that we were on opposite sides."

Shrugging, Khalil replied, "Doesn't matter right now. I think a walk will do you a lot of good."

Beneath the burning gaze of her mother's watchful eye, Blythe nodded. "You're probably right. I need to get out of here." She felt like Nadine's constant rejection would consume her whole. Blythe silently chided herself for caring. After all, it had been like this her entire life.

Khalil watched Blythe out of the corner of his eyes as she strolled briskly toward the door. She looked straight ahead, not speaking to anyone. He quickened his pace to keep up with her. His hand locked against her spine. "Are you sure you're okay?"

Her expression guarded, she asked, "Why do you keep asking?" Blythe stepped through the open doors and leaned her body against the whitewashed banister. Feeling the chilly night air on her face, she inhaled deeply. "Do I look like I'm not?" she asked in a flippant manner.

"Well you do seem a little tense."

Staring fixedly out into the moonlit sky, Blythe folded her

arms across her chest. "I'm always a little tense when I'm around my mother," she mumbled almost to herself.

His eyes never leaving Blythe, Khalil inched closer to her. "Excuse me?" He fought back an urge to touch her.

Blythe blinked and her mouth parted. When Khalil tilted his head wearing a look of confusion, she shrugged and replied, "I'm sorry. It's nothing. I guess I was thinking out loud." Nervous energy caused her to finger the intricate embroidery of her dress. "I'm surprised to see you here."

Khalil smiled. "Why is that? Am I out of my element?"

Blythe looked at him in astonishment. "I didn't mean to imply anything like that. I just meant that . . ." She wasn't sure what she meant. "I'm sorry."

Khalil's laugh was rich. "It's okay. Actually, I usually don't attend functions like this, but a friend of mine invited me." For a moment he pushed his better judgment aside and allowed his gaze to travel appreciatively over her. In the moonlight, Blythe was strikingly beautiful, her short curly hair glistening in the saffron light of the street lamps positioned outside the mansion.

"My mother loves events like this." Blythe frowned. "She's in her glory mingling with the rich and famous."

"What about you?"

The corners of her mouth turned downward. "Believe me, I'm only here because I was *ordered* to attend." Glancing around, Blythe stated, "My sister should be arriving soon. When she gets here, I plan to make good my escape."

"I'd like to know something. Why are you so hard on your mother?"

"It's obvious you don't know my mother. Status and money are the things most important to her. The Bloodstones have to appear the perfect family in public. Mind you, it doesn't have to be true. We just have to appear as such."

"You sound very bitter."

"Call it what you want." She stared out into the night.

"No family is without flaws, Blythe."

She was quiet, probably cursing herself for opening up to

him—a man she barely knew, Khalil thought. He gestured to his left. "Your sister has arrived."

Blythe released a deep sigh. "Now, I can leave." She turned to face Khalil. "It was good seeing you again. I only wish we were on the same side."

She was gone before he could reply.

Curious, he leaned against the whitewashed column, watching Blythe greet her sister. He pondered what it was that made her different from any other woman he'd ever known. She was always well-dressed and wore only a hint of makeup. Then it came to him. He'd never seen her smile.

Not even in her photos.

Blythe Bloodstone had a chip on her shoulder the size of this house. Khalil was surprised when Blythe discreetly wiped away Moira's kiss. He wondered about their relationship. He and his sister were extremely close. Khalil couldn't imagine not having Kuiana around. She was his best friend.

As Blythe entered the ballroom, her mother appeared out of nowhere. "Who is that man you were talking to?" Nadine demanded.

Pretending not to know to whom her mother was referring, Blythe asked, "Which one? I've talked to quite a few men tonight."

"You know which one I'm talking about. *The dark one.* The one with the Afrocentric bow tie and cummerbund."

"Oh him."

"Well?" Nadine persisted.

"That was Khalil Sanford."

"*He's the one . . .*" Her mother sputtered. "He's the publisher of that no-account newspaper?"

Blythe announced grimly. "The one and only."

Grabbing her roughly by the arm, Nadine hissed, "How could you betray the family like that? Where is your sense of loyalty?"

Blythe pulled her arm away, replying caustically, "Mother, I was trying to get him to print a retraction. I thought that's what you wanted me to do. Isn't that proof enough of my loyalty?''

"Well, I certainly didn't mean you had to sleep with him . . .''

Blythe opened her mouth, then snapped it shut. There was no point in responding to Nadine's ridiculous accusation. Hurt and angry, she swept past her mother.

Nadine caught up with her. "Blythe, I'm sorry. I—"

She held up her hand and backed away from her mother. "I'm leaving. *I've had enough.*"

"Blythe . . .'' Nadine's tone was pleading. "We mustn't cause a scene. People are watching us. I can only imagine what they're thinking. We have—"

"No, Mother," she interjected. "I don't care what these people are thinking. I'm leaving. I should've stayed home with Father in the first place. I can't believe . . .'' Blythe shook her head, unable to finish. Tears in her eyes, she dashed off as quickly as she could. Khalil was standing a few feet away from them, and she was mortified by the thought of his witnessing the nasty scene between her and Nadine.

She wasn't aware that he'd followed her outside until she heard him call her name softly. Wiping her tears, Blythe turned around slowly, averting her gaze. "What is it, Mr. Sanford?''

"Are you going to be okay?'' he questioned anxiously. "And please call me Khalil. Mr. Sanford is my father.''

Wiping a lone tear from her eye, Blythe said in a low whisper, "I really wish you'd print a retraction.'' She felt the despair that weighed on her spirit. "You've got it all wrong about the store.''

Silence engulfed them as Khalil moved closer. "Blythe . . .''

"I've spent the last couple of days on the sales floor in various departments and I haven't seen any incidents such as you've mentioned.''

"You're going to have to spend more than a couple of days down there. I'm sure you've noticed that very few black customers even come into the store anymore.''

She held up her hand and backed away. "I can't debate this

with you right now.'' Blythe looked away from him. ''I have
to go.''

''Is there anything I can do?''

She shook her head. ''You've done enough.'' She rushed
off.

Alone in her car, Blythe allowed her tears to run freely. The
evening was over, at long last. She drove quickly, wanting to
get home to her father.

A waiter offered Khalil a fresh flute of champagne. As he
sipped his drink, his thoughts meandered back to Blythe. For
some reason, it had bothered him to see her cry. A part of him
had wanted to reach out and comfort her.

Remembering her parting words, Khalil wondered if the
argument he'd witnessed between Blythe and her mother had
something to do with him. The last thing he wanted was to be
a source of friction between them. If so, he was a small part,
he reasoned. He had a feeling that there was something more
going on in that family.

Adam looked up from his reading. ''You're home early.''

When Blythe entered the house, she tried to present a con-
vincing smile. ''I wanted to spend the rest of my evening with
you.'' She smoothed her long, straight skirt before sitting down.
''Anything wrong with that?''

If he noticed that anything was wrong, Adam didn't comment
on it, instead saying, ''Blythe, you're a young woman. You
shouldn't spend all of your time with me.''

''It's something I want to do.'' Dropping down into the chair
near her father, she said, ''Besides, Mother and I just can't
seem to get along. Father, she . . .''

Adam stroked her cheek lovingly. ''Give your mother a
chance, dear. Nadine can't help who she is. She had a real hard
life growing up.''

''A lot of people grow up poor but it doesn't make them
heartless. Mother's always talking about how we should forget

the past and move on. I guess it doesn't apply to her." She settled her head back onto the soft oversized pillows, loving the cushiony feel.

"Her parents weren't affectionate people, Blythe. Do you know that they never once told her that they loved her. Your mother used to tell me that I was the only person in the world who loved her. Love is very important to Nadine."

"Then why does she treat you so bad now?" She countered. "Because you made a mistake. One mistake!"

"I hurt her, Blythe."

"But Father, look at you. You need her." She pursed her lips into a displeasing line.

Adam shrugged. "I'll be fine."

"No. You never leave the house or anything. You're not fine, so don't tell me that. I don't know why she can't see it."

"Your mother and I will work our problems out in time." Adam's thin hand moved to cover hers. "And you, young lady, I want you to listen to me and hear me good. You need to do the same."

"I've tried. Mother doesn't love me—she never has. I know you don't agree, but sometimes I can see it in her eyes. She hates me."

Adam shook his head. "No, Blythe . . ."

"Father, I can see it. When she looks at Moira and Justin, it's different." Blythe shook her head sadly. "I don't know what I could have done . . ."

He reached for her. "Come here, sweetheart." Adam pulled her onto his lap with arms that were surprisingly strong. "You did nothing wrong. Nadine loves you. I know she does. I remember the first time she held you in her arms." Adam smiled. "It was love at first sight."

Blythe lay her head on her father's shoulder. "You don't know how much I want to believe that, Father. I'm thirty-four years old and I still want so desperately to have my mother's love."

"And she does," Adam assured her. "I know she doesn't show it but that's just your mother's way. Moira and Justin simply accept her the way she is. You've always wanted more."

Sitting up, Blythe's eyes widened in disbelief. "So, I'm the bad guy here."

"Honey, you know that's not what I'm saying at all. I'm only saying that you needed her more than your brother and sister. There's nothing wrong with that."

"Father, I'm glad that I have you. I don't know what would've happened if I didn't have you or Grandfather."

"Well, if I have anything to say about it, you'll always have the two of us."

Kissing his cheek, she embraced him. "I love you."

Adam smiled. "I love you too, sweetheart. Now I know you're tired. Why don't you go on up to bed? I'm going to finish this chapter and then I'm going to call it a night."

Blythe stifled her yawn and stood up. Smiling, she made her way to the door. "Good night, Father."

She greeted Winston as she passed him on the way to the curving stairway. "Could you do me a favor?"

"Sure, what is it?"

"Would you try to get Father out for a brief stroll tomorrow?"

Winston nodded. Lowering his voice, he said, "I've been trying for weeks to get him to leave the house, but he always refuses. I'm not going to give up on him."

Blythe smiled. "Thanks, Winston."

"It's no problem. You have a good night."

"You, too."

In her room, she sighed with relief as she pulled her nightgown over her head. Tonight was over. Now she just had to find the strength to make it the next day.

In bed, Blythe recalled the feel of Khalil's touch and how she'd felt wrapped in an invisible warmth being so close to him. Even now she felt an unwelcome surge of excitement where he was concerned. Part of her had been disappointed that he seemed to let her go so easily, and the other part was moved by his gentlemanly qualities.

She felt a tightening in her groin as she thought about the way Khalil's gaze had roamed over her body. Blythe had enough experience to recognize the signs. Khalil Sanford was interested in her—but for a fling. He didn't want a serious commitment.

Blythe chided herself for the way she'd easily confided in him. She prayed that he wouldn't find a way to use what he'd learned against her. Telling herself that she was being irrational, Blythe turned her thoughts to the conversation she'd had with her father. As she stared into the darkness, she pondered over what he'd told her. He was wrong. Her mother couldn't stand her. Blythe knew that Nadine's whole demeanor changed whenever she was around.

Lying there, she could hear the faint rustle of wind whistling through the trees. She heard a car pull into the driveway. Blythe jumped out of bed and stealthily peeked out her window. It was her mother. Moira pulled in behind Nadine and parked. The two of them walked into the house. She could hear Moira's soft giggle as they climbed the stairs.

Sitting on the edge of her bed, Blythe held her breath when Nadine's footsteps paused outside her door. Although she breathed a sigh of relief when she heard her mother walk away, something akin to disappointment flowed through her like a river.

Chapter 4

After a week of spending time in various departments, Blythe could find none of Khalil's accusations to be true. She strongly disagreed with him. What made Bloodstone's the great store that it was could be measured by its high-fashion, unique merchandise offerings, the Personal Shoppers who were available to satisfy any customer's unusual requirements, and the store's Couture Salon and in-house designer.

After looking over the ad for the after-Christmas sale, Blythe approved it and gave it back to the copywriter. "It looks great."

She was distracted by a commotion down the hall from her office. Curiosity getting the better of her when it sounded as if a scuffle had ensued, she rose to her feet and rushed to see what was going on. Four members of the security team were struggling with a black man who appeared to be in his late thirties.

"What's going on?" she asked.

"We've got everything under control," one of the store detectives assured her.

"That's not what I asked." Blythe followed them into the security office. "I'll repeat the question. What's going on?"

Charlie, the security manager, spoke up. "We found this

gentleman downstairs trying to return a leather jacket that had
been stolen earlier.''

The man spoke up then. ''My son came home with this
jacket. He said he bought it for fifty dollars from one of his
friends. Well, I didn't believe that for a minute. Finally, I was
able to get the truth. His friend had stolen the jacket from this
store. All I was trying to do was bring the jacket back and keep
my son on the straight and narrow. I come in here to do the
right thing and these people attack me. I've known Mr. Bloodstone for years. I can't believe he'd treat me like this.''

''What is your name, sir?'' Blythe asked softly.

''It's Sam Peters.''

''Mr. Peters, are you talking about my father or my grandfather?''

''I know them both but I'm talking about your grandfather.
I've known him a real long time. Since I was a boy. Is he
here?''

Before Blythe could respond, Nadine entered the office asking, ''Charlie, have you called the police? I want that man
arrested.''

Turning to face her mother, Blythe lowered her voice.
''Mother . . .''

''Stay out of this, Blythe.''

''No! Mr. Peters was trying to return a leather jacket his son
bought from one of his friends. He didn't steal it.''

Nadine peered around Blythe, eyeing the man with distaste.
''The clerk said he was trying to return it for money.''

Sam Peters spoke up. ''I was not! All I did was tell that
woman I wanted to return the damn jacket. She didn't even
ask me nothing—just went and got on the phone. I thought
she was calling a manager or something. I didn't tell that woman
I wanted a cash refund or nothing.'' He shook his head. ''Man,
I don't believe this. Try to do the right thing . . .''

Blythe could hear the fear in his voice. She pulled her mother
to the side. ''Can I speak to you outside?''

Nadine followed her to the door. ''What is it? And please
don't say anything about letting him go in the spirit of Christmas. He's a thief and if we don't press charges . . . well you

know what kind of message we'll be sending to other shop-lifters.''

After making sure they weren't overheard, Blythe said, ''If that were the case, Mother, I'd agree wholeheartedly with you, but that's not. Mr. Peters is not guilty. He was just trying to give it back. Did you get a good look at him?''

''I have looked at him. And from where I was standing, he looks nothing more than a bum. That man is lying through his teeth.''

''It was a misunderstanding,'' Blythe argued. ''I don't think he's lying. I'm going to call Grandfather. I think he needs to know what's going on.''

Nadine blocked her exit. ''You'll do no such thing. What's going on around here, Blythe? Did Harwood give you this job so that you could spy on me?''

She was stunned momentarily by Nadine's question. ''No, Mother. However, in this situation, he should be informed.''

''Well, I don't agree.'' Nadine stepped aside. ''But if you feel you must tell Harwood, go ahead. In the meantime, I'm going to make sure this man gets what he deserves.''

Frustrated, Blythe headed to her office. Closing the door, she reached for her phone. ''Grandfather, please be home,'' she whispered as she dialed.

Tapping her fingers on the desk, Blythe silently counted the number of times the phone rang. After several attempts, she gave up.

Blythe paced back and forth in her office, trying to come up with a solution. She couldn't override Nadine's decision—only her grandfather could do that.

Half an hour later, she tried her grandfather again. Still no answer. ''Where are you?'' Blythe called her father. ''Have you talked to Grandfather?''

''About an hour ago. Is something wrong?''

Blythe related the events to her father.

''Did you try calling him in the car?'' Adam asked.

''Yes and he's not answering.'' Her lips puckered with annoyance.

"Well, keep trying. If I hear from him, I'll have him call the store."

"Thanks, Father." Gritting her teeth, Blythe hung up.

Three hours later, Harwood called her back.

"Grandfather, I'm so glad to finally hear from you. I need you to come to the store."

"Hold on, honey. Now what in tarnation is going on?"

"Where are you?"

"I'm on my way to the store. I should be there in about ten minutes. Now what's going on?"

"A man came in to return a leather jacket that had been stolen—"

Harwood's voice was sharp. "He's trying to get a refund on something he stole?"

"No. He didn't steal the jacket. He says his son bought the jacket from a friend for fifty dollars. His name is Sam Peters."

"Sam just wanted to return the jacket? What's the problem?"

Blythe told him what happened. "He didn't want anything. He was only trying to do what's right."

"Then what's the problem?"

Blythe took a deep breath. "Mother's pressed charges. The police took Mr. Peters down to the station."

"Transfer me to Charlie. No never mind. I'll get there as soon as I can. I'll straighten this mess out."

Blythe hung up and pushed away from her desk. Standing up, she squared her shoulders. "Might as well go on and get this over with." She headed to Nadine's office.

She rapped lightly on the door and entered. "Mother, I just spoke to Grandfather. He's on his way here."

From behind her desk, Nadine glared at her daughter. "I suppose you're pretty pleased with yourself."

"Mother, I'm not trying to do anything behind your back. I believe that Grandfather needed to be aware of what's going on."

"So you've said. Now if you will excuse me ... I have

some work to do.'' Nadine dismissed her with a wave of her hand.

Swallowing the hurt in her throat, Blythe returned to her own office. Once again, she'd let Nadine get to her. When would she ever learn? Closing her eyes, she tried to shut out the pain that was ever-present whenever she allowed herself to feel.

''Why are you looking so down, honey?'' Harwood was standing in the doorway of her office.

''Grandfather, hi. Come on in.''

Harwood sank down into a chair. ''I just left Nadine's office. I have to tell you, we really tied one on.''

''Guess I'd better stay out of her path for the rest of the day.''

Harwood laughed. ''You just let me know if she gives you any flak about this.''

Blythe shrugged in mock resignation. ''I'll be fine. Mother and I never see eye to eye on anything, so this is nothing new.''

He stood up slowly. ''I'm on my way down to the police station to straighten out this mess.''

''I'm glad to hear it. That poor man was only trying to do the right thing.'' Standing up, Blythe moved to walk Harwood to the door. ''Thanks, Grandfather.''

He was watching her intently. ''You know, Blythe, I really hate the way Nadine treats you. It's a shame.''

Shrugging, she said quietly, ''I must have done something really bad. I just wish I knew why she hates me so.''

Harwood looked surprised. ''Hate you? Little darling, I don't cotton to your mother's ways, but I'd never say she hated you.''

''She does. I can feel it.''

''Honey, I don't know about that. I have to go right now, but I want to continue this conversation—''

''Grandfather, it's fine. Really,'' she quickly interjected.

''No. Blythe. We need to discuss this further.'' He kissed her quickly. ''I've got to go.''

She returned to her desk, her jaw tightening. No matter what her grandfather or her father said, she knew the truth. *Her own mother didn't love her.* And she had no idea why.

* * *

"Dinner will be ready in a few minutes, Blythe. Where are you going?" Moira asked. She caught Blythe as she aescended the stairs.

"No, I'm going out to dinner."

Following her back down to the living room, Moira asked, "But why?"

Her lips thinned with irritation. "I don't feel like eating at home. I'll see you later."

"Blythe—"

"I'll be back in a couple of hours."

Moira gave Blythe a penetrating look. "Well, have a nice time."

"I'm going to try." Blythe walked briskly out of the house and headed to her car. She didn't want to run into her mother.

Half an hour later, she sat alone at the Cheesecake Factory, poring over the menu. Blythe hated to eat alone, but she couldn't bear her mother's look of pure disgust anymore.

While she waited for her dinner to arrive, Blythe watched the two women sitting at the table next to hers. They were obviously mother and daughter and very close. As they laughed and gently teased each other, she secretly yearned for a relationship like theirs. For years she'd tried, but all of her efforts were met with rejection.

Before Parker dumped her, he'd told her that nobody could love her—not even her own mother. That one statement had hurt her more deeply than his betrayal ever could. Yet it was true. Every man she'd allowed herself to care for had betrayed her, and they all said the same thing. They just didn't love her.

After that, Blythe decided to harden her heart, but somehow Nadine's rejection of her could still penetrate, cutting her to the quick.

Drawing her attention back to the woman and her daughter, she continued to watch them, her heart filled with envy. When a tall, handsome man joined them, she surmised that this man was the younger woman's husband. He, too, stared adoringly

at her. Blythe shook her head with disgust. Life couldn't have
been more unfair.

The next morning, Blythe jumped out of bed, narrowly missing knocking the clock to the floor. She was afraid that she'd
overslept after getting to bed late. Last night, after her dinner,
she'd decided to take in a movie.

Beneath the hot running water in the shower, she mentally
prepared herself for dealing with her mother. Nadine was still
no doubt fuming over the events of yesterday. Blythe decided
that today, she would not let her mother's barbs get to her. She
dressed quickly and was on her way out the door before anyone
came downstairs.

"What in . . ." Blythe was not prepared for the people
marching back and forth in front of the store. She parked in
her designated space and rushed out of the car. She had to find
out what was going on.

Blythe waded through the sea of people milling about in the
front of the arcade-type windows. As soon as she spotted Khalil,
she rushed over to him. Pulling him aside, she asked, "Khalil,
what is going on?"

"Bloodstone's is being boycotted."

"But why?" A faint thread of hysteria was in her voice.
Nadine would no doubt blame her. "What is the meaning of
this?"

"Surely you're aware of what happened yesterday." Khalil
handed her a copy of his paper.

Her mind was spinning with bewilderment. "But I've spoken
to my grandfather. He's going to drop the charges. Make these
people leave. They will listen to you."

"I can't do that, Blythe."

She was baffled by his attitude. "This is wrong, Khalil. It
was all a misunderstanding." She paused. "Did you set this
up?"

"No, I didn't. I'm here as a reporter. I was told by Mr.
Peters that after security practically dragged him upstairs, he
hadn't been allowed to explain. However, he did mention that

you were the only one who tried to help him. He feels that a white man never would've been treated this way.''

''Why does everything have to become a racial issue? If he had been anybody else, security still would've treated him the same way.''

Nadine screamed. ''Blythe!''

She closed her eyes in frustration. ''Dear Lord. Can this day get any worse?'' Blythe waited for her mother to catch up.

Ignoring Khalil, Nadine asked, ''What are those people doing outside of the store? Why haven't you made them leave. They're scaring the customers.''

Blythe's temper snapped. ''Why don't you go over there and talk to them yourself?''

''Because it's your job.'' Glancing up at Khalil, Nadine stated flatly, ''This is all your fault. Did my daughter call you with this little story?''

Brushing past Nadine, Blythe stated, ''Mother, I don't have time for this. I've got to figure out something.''

Khalil blocked Nadine's path. ''Mrs. Bloodstone, Blythe had nothing to do with this article. Mr. Peters contacted a member of my staff directly.''

''I see. Well, it was a misunderstanding. So print that in that newspaper of yours.'' Nadine stomped off.

Khalil walked briskly, trying to catch up with Blythe. ''Will you slow down a minute?''

''Khalil, I have to go. I have to find a way to handle this problem.''

''Blythe . . .''

She regarded him with impassive coldness. ''Please leave me alone.'' She started walking faster. ''I have to go. In case you haven't noticed, I've got a mess on my hands.''

Khalil watched Blythe get on the elevator. It was clear that she was upset. He wasn't sure of the reason. Was it her mother or was it the people protesting outside? Against his better judgment, he stepped on the elevator and headed up to the management offices. He found Blythe in her office.

She glanced up from her monitor, frowning. ''Can't you take a hint? What do you want, Khalil? I have a lot of work to do.''

He sat down without invitation. "I'm going to give you a chance to tell your side of the story." His steady gaze bore into her in silent expectation.

"What good will it do? Those people have all made up their minds about what happened." Blythe regarded him with a speculative gaze.

"I don't know, Blythe, but it might help." His eyes darkened with emotion. He had no idea why she affected him the way that she did. It was going to be a struggle to keep their relationship on a strictly business level.

She leaned back in her chair, her arms folded across her chest. Her head was puzzled by new thoughts. "And you suddenly want to help me. Why?"

Khalil stated simply, "I don't want to be your enemy."

"All we've done is move our store to Beverly Hills, Khalil. Why are we being attacked? Everything that goes on in the store is suddenly turned into something to do with race. What are we supposed to say to defend ourselves against people who refuse to move on past slavery?"

Her eyes held him totally mesmerized. Khalil felt he could become lost in their soft brown depths and never want to escape. He pressed himself to pay attention. "Blythe, I really don't think you're seeing the clear picture. You're not being fair."

"I'm not being fair." She shook her head. "I really don't believe you. You know what? This is what I have to say—"

"Do you mind if I tape our interview?" In his hand, Khalil held up a tiny recorder.

She flung her hand in simple despair. "Fine with me. It's not a simple matter for stores to be on the lookout for the stereotypical shoplifter. The most significant month for shoplifting is December. And there's no age that is considered typical. Our store security watches *everyone.*" He watched as she moistened her lips with the tip of her tongue and wondered why she seemed so nervous.

Blythe continued. "Our employees are given strict instructions to notify security on suspicious returns. The leather jacket had been stolen. However, the employee made a rash judgment and so did the store detective.'' As she talked, Blythe played with the pearl necklace she wore.

"And so you're saying this could have happened to *any* customer, regardless of race?''

Blythe nodded. "Exactly. I'm not saying this excuses what happened, but we, as retailers, have to do what we must to deter or minimize the amount of merchandise that is stolen. And due to the fact that we have such a liberal return policy, we have to be extremely careful there as well.''

"Why do your store detectives follow black customers around?''

Blythe glared at him before responding. "Our employees are trained to be aware of what's going on in their departments. They are instructed to make customers feel that they are not alone but very much in view. That privilege extends to our black customers as well.''

"You call that a privilege?'' Khalil asked, his tone mocking.

"Consider it good customer service. If the customer's action arouses suspicion, a certain procedure is followed.''

"Is that when the salesperson discreetly alerts security?''

There was an edge to his voice. Khalil stared at her with wide, questioning eyes. When his gaze froze on her lips, she asked softly, "What would you have us do?''

He was stirred by her emotional plea. "I don't think anyone is upset over the fact that you have to protect your store. It's that blacks seem to be targeted as shoplifters. Stealing is not limited to blacks by any means. It was recently reported in a major newspaper that a mayor in Washington somewhere was arrested for stealing. There are always stories of affluent people caught trying to take merchandise from stores without paying.''

"I know what you're saying. I will admit that there is a possibility that maybe some of our security may be a little overzealous but—''

"Overzealous?'' Was she serious, he wondered.

"Yes. This Friday we're going to have a store-wide meeting and we will be addressing this issue. We're going to insure that nothing like this happens again.''

"What will you all do if Mr. Sam Peters decides to file a lawsuit for false arrest?"

Blythe took a deep breath. "I hope it doesn't come to that, but should it . . . we'll have to just wait and see what happens. Anything else?"

Khalil asked a few more questions before turning off the tape recorder. "One last question. Can we have dinner sometime?" The expression in his dark eyes seemed to plead for friendship.

"Are you asking me out on a date?"

He nodded, his eyes never leaving her face.

"I don't think so, Khalil. I don't date."

"Why not?" He wanted to know. "Are you engaged or something?"

Blythe shook her head. "No, it's nothing like that."

"Then what is it?" he persisted.

"You're nosy."

"Well, what is it?"

Blythe looked away hastily, then shifted restlessly in her chair. "Let's just say that love hasn't been very kind to me. I feel it's best if I just leave it alone."

"That sounds like a lonely existence."

Blythe swallowed hard, trying to manage a feeble answer. "Maybe, but at least I won't be . . ." She stopped herself.

"You were saying?" Khalil prompted.

"It's nothing. I'm iust not interested in going out."

"Not even dinner between two friends?" he suggested.

She said softly, "But we're not friends."

Even as she spoke, the yearning in her eyes locked with his. "We could be," he said softly.

"Good day, Mr . Sanford."

For a moment, Khalil wondered what it would feel like to kiss her. But just as quickly as it had come, he squelched the thought. He gave her one last glance before leaving.

* * *

How strange, Blythe thought. This was the same man whose paper had trashed the store's reputation, and now he wanted to help her. On top of that, Khalil had asked her out on a date.

She stood up and turned, looking out of the window and wondering at her inability to be loved.

Love . . . she had the love of her father and her grandfather. Why wasn't that enough? She still craved the love of her mother and the love of a man. She wanted a family—a loving family and children.

Blythe had grown up with everything money could buy, but nothing compared to the happiness that only love could produce. As a child, when her parents were gone, she would sneak into their room. Hiding in the closet, she would often fall asleep there, one of her mother's sweaters or expensive blouses wrapped around her. It was the only way to feel close to her mother.

Once Nadine had found her there. She had gathered her up in her arms, but Blythe stiffened and pulled away from her. In her mind, she had been ashamed because her mother had seen her great need to be loved. After that, she'd gone deep inside of herself where she vowed she would never allow herself to appear so pathetic.

Just for a moment, she wished desperately that she were still able to hope, dream and love. But it wasn't to be. She sighed in resignation and continued to stare out over the city.

Chapter 5

"Come on in, Son. You look like you've been to hell and back."

Khalil's laughter floated up from his throat. "No, Dad. Just had a real long day."

James Sanford followed his son into the family room. "Kuiana stopped by earlier today. I'm so glad to see she's putting on some weight finally. That girl was too skinny.

"She told me that Mom asked her if she was pregnant."

James's smile deepened into laughter. "I wouldn't doubt it. She's been having some dream about fish."

Iris met them in the living room. Rolling her eyes at her husband, she stated, "Every time I dream about fish, someone close to me is expecting. I've never been wrong in the past. Anything you want to tell me, Son?"

"Mom, I'm not pregnant." Khalil kissed her cheek. "Happy birthday."

Iris burst into laughter. "Why, I ought to take you over my knee . . ." She picked up a pillow and threw it at Khalil.

Dodging the pillow, he grinned. "You can relax. I'm not going to have any children. At least not right now. I'm not even seeing anyone right now."

Her usually clear, observant eyes were now clouded with confusion. "Well if not you or Kuiana, then who is it?"

Khalil eyed his father. They both shrugged.

Iris waved her hands. "Well, whoever it is, it'll come to light."

Reaching into his pocket, Khalil pulled out a small, gift-wrapped box. "This is for you, Mom." Watching his mother tear into her present brought a smile to his face. Iris loved receiving presents and it thrilled Khalil to see the look of pure joy on her face each time he bought her one.

Her eyes were tear bright. "This ring is beautiful, Son. And it's my birthstone."

"I'm glad you like it."

"Like it. Honey, I love it."

"Well, why don't we head into the kitchen," James said. "I'm starved." He helped his wife stand. "Come on, honey."

Khalil laughed. "I'm right behind you, Dad."

"I fried some catfish, made some cole slaw and some hush puppies."

"Kuiana's going to wish she'd come for lunch."

"I'm going to send her a plate back with you."

After stuffing himself, Khalil pushed back from the table. "I don't feel like going back to work. I'm so full that all I want to do is lay around the house."

"If I must say so, I outdid myself today," James announced.

Iris smiled. "You sure did, hon. Lunch was wonderful. I don't know how you're ever going to top this."

James grinned and winked at Khalil. "Oh, just you wait. Tonight, we're going to have a real good time. You're only fifty-five once. We're going to make it a night to remember."

Iris looked from Khalil to his father. "What have you all gone and done?"

"It's a surprise," Khalil whispered as he leaned down to kiss her cheek. "I hate to leave but I've got to head back to the office."

His parents walked him to the door. "Don't forget the plate for Kuiana. We'll see you tonight."

Khalil waved to them as he drove away. He was looking forward to the party tonight.

Justin was standing in the driveway when Blythe pulled up. Resisting the urge to run him down, she turned off her car and parked. Getting out, Blythe asked, "What are you doing here?"

Leaning over, Justin attempted to kiss his sister on the cheek. He looked away in anguish when she recoiled. Straightening his tie, he mumbled, "I'm still your brother." In awkward silence, he waited for her to unlock the front door. "I came to see Father and I want to talk to you."

Blythe held the door open, stepping aside to let him enter. "Talk to me about what? I can't imagine what you would have to say to me."

"Don't do this." His inflection was adamant.

"Well, what is this all about?" Blythe ripped out the words impatiently.

"I'll tell you when Moira gets here."

"Moira? Justin, what's going on? Is this about Mother?"

They stared at each other across a sudden ringing silence. Finally, he replied, "It's about all of us, actually."

Blythe's medium brown eyes darkened as Justin held her gaze. "I see. Well, I'm not planning to hang around the house this evening, so you'd better hurry up and tell me whatever it is you have to say."

The corner of his mouth twisted with exasperation. "Blythe, we'll talk when Moira gets here."

Winston entered the room. "Hello, Blythe, Justin. How are you both?"

"I'm fine, Winston. Justin is here to visit with Father. Is he awake?"

"He's up. In fact, he should be coming out in a moment."

"Thanks, Winston." When the nurse left the room, Blythe glared at Justin. "You could at least pretend to be civil."

An expression of contempt slid over his face. "I don't like the way he looks at you. You'd better watch yourself around him."

"You've got a lot of nerve," Blythe responded. "Winston has been nothing but kind to me. Besides, I guess in your eyes, Parker is one to be trusted, right?"

"This is not about Parker. All I'm saying is that Winston's attracted to you," Justin stated flatly.

"Well it's none of your business. I can find my own man, thank you." Blythe headed to the stairs. "I'm going upstairs to change. I'll come down when Moira gets here."

Upstairs, Blythe wondered what Justin and Moira could possibly want to discuss with her. Standing before her mirror, she fingered her hair. She could hear Moira's voice and her laughter. Sighing, she headed to her door. "Let's get this over with."

Moira and Justin were seated side by side on the sofa.

Her arms folded across her chest, she said, "Okay. What do you two want from me?"

"Why don't you just sit down and hear us out?" Justin suggested. "You know you really need to lose that attitude."

"You need to—" Blythe began.

Moira held up her hand. "Will you two please stop fighting? Justin, you came here to talk."

"Talk about what?" Blythe asked impatiently. "Why is it such a big secret?"

Moira spoke up. "Blythe, we've been thinking that you should spend Thanksgiving with us."

Shaking her head, Blythe said, "No way! There is no way I'm going to Barbados. Thanksgiving is a day for families and—"

"Your family will be in Barbados, Blythe," Justin stated.

"Our father won't," she countered. "Or is he not a part of this family anymore?" Blythe gazed at her brother and sister. "Well?"

Moira flushed red. "I didn't think Father wanted to go." She leaned forward and lowered her voice. "He never wants to go anywhere anymore."

"Did anybody bother to ask him?"

Justin and Moira exchanged looks, but neither said anything.

Easing down on the arm of the sofa, Blythe said, "The only way I'll even consider going to Barbados is if Father goes."

"I suppose that's reasonable," Justin acknowledged.

Moira smiled. "See, it wasn't so bad. Us talking like this."

Rolling her eyes heavenward, Blythe didn't respond.

Peeking out of the window, Moira announced, "Mother's home."

Standing up, Blythe said, "Well if we're done, I'm going back upstairs. I need to work on the window schedule before I leave."

Justin stood up swiftly and looped his hand around Blythe's arm to keep her from leaving. "You can have someone else work on window displays. Why do you always disappear when Mother's around?"

Blythe's animosity toward her brother burned hot within. Snatching her arm away, she sniped, "Lay off me, Justin. Now I said I had some work to do. That's it."

Nadine entered and the room grew silent. Surveying the faces of her children, she asked, "Has something happened to your father?"

"No, he's fine," Blythe responded. She brushed past her mother saying, "I was just on my way upstairs."

Bewildered, Nadine watched as Blythe took the steps two at a time. Turning to face her other children, she asked, "Okay, what's really going on?"

"Khalil, this must have cost a fortune!" Iris whirled around slowly, admiring the elaborate decorations of the private dining room at Gina's. "This place is incredible."

"I can't take all of the credit. Actually it was a joint venture between Dad, Kuiana and myself."

"You all are so sweet." Iris wiped at her eyes with a tissue.

"I thought we were just going to have a small family dinner."

Kuiana joined them. Hugging her mother, she said, "Happy birthday, Mom. You look beautiful."

"Hey baby. I can't believe you all did this for me. All of my friends are here . . ." Iris waved at a passing couple. "This is so nice."

Khalil ran his fingers through his sister's hair. "You look beautiful yourself."

She smiled. "Thanks, big brother. Oh, did you speak to the caterer? About the special plate for Grandpa?"

Khalil nodded and scanned the room. "Where is Grandpa anyway? I saw him earlier."

Turning around, Kuiana searched the crowd. She pointed. "He's over there with Aunt Maida."

James Sanford cleared his throat and offered Iris his arm. "I'm gonna take your mom to our table, Son. They're ready to start serving."

"Okay. I'll be over there in a minute. Sis, you go with them and I'll be right back."

"Where are you running off to?" Kuiana wanted to know.

"I'm going to get Mom's present out of the car."

Lowering her voice, Kuiana asked, "Do you think she has any idea?"

Khalil shook his head. "She doesn't."

"Perfect." Kuiana rubbed her hands together gleefully. "I can't wait to see Mom's face when she sees her brand-new computer and printer. She's always wanted to write. Now she can."

He nodded in agreement. "Dad's built her an office of her own."

Kuiana's mouth dropped open in shock. "He did? I thought he was building that room for himself. He never told me."

Khalil laughed. "That's because he didn't want you to tell Mom."

"I wouldn't have."

Wrapping his arms around Kuiana, he led her toward their table. "Go on, Sis. You join them at the table and I'll be right back before they miss me. Let's give Mom the time of her life."

"If you happen to see Danny outside, would you please send him in this direction. He seems to have gotten lost."

"Sure." Khalil laughed. "You are always losing your boy-friend."

"No, I'm not. He just seems to know everybody in town. Every time we go somewhere, he ends up talking."

Khalil stepped outside into the cold night air. Seeing couples coming in and out of the restaurant made him realize that he was tired of being alone. He wanted a woman. Blythe Bloodstone crossed his mind and she'd made herself as unattainable as a dream.

From the excuse that she'd given him, it was obvious to Khalil that she had been hurt in the past. Rubbing his chin, he wondered at the reason she was beginning to figure so prominently in his life—it was clear as day that they were from two different worlds.

Spotting Danny, Khalil enlisted his help in bringing in his mother's presents.

After another quiet dinner alone, Blythe returned home and headed up to her room. She had just stepped out of the shower when she heard a knock on her door. Rushing into her robe, she quickly opened the door to find Nadine standing there. "Mother?"

"May I come in?"

Nadine looked as uneasy as Blythe. Wrapping the belt of her robe tightly around her, she replied quietly, "It's your house, Mother."

Nadine eased by her, wringing her hands. "I'm s-sorry about the things I said earlier today at the store. I never meant to hurt you."

Blythe shrugged nonchalantly. "It's over and done with."

Leaning against the pine dresser, Nadine said, "After you left, I spoke to your father about Barbados. Would you believe that he's agreed to come with us? We'll be a real family. That is, if you'll also join us. It's been a long time since we've all been together on a vacation." A wry smile curled her lips.

Hope sprang into her chest and Blythe's body tingled with excitement. "Really? Father's really going to come?"

Nadine smiled. "Yes. Now will you agree to join us?"

Blythe nodded slowly. "If Father goes."

"Dear, I'm sorry about the way I've been acting. It's just that I've been under a lot of pressure with the store and . . ." Nadine's voice faded to a hushed stillness. Flinging her hands in resignation, she sank down on a fabric-covered bench positioned at the foot of Blythe's bed. "It seems that I'm always apologizing to you about something. Why is that?"

Blythe turned away from her mother, closing her eyes in an effort to control her temper. Finally she managed to say, "I don't know, Mother. Why on earth should you apologize to me?"

"Blythe, I don't think I like your tone. I caution you to remember that I'm still your mother."

"As if I could ever forget." She turned, facing Nadine. "However, it seems that you only remember that little fact whenever you feel I'm being disrespectful. It would be nice if you'd remember more often."

Nadine's eyes sparkled with her anger. "I've tried so hard to be here for you, Blythe, but you continually push me away. I don't have any idea what you want from me."

"Nothing. I don't want anything from you. Actually, I take that back. You're always demanding that I respect you—well, I would like the same. I would appreciate it if you'd extend me the same courtesy."

Nadine was silent. She stood up slowly. "You were always a difficult child to understand."

Blythe blocked her exit. "Mother, I want to know something."

"What is it?"

"Did you ever really try to understand me? Can you honestly say that you tried?"

She nodded. "I will be honest with you. I did, but after a while, it became much too hard, so I stopped." Nadine kissed her cheek somewhat formally. Reaching for the doorknob, she said, "Rest well."

"You, too."

Just as Nadine opened the door, Moira was passing by. "Mother! I thought you'd be in bed by now. Hi, Blythe."

Nadine smiled. "I'm on my way there."

Moira wrapped her arms tightly around her mother and kissed her cheek long and lovingly. Blythe winced and looked away. She fought back the tears that burned against her eyelids.

"Good night," she whispered as she closed her door on the affectionate scene between mother and daughter.

Blythe wandered slowly around her room. This room with its elegant furnishing was not her room. Her focus lingered on the bed. That cold, lonely bed was not hers either. This house would never be her home. She would never be happy here. Sighing, Blythe sadly acknowledged that this beautifully decorated house was only a very small part of the problem.

Blythe fell on her bed in tears. How much she wished her mother loved her. In her mind, the child in her cried, *What did I do wrong? Why does she hate me so?*

Chapter 6

Khalil was transported to the fifth floor in Bloodstone's glass-walled elevator. He noticed that the materials used in constructing the store included lots of brass, travertine and other luxury elements. He assumed that they were used to distinguish the store from all others. Each floor was unique in that each was given a specific street name.

He walked along the narrow hallway to where the merchandising offices were located. Standing in the outer office, Khalil stopped to think. What was he doing here? He'd originally believed that coming over here was the right thing to do, but now his better judgment intervened. Maybe Blythe didn't want his help. Khalil was about to leave when he heard her call out.

"Peggy, is that you?"

Blythe's assistant wasn't in her outer office. Khalil waited a few minutes before he made his decision. *Well, I'm here now . . .* He strolled straight into her office.

She glanced up briefly. "I thought we said everything yesterday. Right now I don't have time to deal with you, Khalil." Blythe glanced down at her watch. "I've got a plane to catch in about four hours, so say what you've come to say. Please make it quick."

He took a seat. "I think you'd better make time. Those people marching outside your store are very serious. Leaving right now is not a good idea."

"It won't do any good. Those people downstairs have already made up their minds. Right now, all I want to do is get out of here. I only came to pick up some papers."

"Where are you off to in such a hurry? Leaving right in the middle of a crisis can only cause more harm to the store's reputation."

She rifled him with an unreadable stare. "If you must know—I'm going to Barbados for Thanksgiving."

Shifting in his chair, Khalil said, "So I guess I was wrong about you." He was disappointed that she would run away like this. He never figured Blythe to back down from a fight. Not after the way she'd charged into his office.

"What are you talking about?"

His eyes bored into hers. "I thought you cared about the store."

"I do." She rose to her feet and grabbed her attache case. Blythe hoped Khalil would take the hint and leave. He didn't.

"You're certainly not acting like it. Running off to Barbados for a vacation." He shrugged. "It doesn't matter what I think."

Blythe's eyes flashed with outrage. "You're right. It doesn't. But for your information, I love this store and I care what happens to it. I can't stop those people from marching outside of the store—even if I canceled my trip. If there was something I could do, I would do it in a heartbeat."

"You don't know what might happen. Are you willing to take the risk?" Khalil wanted to know.

After a moment of uncomfortable silence, Blythe threw down her attache case. "You win. I'll delay my trip."

"I think you've made a wise decision."

She sat on the edge of her desk, her arms folded across her chest. "I'm so glad you're pleased."

Khalil bent his head slightly forward. "I detect a tinge of sarcasm. Why is that? In fact, I've noticed that you seem to be in a permanent state of bitterness."

Stiffening, Blythe stated, "I don't have to listen to you bad mouth me." She stood up as if ready to take flight.

He rose quickly, blocking her path. "Do you always run off when you don't want to face the truth?"

She lifted her chin, meeting his icy gaze straight on. With hands on her hips, Blythe demanded, "Khalil Sanford, move out of my way or—"

He raised an eyebrow. "Or what? Are you violent, too?" Blythe disturbed him in a way that he'd never experienced. She radiated a vitality that drew him like a magnet.

"Why are you harassing me? What have I done to you?"

"Nothing. I'm just curious. Why are you always in such a rotten mood? You do know that you're going to be a wrinkled old prune if you keep frowning all of the time. I have yet to see a real smile on your face."

"Maybe I have nothing to smile about," Blythe snapped. "Besides my gums show and I hate that."

A wry smile touched his lips. "I didn't say you had to go around with a wide grin on your face."

Blythe's mouth dropped open in surprise before she gave way to laughter, holding a hand over her mouth. She went back to her chair and sat down.

"You have a beautiful laugh. You should do it more often." He fought the sudden urge to draw her into his arms.

Looking away, Blythe mumbled, "Thanks, I guess."

Their eyes locked and both could see the attraction mirrored in the other's gaze.

Drawing a mask over his emotions, Khalil asked, "You know what I think?"

"I'm sure you're going to tell me."

"I think you need to stop being so serious. You need to loosen up and have some fun." He crossed the room slowly and stood before her desk.

Blythe looked up at him. "So how much do I owe you, Dr. Sanford? Or is the clock still running?"

"This session was on me."

"When does the article come out?" she asked as she pushed

herself to a standing position. Blythe grabbed her things once more and came around the desk.

"It'll be in Friday's paper," Khalil replied as he walked her out.

"Will I get to see it beforehand?"

He nodded. "I'll have a copy sent over here tomorrow morning." Heading toward the elevator, he asked, "Are you going down?"

"Not just yet. I need to speak with my mother and let her know there's been a change in my plans."

After Khalil left, Blythe wandered into her mother's office. Her mother was packing up to leave, too.

Nadine glanced up and said, "I'm on my way home. How about you?"

Blythe took a seat. "Do you have a minute, Mother? I need to talk to you about something."

Dropping down into her chair, Nadine asked, "What is it?"

"Khalil just left here. He interviewed me yesterday for an article on the Peters incident and the boycott. He's going to send an advance copy over tomorrow."

A soft gasp escaped Nadine. "You actually gave him an interview?"

Blythe took a quick sharp breath. "What would you have me do? He's promised to send me an advance copy."

"He's going to twist your words around. Make you look like an idiot."

"I don't think so. Also, I've been thinking about staying here and trying to talk to the people that are outside marching."

Nadine was aghast. "What on earth for?"

"I want to put an end to this. We're into the Christmas season. A boycott is the last thing the store needs."

"Are you backing out on our trip to Barbados?"

She was clearly surprised that her mother had asked her that. "No. I'm delaying my trip for a day—two days at the most." Gazing into Nadine's eyes, she replied, "It might be a good idea if you'd delay your flight also. I think you should be here—we'll meet with them together. It's good PR."

Nadine shook her head. "Oh, no. I can't do that. I simply

don't think I'd be any good here. You were always so much better with people like that.'' She stood up and straightened her suit. "I'll have Peggy change your flight arrangements.''

"I'll take care of them, Mother. I'm not real sure when I'm leaving.''

"Are you going to join us? You're not trying to back out on us, are you?''

Their eyes met. Blythe felt something unidentifiable run through her. "I wouldn't do that.''

Nadine relaxed. "Why don't you call Harwood and let him know what you've planned. He'll probably fly home to be with you. As he always throws in my face—it's his store.'' She grabbed her purse and stood up. "You can use my phone.''

After Nadine left, Blythe picked up the phone to call her grandfather. She knew her mother hoped that he would be upset and blow up at her. Blythe prayed that Nadine was wrong.

After her call she felt much better. Her grandfather supported her one hundred percent—even offering to fly home to be with her tomorrow. Blythe had assured him that he should stay and enjoy his visit with his sister.

Khalil crossed her mind, and she hoped he would be there. Standing up, Blythe gathered her courage and headed downstairs. It was time to face the men and women who were outside marching.

The next morning, when Blythe arrived at her office, she found a large envelope on her desk. It was from Khalil. She turned around at the sound of footsteps.

Peggy announced, "The messenger brought it this morning. I knew you were expecting it so I brought it straight to your office.''

"Thanks.'' Blythe dropped down into her chair and opened the packet. It was a copy of the *Heritage Reporter*. Khalil included a note that said: *I wanted you to see this first. Tell me what you think. The newspaper will hit the stands this evening.*

She read the article, taking everything in. Khalil had done

as promised. He'd written an article that clearly stated Blood-stone's position on the Peters incident. While he didn't take one side over the other, Khalil was very objective in suggesting ways that the whole episode could have been avoided. Although it didn't absolve the store of any wrongdoing, she had to admit the article was a good one. Blythe was pleased. She reached for the phone.

"Hello, this is Blythe Bloodstone. May I speak to Khalil Sanford, please?"

"Just one moment," Caryn stated flatly. "I'll see if he's in."

Blythe smiled. She knew the receptionist didn't like her. She made a mental note to apologize to Caryn the next time she saw her. She felt an apology on the phone wouldn't be enough. Khalil's bass voice came on the line.

"Hello, Blythe."

"Khalil, I just read the article. It was very positive and it gave me an idea. I've invited all of those people to come upstairs for a meeting. I think I should talk to them or, better yet, listen to what they have to say. I'm going to ask Sam Peters here, too. We're meeting in an hour. I'm hoping you'll be here, too."

"What are you trying to accomplish by doing that?" Khalil questioned.

"Well, obviously there's a problem and I need to find out what it is. Hopefully I'll be able to come up with a solution that will make everyone happy."

"I see."

"You don't think it's a good idea, do you?"

"I didn't say that, Blythe."

"You didn't have to. All I'm trying to do is salvage something from the damage that's been done. I need to find out what's wrong."

"Well, I think you're doing the right thing. I guess you couldn't convince your mother to delay her flight."

"No, she left me here to face the lions alone."

"I'm sure you can handle it."

Khalil's voice was soothing. "I guess. I'll just be relieved to get this public apology over with. Grandfather offered to fly back but I told him it wasn't necessary.''

Khalil smiled. ''You'll be fine. And I'll be there.''

''Is that supposed to make me feel better?'' Blythe was not about to let him know that it did. She smiled at his laughter.

''I've got a call coming in and I've got to take it. I'll see you in an hour, okay?''

''Thanks, Khalil.'' Still smiling, Blythe hung up. Peggy, her assistant, entered the office. ''I have everything set up in the cafeteria.''

''Thanks, Peggy. I hope this works.''

''I don't think you'll have a problem. They've agreed to hear what you have to say. That was the hard part, I think.''

''I suppose you're right.'' When she was alone, Blythe closed her eyes, praying for the right words to come.

An hour later, Sam Peters and Khalil arrived. Knowing that Khalil was there made her feel better. Blythe mentally prepared herself for her meeting.

She met with the men and women for more than two hours.

On her way back to her office, Khalil approached her. Against his better judgment, he put his arms around her, drawing her flush against him. ''For whatever it's worth, I think you did a good job. Sam Peters seemed to be pleased.'' Drawing a mask over his emotions, he released her with reluctance.

''That's all that matters, isn't it?'' Blythe asked as she sat down at her desk, looking as shaken as Khalil felt.

''I wouldn't say that. What's wrong? Are you upset about something?''

Blythe shook her head. ''No, it's just that I think my mother should have been the one doing the apologizing.''

''I agree. But the fact is, she wasn't.'' Khalil stood up slowly. ''I'm starving. Would you like to have lunch? Sort of a little celebration?''

Smiling, Blythe leaned forward, her elbows resting on her desk. ''You don't give up, do you?''

''It's just lunch. I'll tell you what. Have lunch with me this one time and I promise that we'll not become friends.''

In spite of herself, Blythe burst into laughter. "I really don't know about you, Khalil."

He reached for her hand. "Come on. Lunch is on me."

Blythe flushed warmly over the touch of his hand on hers. As they headed out of her office, she said, "We can eat in the private dining room."

"You don't have to worry. Having lunch with me won't bind us together in any way. I meant what I said. You are under no obligation to become my friend. However, I feel I must warn you that you're missing one hell of a good time."

She laughed. Blythe had to admit it felt good to laugh. She hadn't done so in such a long time. "You're crazy."

"I've been called that a time or two. I just love having a good time. Life is too short to be so serious all of the time."

Over her menu, she eyed Khalil as he studied the selections. Blythe couldn't deny the spark of excitement at the prospect of getting to know him. What harm could it do? She found him charming, funny and comforting—all at the same time. His voice cut through her reverie.

After the waiter took their orders, Khalil broke the silence. "I remember reading that you'd moved to England or somewhere a few years back. When did you return home?"

"I was living in Paris. I moved back here about four months ago."

"How do you like being back?"

"It's good. I miss Paris and my best friend, but it's good to be home. I really missed my father and my grandfather." She was relieved to see the waiter bringing their food.

Khalil noted that she'd said nothing about her mother or her siblings. He longed to ask her why, but thought better of it. He didn't want to put Blythe on the defensive. He sliced off a piece of his baked chicken.

"So what about you?" Blythe asked. "Have you always lived in Los Angeles?"

He nodded. "Born and raised. My family's originally from Mississippi though. There have been a few occasions that I've thought about moving away, but things never really worked out.''

"I see."

They exchanged a subtle look of amusement.

"I gather you never married, then?"

Blythe nodded. "You gather right. I've been a bridesmaid but never a bride."

"I almost made it to the altar once."

Blythe looked up at Khalil. "What happened?"

He smiled, seeing the gleam of interest in her eyes. "We decided that although we wanted to get married, we didn't want to be married to each other."

"I was engaged when I moved to France. He was an artist and the picturesque city of Paris was his inspiration."

"Why did you two break up?"

"He met someone else. A few months after we moved there, he decided my purse was not as large as he originally thought, so he dumped me for a bigger purse."

"You're still angry about it," Khalil observed. "Do you still love him?"

"No, I don't love him," she replied quickly. "I guess I'm still very angry because I never saw it. I've met his type many times before." Blythe reached for her water glass. She drank slowly. "He and my brother are best friends. I guess I thought knowing him all of my life made him different."

"He was more interested in your money than your love."

"You've summed it up nicely. The only thing is—I don't have any money. I had to work for a living just like the next person. Parker refused to believe that."

"I've met a few gold diggers in my day. I know how you feel."

Blythe took a frank and admiring look at Khalil. "What ever happened to old-fashioned love?"

His dark brown eyes were tender. "I think it's still out there."

"Well, it obviously doesn't know my address."

"I think people should just take time and really get to know each other. Too many times, fools rush in."

"You're probably right." Blythe stabbed at her food. "I've

done that, too. I've come to the conclusion that love is just not for me.''

When they finished eating, Khalil walked her back to her office.

Outside of her door, Blythe paused and said, ''Thank you for lunch. I have to admit I had a wonderful time. I haven't enjoyed myself like this in a while. I almost hate going back to work.''

''Then why go back? Since you're leaving this evening, just take the rest of the day off.''

''Actually, I'm only going to put in another hour or so and then I'm calling it a day.''

''When does your plane leave?''

''Three thirty.''

''I hope you have a good time in Barbados. Relax and enjoy yourself, okay?''

She smiled. ''Yes, doctor. Anything else?''

''Yes. Happy Thanksgiving to you and your family. Remember what the day is all about. It doesn't matter where you are— just be thankful.'' Khalil checked his watch. ''I'd better get going. You have a safe trip.''

''Happy Thanksgiving to you and your family, Khalil. And I'll keep everything you've said in mind.'' Blythe held her hand out to him.

He laughed and embraced her. ''I'll see you when you get back.''

Blythe entered the huge empty house. Everyone was gone, including her father. The grandfather clock located in the living room struck two o'clock, and its chimes sounded musically throughout the quiet house. She rushed up the stairs to her bedroom.

Thoughts of Khalil Sanford kept filling her head. Before leaving her, he'd asked for her phone number. Blythe hoped he would call her upon her return. Although she'd originally balked at the idea of getting to know him, being around him today had given her cause to change her mind.

Grabbing her luggage, Blythe headed downstairs and to her car. She needed to be on her way to the airport. Her plane wouldn't be leaving for another hour and a half, but there could be traffic and other unforeseen delays. If she missed this plane, Blythe knew she would not go to Barbados.

An hour later, she was seated on the plane. Blythe searched her travel bag for something to read. In truth, she was not looking forward to this trip, but she would enjoy spending time with her father.

Chapter 7

Barbados

After her nap, Blythe found her father staring out of the patio doors. She joined him in admiring the view. The silver sand beaches contrasted against the rugged Atlantic coastline. "Are you having a good time?"

Adam turned his wheelchair around facing her. "To tell you the truth, I would have had a better time if I'd stayed at home. I'm glad you didn't chicken out on me."

Blythe laughed. "I was tempted to miss the flight yesterday. You know, we can leave right now if you're not happy. I don't mind. Mother, Moira and Justin are off seeing the Andromeda Flower Gardens in Bathsheba."

"We're back," Nadine announced as she flounced into the room. "You two should have joined us. It was wonderful. There were individual gardens of hibiscus, orchids, cactus, ferns, palms and a host of other plants."

"We weren't invited. You all were on your way out when Father and I came to breakfast."

"You could have said you wanted to come. We would have waited on you." Nadine sat down prettily on a rattan sofa. "By the way, in case you both have forgotten, we came here to be a family, so you two are not going anywhere. I overheard what you were saying."

"Nadine . . ."

"No, Adam. We're going to stay," she said with a slight smile of defiance. "We'll just have to make the best of our vacation."

"I'm sure we won't be missed," Blythe interjected. "You, Moira and Justin seem to be having a wonderful time of it."

"Blythe, you don't have to stay holed up here. That was your choice." A sudden thin chill hung on the edge of Nadine's words.

"And what about Father? What choice does he have?"

Nadine glowered at her. "Why must you challenge me so?"

Blythe gazed at her father. She could read the pleading in his eyes. Her eyes downcast, she said, "I'm sorry, Mother."

"It's fine, Blythe. No need to fight over this. Turning to her husband, she asked, "Adam, why don't you join us on the beach? Winston can assist you into a lounge chair."

"Please, Father?" Moira pleaded from across the room as she entered. "You haven't been outside of this cottage. The weather's so pretty."

A shadow crossed Adam's face. "I'm feeling kind of tired. I think I'll lay down for a nap."

"Can't you come out for a little while?" Blythe pleaded. "It'll be nice, don't you think?"

He stroked her cheek. "I'm really tired."

"What about you, Blythe? Will you come with us?" Nadine asked.

"Sure. Just give me a minute to change into my swimsuit." Blythe ran to her room, her heart filled with hope. Maybe this time she and her mother would bond.

Putting on a black one-piece, Blythe searched frantically for the matching wrap skirt. By the time she made it downstairs, her mother and siblings were heading down to the beach. She rushed after them.

"What took you so long?" Moira asked. "I thought you'd changed your mind."

"I couldn't find my skirt."

"You look good in that. I tried that suit on but it didn't do anything for me."

Nadine frowned. "Why do you wear so much black, Blythe? One would think that you are in a constant state of mourning."

"Black is my favorite color," she stated simply.

"You should add some color to your wardrobe."

Blythe said nothing. Moira glanced over, imparting a sympathetic smile. "I think you look great in black."

They found a spot and set about laying the huge blanket down and the basket of food. Instead of sitting with them, Blythe chose to lay her towel a few feet away and sit down. Nadine had already started in on her, so she decided to take herself out of the line of fire.

"You never told me how your little meeting went."

"I wasn't sure you'd be interested, Mother."

Nadine sighed loudly. "I'm interested in anything that has to do with the store."

Blythe couldn't refute her on that point. She could feel her siblings' eyes on her. They were all waiting to hear what happened.

"Well," Nadine prompted.

"The meeting went well, I think. Our black customers had a lot to say. They feel that we've changed since moving to Beverly Hills."

"Changed? How?" Nadine asked. "If we've changed then it's certainly for the better."

"They don't seem to think so. For one thing, they don't like the fact that we have a predominantly white staff now. And they don't like being watched or followed by security whenever they're in the store. They would like to see more black employees hired."

"That's so ridiculous. As far as the staff goes ... well I'm sure Human Resources hired the people who were most qualified."

"It was suggested that we hire more blacks, Mother. What's wrong with that?"

"We only want the most qualified, Blythe. Color of skin shouldn't matter."

"We both agree on that point."

"So what did you tell them?"

"I told them that I would give you and Grandfather a full report and that we'll consider all suggestions. I also apologized to Sam Peters on behalf of Bloodstone's."

Nadine looked like she had a bitter taste in her mouth but kept quiet.

Blythe glanced over at Moira and Justin and shrugged in resignation.

Moira gave her a reassuring smile.

Moira and Justin readied to test the water. Her brother rushed in and yelled, "Are you coming, Blythe? The water feels good."

"You know I can't swim," she yelled back.

"Why don't you join them, Blythe? You don't have to go out very far."

She eyed her mother. It was obvious Nadine didn't want to be alone with her. Standing up, Blythe nodded. "I think I'll do just that." She flounced off.

Walking along the edge of the water, she admonished herself for getting her hopes up. She'd anticipated having a few minutes alone with her mother—just to talk . . . Blythe shook her head. *Just give it up,* she silently railed.

Later that evening, Blythe found Nadine sitting by the huge bay window, her fingers knitted in boredom.

"Mother, why won't you spend time with Father?" Blythe suggested. "Can't you see he needs you? The only reason he came is because he wanted to be with you."

Nadine gave her a disapproving stare. "Blythe, this has nothing to do with you. Stay out of it."

Anger welled up in her. "Fine. I'll just take Father home. I'm not going to let you humiliate him like this." She turned to walk away.

Nadine jumped up, following her. "You're not going anywhere."

Blythe stopped mid-stride. "Yes, I am. And there's nothing you can do to stop me," she challenged. "Father is not happy here. Are you so selfish you can't see it?"

A glazed look of despair began to spread over Nadine's face. "I'm trying, Blythe. I'm really trying."

Resigned, she said, "I know, Mother. I just think it's best if we leave."

Nadine wrung her hands. "I'm sorry. I really wanted us to rebuild some semblance of a family."

"You tried and so did Father. Maybe it's much too soon."

Heading back to the bay window, Nadine said, "I'll have Winston start packing."

The phone rang, startling them both.

"Do you want me to get it?" Blythe asked.

"No, you go on up and pack your things. I'll make the plane reservations."

Nadine stood in the doorway of Blythe's room a few minutes later. "Well, it appears that I'll be joining you on the flight tonight."

Blythe turned around to face her mother. She was shocked that her mother would actually be joining them. "Why?" She could tell that something had happened.

"Carol just called. David Garsone just quit."

She was disappointed. Blythe had actually thought Nadine was joining them because she wanted to be with them. "I'm sorry," she murmured.

"Oh Blythe, it's not your fault. For goodness sake, quit apologizing," Nadine snapped. "I had to call Harwood. He's the last person I wanted to deal with. He's called an emergency meeting." She gave Blythe the details.

After finishing with her own packing, Blythe headed to her father's room to see if he needed assistance.

"Mother's fit to be tied. David just quit," Blythe announced to her father. She remained standing by the door in an effort to stay out of Winston's way as he moved around the room gathering her father's medicine and equipment.

Adam looked up from his packing. "I'm not surprised. He and Nadine never got along."

Blythe nodded. "His timing is lousy though. Now we don't have a designer for the Couture Salon."

"When will Dad be back from North Carolina?" her father asked. "Or does he even know yet?"

"Oh he knows. Grandfather will be home sometime tonight. We're having a meeting the day after tomorrow."

"Any ideas?" Adam asked.

"Not at the moment. I'm going to give it some serious thought on the plane, but I'm sure it's much too late to find someone else."

He patted her hand. "Well, honey. Everything will work out for the best. I'm sure of it."

Blythe smiled and stroked his cheek. "I hope you're right, Father."

Within an hour, they were ready to leave. Moira and Justin had decided to stay in Barbados, but they saw them off at the airport.

On the plane, Nadine was in a foul mood, not saying anything to Blythe or her father. Blythe and Winston sat side by side.

Tired of reading, she closed her book. "How is Father doing?" she asked Winston.

"He's doing just fine, Blythe. Healthwise anyway."

She nodded her understanding. "I keep hoping that he'll return to being the man that he used to be."

"Adam's been through a lot. He keeps a lot within, but I believe that everything will work out. He needs all of you. He needs his family."

"Don't we all?" Blythe murmured before turning to look out of the window. They were nearing Kennedy Airport in New York and would be changing planes there.

"I'm so glad to finally be home." Blythe announced. She sat her luggage near the stairs. "That eight-hour layover was a killer. I hate sitting in an airport for that long. Especially with Mother sulking the whole time."

"Me, too," Adam agreed. "Well, I think I'm going straight to bed."

Stifling her yawn, Blythe mumbled sleepily, "Well good night, Father. I'll see you in the morning." Before going upstairs, she sorted through the mail. She smiled when she came across the familiar scrawl of her best friend, Alda Forrester, on an envelope.

Suddenly, a light went off in her head. She could hardly contain her excitement as she readied for bed. Blythe longed to rush to Nadine's room with her idea, but she restrained herself. It would have to wait until the meeting.

"... without a designer, we are just like any other department store," Nadine stated. "We need to hire someone immediately."

"I hear you, but I don't think we have much choice in the matter," Harwood countered.

"I've been doing some thinking," Blythe interjected. "I have a friend in Paris. Her name is Alda Forrester. She's one of the most exciting young designers in the world, according to *Women's Wear Daily.*"

Nadine frowned. "I've never heard of her."

"She's worked at the Couture houses of Dior and Yves St. Laurent."

Nadine was excited. "Do you really think she'll come to the states and work for Bloodstone's?"

"I think she might. It's always been a dream of hers to have her own line of clothing."

Harwood nodded. "We've got nothing to lose, so give Miss Forrester a call."

Pleased, Blythe rose to her feet. "I can't wait for you all to meet her."

As soon as Blythe entered her office, she got on the phone. She smiled when Alda came on the line.

"Blythe? Blythe, is that you?"

"Yes, it's me. How are you, Alda?"

"I'm fine. This is a pleasant surprise. Are you coming back to Europe?"

"No. Actually, the reason I'm calling is to invite you to Los Angeles. I received your letter and I was sorry to hear what happened. However, we've had a crisis at the store and we happen to be looking for a designer for the Couture Salon."

"Really?"

"I'm hoping you'll fly here for an interview. My family's eager to find another designer. I know you have a complete line ready. It would be perfect for the store. We'll pay for your trip, of course. Please tell me you'll come. I can have my assistant make all of the arrangements."

"Well, I've got no job and soon no home, so why not?"

"Oh, in the meantime, fax over a copy of your resume." Blythe gave her the number.

"As soon as the arrangements are made, fax me a copy of the itinerary. This is really a godsend."

"If you decide to take the job, it's going to be fun having you here." They talked for a few minutes more before Blythe hung up, a smile plastered on her face. She was exhilarated over the thought of having her best friend nearby. She prayed fervently that all would work out and Alda would decide to stay. She was tired of being alone.

Nadine interrupted her thoughts. "Were you able to reach your friend?"

"Yes, Mother. I'm going to have Peggy make her travel arrangements. She should arrive in a week."

"That long?"

"Alda lives in Paris, France. She can't just pick up and leave."

"Does she have something ready? A line that's uniquely hers."

Blythe nodded. "She does. Alda's going to fax her resume. We should get it any time now."

At that moment, Peggy strolled in carrying a piece of paper. "Excuse me, but this fax just arrived for you, Blythe."

"We've been expecting that." She took Alda's resume from

her assistant. "Thanks, Peggy." After glancing through it, she handed it to her mother.

Nadine read it gingerly. "This is impressive. I can't wait to see her designs." She smiled at her daughter. "I think I'm going to like your friend."

Blythe prayed that was the case. She wasn't sure of how Nadine would react when she met Alda in person.

Chapter 8

Alda stepped off the plane, her neat, shoulder-length dread-locks waving in the air. Her smooth, dark chocolate complexion was devoid of makeup.

Blythe raced toward her friend. *"Ma cherie,* I'm so glad you're here." Seeing Alda gave her complete joy. She prayed Alda would decide to stay in Los Angeles.

"Girl, I am so grateful to be off of that plane. The trip was trying. I feel like I've been on that plane for days."

Laughing, Blythe nodded. "It *is* a long flight." Looping her arm through Alda's, she asked, "Do you feel like having dinner?"

A frown crossed Alda's face. "Can we do it another night? All I want to do is take a long, hot bath and go to bed."

Blythe nodded. "I understand. Your interview isn't until tomorrow afternoon. I knew you'd be tired from the trip."

"Merci."

Blythe embraced her once more. "I'm so glad you're here. I hope you'll take the job."

Alda laughed. *"Ma cherie,* they may not offer it to me."

Waving away the comment, Blythe stated, "Once they see your designs, my family's going to go wild. Just wait and see."

"It sounds like a great opportunity, and I've always wanted to see Los Angeles."

As they headed to Blythe's car, she asked, "What's Wilma up to these days?"

"My sister is still the same. She has not changed one bit."

She opened the door for Alda. Blythe stuck her garment bag into the trunk of her Mercedes. "We used to have some splendid times, the three of us."

Alda nodded. "We sure did. Wilma and I were just talking about that over Thanksgiving."

"How will she feel about you living in Los Angeles?" Blythe asked as she stepped into her car. "I know she's going to miss you like crazy."

"She's excited for me. In fact, she's packing up my things. Wilma's like you—she's positive I'm going to get the job."

Blythe started the car. "You're going to get it. I just know it." She drove out of the parking garage.

When they were on the freeway, Alda said casually, "I saw Parker before I left. He was on the Left Bank painting the Cathedral of Notre Dame." She laughed. "He fancies himself a great painter but he cannot paint."

Blythe tried to sound uninterested. "Oh. How are he and his wife doing?"

"They are no longer together. Parker wants a divorce. He says that breaking up with you was a big mistake."

Blythe shrugged nonchalantly. "Well, it no longer matters. It's over between us. Has been for a long time."

Alda stopped and stared at Blythe. "I almost believe you."

"It's true. I could never trust Parker again after the way he hurt me. Not ever."

"He has been talking about coming back to California."

Shrugging again, she said, "Doesn't matter to me." Blythe meant it. Parker was out of her life, but more importantly, he was out of her heart.

"So who is this new man in your life?"

Blythe turned to face her friend. "Why does there have to be another man?"

"It usually takes finding someone new to mend a broken heart."

"I don't believe that."

"You walked around Paris for three years like a zombie. One mention of Parker and you would burst into tears. You would not let a man get within two feet of you, *ma cherie.*" Alda surveyed her for a moment. "Blythe, you have met someone. I know it like the back of my own hand."

The next day, Blythe picked up Alda and brought her to the store. She walked around in awe. "This store is incredible, Blythe. I can't believe you made all the mannequins to resemble famous people." She stopped and pointed. "Is this who I think it is?"

Nodding, Blythe said, "Yes, it's Joan Collins. She's wearing a dress from our Dynasty collection."

Alda walked around the platform, surveying the mannequin. "You know, Blythe, I think using a red spotlight on the dress would intensify the color. Drama is always an attention-getter."

Blythe considered her suggestion. "Hmmmm. I'll have the display department change the bulb."

"Do you miss working at Printemps?"

"At times. But I'm glad to be home with my father."

"I was offered a job with Kenzo a couple of days before you called me."

"Kenzo. Isn't that the designer of honor with the Limited stores?"

Alda nodded. *"Oui,* but after working all those years at couture houses . . . I really want to see my name on the labels. I'm tired of working in the houses of Dior, Hechter and Yves St. Laurent. The money was good but I turned Kenzo down anyway."

"Kenzo's loss will be our gain, I hope." Blythe hugged her friend. "I missed you so much."

"I missed you, too. I know this sounds selfish but I kept hoping that you would return to Paris."

"I probably would've considered it if Parker wasn't there.

I saw him more than I cared to. His wife, too." Blythe led Alda to the elevator. "It's almost time. The models you requested are already upstairs."

Smoothing back her hair, Alda chewed her bottom lip.

"Stop that."

"Blythe, I am so nervous. I hope your family will like my designs."

"I'm sure they will. Don't worry so." She guided Alda into the conference room. Her mother, grandfather and the Human Resource manager were already seated. "Everyone, this is Alda Forrester."

Nadine's eyes opened wide. Standing up, she said, "Excuse us for a moment. I need to speak to my daughter." She led Blythe into an empty office. Closing the door, Nadine ripped into her.

"Have you lost your mind? What could you be thinking— bringing that woman here."

Blythe had hoped to avoid a confrontation like this. "Mother, she's the designer. Remember the one I told you about?"

Anger flashed in Nadine's eyes. "I'm not losing it. You really should have told us everything."

"Everything?"

"Why didn't you tell us that she's black?"

Blythe frowned. "What does her skin color have to do with anything? You're going to love her collection."

"We have to think about our clientele, Blythe."

"Mother—"

"She won't do. We'll look at her collection, but after that she returns to Paris. Understood?"

Blythe glared at Nadine, her eyes full of reproach. "I can't believe you just said that. Have you actually lost sight of who you are, Mother?"

"What do you mean by that?"

"You're ready to put Alda on the next plane back to France just because she happens to be black. Have you forgotten that you are black as well?"

"I'm not going to listen to this nonsense."

"What—"

Harwood knocked and entered. "Are you two going to join us?"

"I'm coming, Grandfather." Blythe headed to the door.

Nadine turned to Harwood. "You can't seriously be considering—"

"I think you'd better stop right there, Nadine. We are in the middle of a business meeting. Would you care to join us or should I make your regrets for you?"

Blythe bit back a smile when her mother followed her back to the conference room without another word.

While she waited for the models to change, Alda showed her sketches for a new spring line.

Blythe covertly eyed her mother and grandfather's faces as Alda showed her designs. The designs were superb. Once or twice, she thought she saw a bright spark in Nadine's eyes.

". . . and this one is what I call my crème de la crème. This silk number is hand-painted . . ." Alda narrated as a tall, rail-thin model paced back and forth. "A palm-frond print is absolutely eye-catching in this stunner of a long dress. Customers will love the fitted, flowing shape."

A second model sauntered into the room and she continued. "Now this hand-painted stripe wrap skirt has tropical appeal . . ."

When the entire line had been shown, Blythe stood up. "Thanks, Alda. Why don't you and the models go up to the cafeteria. There are some refreshments. We'll join you in a few minutes."

"Sure."

As soon as the door closed, Harwood said, "Well darling, Alda's designs are remarkable. Lots of color. Unique, too. I think we've found our designer."

Nadine almost choked on her coffee. After a brief coughing spell, she sputtered, "You've got to be kidding."

Harwood glared at Nadine. "I'm very serious."

"But . . ."

"Mother, why don't you want Alda to be the designer? What is your problem with her?"

"Think of our clientele, Blythe. They aren't looking for a . . . a funky—"

"What the hell are you talking about, Nadine?" Harwood asked. "You saw her designs. They are the type of clothes that our customers want. They want one-of-a-kind, fresh, bright . . . you know what I'm talking about."

"Her designs are magnificent. It's just her look . . . well, she looks so . . . she looks so ethnic." She wrung her hands. "I don't know any other way to put it. Look at the way she was dressed."

"I liked her dress," Blythe contended. "It was hand-painted on the finest quality rayon. I have one similar that she designed for me. Matter of fact, you complimented me when I wore it."

"Does she have to look . . . I mean, it's quite obvious that she's black. Does she have to wear her hair that way? People may not think she's clean."

Blythe burst into laughter. "Her hair is clean, Mother. Alda is clean. You just don't like the fact that she wears her hair in dreads."

"Why does she have to? Our store has a certain reputation—"

"That's going to hell in a hand basket if we aren't careful," Harwood stated. "I don't think anybody'll have a problem with Alda's hair."

"I'm not so sure."

"Once they see her couture line, nobody will care if she's blue, green or purple," Blythe assured her. Standing up, she said, "I think we should join Alda upstairs. I can't wait to tell her that she's got the job."

Nadine wisely kept her mouth shut. As soon as they entered the cafeteria, Blythe and Harwood advanced to tell Alda the news.

"Welcome to Bloodstone's, Alda. We're very happy to have you on board," Harwood announced. "We'll have the contracts drawn up immediately."

"*Merci, Monsieur* Bloodstone."

Blythe hugged her. "Congratulations, Alda. I'm so glad you're going to be here with me."

"We're all very happy to have you with us," Nadine stated. "Welcome."

Later, Alda and Blythe sat in her office catching up. "So, what do you think?"

"Your grandfather is a very generous man. And I love the store. However, I don't think your Mom's too thrilled with me."

"She'll get over it. I hope you're still going to take the job."

"Of course. I think I'm going to like it here."

Blythe stood up then. "We're going to celebrate. I'm taking you to dinner tonight."

She took Alda to a restaurant that served African specialties, much to her friend's delight. They were seated and served quickly. They had already ordered and were quietly surveying the room.

"This place reminds me so much of home . . ."

"When was the last time you visited Ghana?"

"Right after you left France. Remember Wilma and I had been planning to surprise my mother."

Blythe nodded. "That's right. I remember now."

Their main dishes arrived and there was a short silence while they began their dinner.

Sipping her wine, Blythe saw a familiar figure coming their way. "What is he doing here?" She refused to acknowledge the way her senses leapt to life upon seeing Khalil.

Alda turned around. "Who?"

"Khalil Sanford. He's the publisher of the *Heritage Reporter.*" Blythe gave Alda a rundown of her first encounter with Khalil.

"Really?" She leaned closer and whispered, "Is he your lover?"

"No. Why on earth would you think that?" As Khalil approached, Blythe smiled. "What a surprise to see you, Mr. Sanford." She gestured toward Alda. "This is my best friend, Alda Forrester. She's also the new designer for the Couture Salon. David Garsone quit."

"I'm sorry to hear that," he teased. "I'm going to miss old Dave."

Alda burst into laughter.

Not amused, Blythe firmly planted her foot on top of Alda's while she glared at Khalil.

"Ouch!"

"What's wrong?" Khalil asked, his expression one of concern.

"Oh, nothing." Alda smirked at Blythe. "I just hit my foot on something."

"Well, it's very nice to meet you, Alda."

"You, too." Eyeing Blythe, she asked, "Won't you join us?"

"Thank you, but no, I'll let you two catch up. I'm meeting someone for dinner." He smiled at Blythe. "I'll talk to you later."

Not bothering to return his smile with one of her own, Blythe asserted, "Enjoy your dinner."

When he walked away, Alda leaned across the table, whispering, "He seems to be such a nice man. Handsome, too. He looks good in that dashiki."

"I guess so. If you like that kind of clothing. He's always wearing something with an African motif."

Alda observed her gingerly. "What's going on between you two?"

"We just got off on the wrong foot, that's all."

"Oh no, it's much more than that. There's definitely something more going on?"

"Why do you say that?"

Alda grinned. "Because of the way you keep looking over at his table. Are you curious to see who he's having dinner with?"

Blythe shook her head. "No, Alda, I'm not the least bit interested in Khalil's dinner companion," she lied. Her heart started to pound faster as she watched the approach of a stunning woman with a shapely body. To Blythe's dismay, she joined Khalil at his table.

Leaning forward, Alda whispered, "She's beautiful, don't you think? He certainly has good taste in women."

Blythe glared at Alda, who only laughed. "Come on, dear friend. Admit it. You're attracted to the man."

"Alda, let's change the subject. Khalil means nothing to me."

Shaking her head, Alda disagreed. "I don't believe that for a minute."

Blythe pointed her fork toward her friend. "Your food's going to get cold." As hard as she tried, she couldn't stop thinking about Khalil and his beautiful date.

"Huh? You're talking about my food getting cold. Look at you. You can barely eat for looking over there. Girl, why don't you pick yourself up and start again. Stop window shopping and dreaming about it. Go on out and get the real thing. You want that man!"

"What on earth are you babbling about, Alda?"

"You know what I'm saying. You are interested in that man over there. Yet you're giving him the idea that you're not wanting a relationship. That could be you over there, having dinner."

"I'm fine right where I am," Blythe said flippantly.

"Do you want to be alone for the rest of your life?"

"No, but I don't really have a say in the matter."

Alda shook her head sadly. "You're talking like a crazy woman, Blythe."

"No, I'm not. Some of us are just meant to be alone. Or haven't you heard? There are not enough men to go around."

"There are baby boys born every minute."

Blythe put her hand to her mouth to hide her laughter. "You are terrible, Alda."

"That man sitting over there is ripe and ready to be plucked."

"And what makes you so sure?" Blythe asked, folding her arms across her chest.

"He's trying not to watch you as much as you're trying not to watch him." Alda laughed. "You two are so funny."

"Just quit it. Khalil and I are as different as day and night. He's pro black and I'm just . . . well, black. Look at the way he's dressed and what do you call the hat on his head by the way?''

"A Kuffi.''

She had to admit that he looked good in navy and gold. His mustache and beard were always impeccably trimmed. Khalil was an extremely handsome man.

"I think he looks good. Dressed like that, he looks like an Ashanti prince.''

Blythe put her hand to her mouth to stifle her giggles.

"I think you've met your match, girl.''

"Alda, be serious. Khalil and I . . . well, I don't wear Afro-centric clothing for one.'' She pointed to herself. "I for one don't need to wear a certain type of clothing to announce that I'm black and proud of it. That's just not who I am.''

"I'm pretty sure that's not what he's doing. Village weavers weave stories into the fabric—long-ago stories of the Ashanti kings and queens. They weave tales of wisdom, hope and harmony. The blue he's wearing tells a parable of peace. Red is the story of struggle and yellow tells the legend of sanctity.''

"I had no idea.''

"There are those that don't acknowledge or respect the religious, moral and cultural values of my people and our kente cloth—they simply want to make a fashion statement.''

"But you don't think Khalil is one of those people?''

Alda shook her head. "No, he wears his clothes with such pride . . . He's a man with a heart of gold.''

Blythe gave a small laugh. "Your food's getting cold.'' Silently, she admitted that she felt an attraction to Khalil. She was actually jealous seeing him with that woman. Blythe had been through so much that she'd decided to forget about relationships altogether.

Her gaze slid over Khalil's profile once more and the pit of her stomach churned. Her mind kept telling her to resist, but her body refused. When Khalil's gaze met hers, Blythe realized that they shared an intense physical awareness of each other.

Blythe felt Alda watching her, so she wrenched herself away from her ridiculous preoccupation with Khalil and his date.

Alda opened her mouth to speak but Blythe silenced her

with a shake of her head. "Don't you dare say it. I mean it—just don't say a word."

Khalil forced himself to pay attention to Pamela. "I'm sorry. What were you saying?"

She frowned. "You weren't listening to me," she accused between bites of her dinner. "That's not very nice."

"You're right. Again I apologize." Khalil eyed her. "You look very nice tonight."

Pam smiled prettily. "Why thank you. I bought this dress just for you."

Shifting in his seat, Khalil suddenly felt uneasy. He hoped she hadn't misinterpreted his invitation to dinner. "Pam . . ." he began.

She suddenly burst into laughter. "Relax, Khalil. I was only teasing you. I'm not trying to go back to the way we used to be."

"We make much better friends, I think."

Pam agreed. "Besides, I have a little news to share with you."

Khalil leaned back in his chair. "What?"

Holding her left hand out to him, she announced, "I'm engaged. Can you believe it?" Pam put her hand down. "I'm actually going to get married."

"I'm happy for you. Congratulations." Khalil was genuinely pleased with her announcement. After they'd called off their engagement, Pam had kind of withdrawn within herself. Although the breakup had been a mutual one, he felt that she'd blamed him somehow. His eyes traveled involuntarily to where Blythe was sitting.

Following Khalil's gaze, Pam asked, "So tell me. When are you going to jump the broom?"

Returning his eyes to her, he shrugged. "Whenever Miss Right decides to show up."

"Judging from the way your eyes keep checking out that table over there, I'd say it won't be much longer."

Khalil's eyes glittered bright with merriment. "You're a funny lady, Pam."

"I see the way you're staring at those two women. Which one are you interested in?" She peered in their direction. "Wait, I bet I can guess. It's the one with the short cut and the conservative suit. She looks like your type."

He raised his eyebrows. "You really think so?"

Pam nodded. "It looks like she's interested in you as well." She grinned. "I wish I had a camera."

"Why?"

"Because I've never seen you have that look in your eyes in all the years I've known you. You're falling in love with Miss Prim and Proper over there." Pamela held out her hand to him. "Welcome to the club."

Khalil shook his head. "You don't know what you're talking about." He motioned for the waiter. "I think I'll have dessert."

After dinner, Khalil headed home. All throughout his meal with Pam, he'd caught Blythe watching them. As if he could read her mind, he knew she wondered what his relationship was with Pam. Khalil decided to take it one step further— Blythe had been jealous and it pleased him.

His smile faded and his spirits took a downward plunge. What was he thinking? Did he really intend to get involved with a woman like Blythe? Khalil wanted to make a difference. He resolved to be part of the solution. Blythe, on the other hand, was part of the problem.

By the time Khalil had undressed and was heading to the shower, he knew what had to be done. He would have to invite Blythe to share and understand his world. Only then could they have any type of relationship.

At home, Blythe recalled Alda's words and smiled. Khalil, *an African prince.* She had been right. He did look like a prince. "I'm not going to keep thinking about you," she whispered. "I don't need another man hurting me."

Yet as she said those words, a sinking feeling of despair swept through her. She was tired of being alone. But how could she ever let another man get close to her? Parker summed up her problem a long time ago. Nobody could love her. And he was right. Even her own mother didn't love her.

Blythe ripped off her clothes and turned on the shower. Why didn't she deserve to be loved? What was wrong with her? Shaking her head, Blythe silently railed at the creator. *What did I do? Was I such a horrible child that I deserved to grow up without a mother's love? Am I destined to go through the rest of my life without knowing the love of a man?*

Beneath the hot running water, her tears of hurt mingled with the soothing stream. Blythe hated when she got this way. For the most part, she tried not to think of the yearning. Or her mother's constant rejection. She stayed in the shower until she felt better. It was as if the hot water gave her strength.

Blythe climbed out and dried herself with a fluffy bath sheet. Feeling much better, she dressed quickly in a pair of satin pajamas. She stood before her full-length mirror, running her fingers through her short hair, fluffing up the tiny curls. She knew she wasn't beautiful and she didn't care. She was Blythe Bloodstone and that would never change.

Chapter 9

"All of our customers are not wealthy, Alda," Blythe stated during their meeting. "I think it would be great to have a line of clothing priced from ... say, one hundred dollars to one thousand. Do you think that's possible?"

"Well, as I've explained, every garment in the new line will be individually designed and sewn to produce distinctive garments that will represent the wearer's individual sense of style. No two pieces will be exactly alike."

"That sounds wonderful, but what about price? What fabrics are you going to use?"

"The dresses, jackets and coats are all pieced from personally selected wool, rayon, cotton, silk and leather. Depending on the fabric, the clothing can be priced according to the customer's budget."

Smiling, Blythe eyed the sketches once more. "I love them. Especially this one." She pointed to a patchwork cardigan and tiered broom skirt in black.

"The cardigan would be a textural mélange of crocheted ribbed and woven tapestry patches to carved bone buttons, swirls of jute and a trio of brass beads."

"That's an intriguing mix. What about the skirt?"

"Suede, silk and I'm even thinking of velvet."

"Can it be done in rayon or cotton?"

Alda nodded. "Sure." She closed her notes. "You know, I've been thinking about what you've told me about the store's reputation in the black community and I think I have an idea how to rectify it."

Leaning closer, Blythe said, "I'm listening."

"I have some wonderful fabrics from Africa. I have a beautiful brocade, some handwoven kente, rab and mud cloth, of course."

"Mud cloth?"

Nodding, Alda said, "Yes, it's made from cotton grown, spun, woven and dyed by a single group of crafters in a tiny village in Mali. I was thinking about saving it for the spring line, but the more that I think about it, I think it'll be perfect for the holidays."

"What exactly do you have in mind, Alda?"

"Well, I could have a complete collection ready in a couple of weeks. I know you don't celebrate Kwanzaa but you might want to consider doing so this year." She held up her hand to halt Blythe's comment. "On a store level, that is. On the fifth day of Kwanzaa we could have a fashion show and debut the Heritage collection. It's perfect because the entire clothing line will reflect our African heritage. As a matter of fact, the entire store's image can be changed to reflect and celebrate our heritage."

Blythe had to admit that it might just be what the store needed to bridge the gap between Bloodstone's and the black community. "I think it's a great idea, but I'd like to talk to someone else about it. Do you mind?"

"No. Just get back to me as soon as possible."

"Go ahead and get started. I'm positive that we could get my grandfather's approval."

Alda stood up. "But what about your mother? What do you think she'll say?"

Blythe rose to her feet and walked around her desk. "Don't worry about my mother. If anybody on earth can handle her, it's Grandfather.'' She escorted Alda to the door. "I'm going by his house when I leave here.''

A few hours later, Blythe left the store and drove to her grandfather's house. She'd called earlier and Harwood was expecting her.

He greeted her at the door. "Well, hey darling. Good to see you.'' Harwood moved to let her enter.

Blythe kissed his cheek. "Grandfather, thank you for seeing me.''

"Honey, you're always welcome here. This is your home, too.''

"I know.'' Blythe followed Harwood into his study. "Alda and I were talking, and we came up with an idea to bridge the gap between the black community and the store.'' She made herself comfortable on a sectional sofa that had seen better days. Blythe knew he kept it because her late grandmother loved it so much.

"Really?'' Harwood joined her on the sofa.

She nodded. "Yes. I think it's a great idea.''

Sitting back, he said, "Well, I can't wait to hear it.''

"Grandfather, what do you think of Bloodstone's celebrating Kwanzaa?''

Rubbing his chin, he was thoughtful. "Hmmmm. Never gave it any thought. I don't know much about Kwanzaa.''

"Well, I'm still learning. Matter of fact, I'm picking up a couple of books on the subject after I leave here.''

"Have you come up with a specific plan?'' Harwood asked.

Blythe shook her head. "I wanted to get your thoughts on the idea before I presented a tentative program.'' She paused before adding, "And before I even mention the idea to Mother.''

"She won't like it,'' Harwood stated.

"Not at all,'' Blythe agreed.

"I'll tell you what, honey. You come up with some ideas and present them on Monday at the meeting.''

She leaned over, hugging him. "Thank you, Grandfather. I knew I could count on you.'' Standing up, she said, "I've got to run. I need to get to the bookstore before they close.''

Harwood rose slowly, using the back of the chair for support. "I look forward to hearing your proposal."

Blythe left her grandfather's house and drove to a nearby bookstore. There she selected a video and two books on Kwanzaa.

In her car, she searched through her purse for Khalil's business card. Finding it, Blythe picked up her cellular phone and dialed the number of the *Heritage Reporter*. She prayed that Khalil would still be there. Her prayers were answered. He answered the phone himself.

"Khalil, this is Blythe."

There was a brief pause. She assumed it was because of his astonishment. She was probably the last person he'd ever expected to call him.

"How are you, Blythe?"

"I'm fine. Look, I have a favor to ask of you. Can you meet me in about an hour for dinner? I'd like to talk to you about something."

"Dinner?"

She heard the surprise in his voice. And something else. Caution. "Yes. Is there a problem? We can do it another night."

"No. No problem. I'm just a little surprised, that's all."

She quickly gave him the name of the restaurant. "Around seven o'clock?"

"I'll see you then."

Blythe hung up, excitement flooding through her body. She drove quickly, arriving home in record time. Blythe raced into the house and almost collided with Moira, who was on her way upstairs.

"What's got you in such a rushed state?" Moira asked.

"I've got to take a shower and change. I'm meeting someone in an hour," she said breathlessly. "Will you give me a hand?"

"Sure," Moira replied, thrilled to assist.

The two women went into Blythe's room. While Blythe removed her clothes, Moira searched through the overflowing closet for the perfect ensemble.

"This man must be pretty special, the way you're carrying on. Who is he?"

"Nobody you would know. It's not a date or anything. We're just meeting for dinner. I have an idea that I want to pass by him," Blythe rambled excitedly. Her medium brown eyes sparkled. "He's very handsome."

Moira peeked out and laughed. "I gathered as much. It's good to see you so happy. It's been a long time."

"Just because I don't go around grinning from ear to ear doesn't mean I haven't been happy," Blythe mumbled. Stepping over to the mahogany dresser, she ran her fingers through her hair. Thinking about the woman with the long tresses she'd seen Khalil with the other night, she grumbled, "Maybe I shouldn't have had it cut so short." Eyeing her sister in the mirror, she asked, "Do you think I look like a boy?" She wanted Khalil to view her as an attractive woman. She wanted him to think she was sexy.

"You look beautiful, Blythe. I like your hair and no, you don't look anything like a boy." Moving to the bed, Moira laid out three outfits. "Which do you want to wear?"

"I think I'll wear the black pantsuit with the zebra-striped shirt."

Moira took the other two and returned them to the closet. "I have some earrings that would look good with this." She headed to the door. "I'll be right back."

Dressed in her robe, Blythe headed to the bathroom. She showered quickly. When she returned to her room, she found Moira sitting on her bed.

"What do you think?" In her hands, Moira held up a pair of zebra-striped earrings and a matching handbag.

Blythe smiled. "Perfect. Thanks for letting me borrow them."

"No problem." Moira rose to her feet. "Well, I'll leave you to get dressed. Have fun tonight."

"Thanks." When Moira left, Blythe put on her bra and panties. She was nervous about facing Khalil. She hadn't exactly been very open to his offer of friendship and now she was asking for his help. She prepared herself for the possibility of his saying no, although she hoped he'd say yes.

Dressed, Blythe checked herself out in the full-length mirror. Satisfied with her appearance, she was ready to leave. Moira was just about to knock when Blythe opened the door.

"You look beautiful," she exclaimed.

Blythe smiled hesitantly. "Wish me luck. I'm going to need it."

Kuiana blocked Khalil's path. "Are you sure you know what you're doing? This woman has something up her sleeve. Maybe I should go with you. I don't trust that wannabe."

He navigated around her. "I'll be fine, Sis. I can handle Miss Bloodstone." Khalil planted a quick kiss on Kuiana's cheek as he left his office. "Make sure Sam walks you and Caryn to your cars after you lock up."

"She's up to something," Kuiana warned as she followed him to the door.

He waved off her comment and headed to his car.

Blythe was already seated when Khalil arrived forty-five minutes later. She smiled up at him as he made his approach across the room. When he was seated, she said, "Thanks for meeting me."

"Well, you made it sound important. What's up?"

"I think I've come up with a way to bring the black community and Bloodstone's together."

"Let's hear it."

"Alda, she's the person I introduced you to. Well she and I were talking earlier and she had this idea. One I think even you'll like."

She had his complete interest. "I'm listening."

"Well, she's going to design a complete line—one that's affordable for all budgets. The line will debut on the fifth day of Kwanzaa. We're going to have a fashion show."

"Hold up." Khalil sat up straight. "Correct me if I'm wrong, but since when do you celebrate Kwanzaa?'' Blythe didn't strike him as a person who appreciated the African-American festival of the harvest.

"Well, I've never celebrated Kwanzaa personally. We were playing around with the idea of the store as a whole participating in a Kwanzaa celebration. A portion of the moneys brought in that week will be donated toward the new community center in South Central."

Khalil said nothing. To Blythe, he appeared to be in deep thought.

"Well?" she asked nervously.

"I think it's a good idea. And a good start. Where are you thinking of having this Kwanzaa celebration?"

"The store of course." Blythe communicated to Khalil what she and Alda had discussed. "Don't you think it's a good idea?"

He was impressed. "I think you may be on to something." He nodded thoughtfully. "It just might work."

Blythe swirled her white wine in her glass, watching the lazy pattern the golden liquid made. She couldn't quite meet Khalil's eyes, her attraction to him was so intense.

He noted that Blythe always seemed on edge around him. "Do I make you nervous?" he asked.

"In a way ... I don't know ... Maybe I just feel a little guilty asking for your help after the way I've treated you."

Khalil broke into a smile. "I don't mind helping, Blythe. I think it'll be good for the store, pure and simple." He moved his chicken around on his plate. He was as nervous as she appeared to be.

She nodded her head, agreeing with him in spite of herself. "You're right, but I think it'll be good for the black community as well." Blythe pointed to his plate. "Are you enjoying your dinner?"

"It's fine. How about you? You haven't really touched your food."

"I'm nervous." She looked up and found his eyes on her. "I hope you don't think that I'm trying to use you or anything—''

Khalil held up his hand. "I'm helping because I want to, Blythe." He grinned. "However, you know that means we're going to have to work closely. How do you feel about that? Since you turned down my offer of friendship."

"You're going to make me say it, aren't you?"

His boyish grin was his reply.

"Okay. Okay. I'm sorry I didn't want to be your friend. If the offer still stands . . ." Blythe covered up her laughter with her hand.

Khalil pulled her hand away. "You really should smile more often."

"So you've said."

He decided to forge straight ahead. "You look very nice tonight. The only thing missing is that million-dollar smile of yours."

Blythe played with her fish. "I guess I just haven't ever had much to smile about."

This was his chance. Khalil wasn't going to let it pass him by. Blythe intrigued him. He knew her to be a spitfire when she felt threatened, but he sensed there were many layers to her personality she kept hidden from view. "We're going to have to change that. If you're going to be a friend of mine, you're going to have to learn to loosen up—have fun."

Giving him a questioning glance, Blythe asked, "Do you think I'm boring?

"No," Khalil replied quickly. "I just think you're much too serious. You probably do a lot of thinking." His glance slid boldly to her mouth. "You also have beautiful lips."

Blythe burst into laughter. "I've never been told that before."

"Sweetheart, women pay a lot of money for lips like yours."

She nodded. "You're right. I guess I've taken them for granted."

They eyed one another before bursting into laughter once more.

When Khalil signaled for the check, Blythe stated, "Remember, I invited you to dinner. I'm paying."

He held up his hands in mock resignation. "I try not to argue with a lady."

She paid the bill and they walked out of the restaurant together. Khalil walked Blythe to her car.

"Thank you for dinner. I had a good time."

"I should be thanking you, Khalil. I look forward to working with you on this project."

Being so close to her like this, Khalil was tempted to kiss her. Resisting the urge, he held out his hand instead.

Blythe looked surprised for a moment before she shook his hand. "Good night, Khalil."

"Drive safe." He waited until Blythe was safely locked into her car before he strolled away. He'd had a good time with her tonight. Blythe could be charming when she wanted to be. Getting to know her was certainly going to be a challenge.

Inside his car, Khalil sat for a moment recalling the charming way Blythe hid her smile. He had to amend his earlier opinion of her looks. She wasn't plain looking—just serious. Very serious.

She had come into his life with the force of a speedboat that first day in the office. He'd glanced up and known without a doubt that she brought out feelings in him that went way beyond getting her into his bed. Khalil had thought her haughty attitude would dim the force of his attraction, but it hadn't. Her cautious nature forced him to continue his silent fascination with her. Khalil was determined to bring her out of her shell.

As he drove away, he decided she was actually quite pretty when she smiled. He resolved to make her smile every chance he got.

As soon as Khalil walked into his house, the phone was ringing. Checking the caller ID, he grinned and picked up. "Hello, Kuiana."

"Just checking to see how things went with Miss Beverly Hills."

He shook his head. "Everything went rather well. As you can see I made it home in one piece."

"Well, what did she want?"

"She wants me to help with the store's Kwanzaa celebration." Khalil gave her the details.

"I can't believe Miss High and Mighty came up with that idea. I bet she doesn't even know a thing about Kwanzaa."

"Her name is Blythe," he interjected. He heard his sister's sharp intake of breath.

"You're attracted to her, aren't you?" Kuiana asked.

There was no reason to lie to his sister. "Yes, I am."

"I hope you know what you're doing. She's not exactly our kind."

"I'll be fine. We've got a long day tomorrow, Sis. Why don't you go on and get some rest?"

She laughed. "This isn't over. Not by a long shot."

Blythe sat on the floor of her bedroom, in front of the marble fireplace for most of the evening, staring at the dancing flames and wondering what it would feel like to be loved. Truly loved. She wasn't afraid of an intimate relationship with a man—she just didn't want to be hurt. That was why she'd cut Khalil off from the beginning.

Having dinner with him tonight had unearthed feelings that she'd sought desperately to keep buried. Her heart accelerated at the thought of making love with Khalil. Tonight she'd longed to have him take her into his arms and kiss her with such deep passion . . .

Blythe sighed. She would have to keep a small but necessary distance between them. She needed the distance because of the way Khalil affected her. She rose up slowly and began to get ready for bed. What she wouldn't give for five minutes of absolute happiness.

Everything was happening so fast. Since taking on the position at the store, Alda hadn't had a moment to spare. Her sister packed her clothes and sent them to her via airplane. Alda and Blythe had finally found an apartment she liked . . . She sighed wearily. The long hours at the store and the time spent looking for a place to live were taking its toll on her. She was exhausted and her nerves taut.

Today she was irritable. Her fists clenched, she slammed down the phone, hanging up on a distributor. Her delivery would barely make it in time. "This can't happen," Alda murmured as she massaged her temple.

Taking deep calming breaths, she forced herself to relax. "Just think, Alda. There is another way to handle this problem." Feeling calmer now, she searched through her list of contacts in France and in Ghana.

Taking note of the time difference, Alda exhaled in frustration. She realized at that point she really needed to take a walk or something. Maybe some fresh air would soothe her. The rumbling sound of her empty stomach reminded Alda that she hadn't eaten since the bran muffin this morning in Blythe's office.

Having decided to take a lunch break, she rose to her feet, grabbing her purse and a stack of fabric samples. Nothing was going to keep her from having that line ready.

As soon as Alda stepped off the elevator downstairs, she collided with someone. She glanced up into a pair of hazel eyes and a handsome face. In her present state of mind, she didn't care one whit what he looked like.

"Why don't you watch where you're going?" Alda snapped.

"Excuse me, I'm really sorry. Let me help—"

He bent down to help her retrieve her swatches. Alda touched his hand to stop him. "No, that's okay. I can do it myself." She picked them up quickly. Alda moved around him, walking fast.

"But wait . . ." Justin began.

Alda turned around. "Look, I don't know who you are but I've got a lot of work to do. Now please go away!"

"Go away?" Who in hell did she think she was? Justin shook his head. It was obvious she didn't know who he was or she just didn't care. He stared after her, wanting to follow her. But even in her anger, he found her breathtaking. "Who are you?" he whispered. She was leaving the store, but Justin decided that she must work in one of the departments.

A woman approached him. "Hello, Mr. Bloodstone. How are you?"

He smiled. "Hello, Cindy. You're looking very nice today."

"Thank you." She blushed and looked away.

"Have you seen Blythe today?"

"She was over in the bridal department a few minutes ago."

"Thanks, Cindy. You have a good day now." Justin knew she had a slight crush on him, but he wasn't interested. Cindy was nineteen years old and silly. To him, that combination was a recipe for trouble.

"You too, Mr. Bloodstone."

Walking swiftly, Justin made his way over to the Bridal Salon, smiling and waving. He stopped the elderly Mrs. Watkins, an employee who'd been with the store as long as he could remember. "Is Blythe still here?" he asked her.

"No, darling. She should be back in her office by now."

He hugged her. "It's good seeing you, Mrs. Watkins. You take care of yourself." Justin headed to the elevators. Backtracking, he stopped at a nearby phone. Calling Blythe's extension, he waited for her to pick up. When she did, he said, "Hey, I'm on my way up to your office. Stay put."

"Come in, Justin." Blythe motioned for him to take a seat.

"How have you been?" he asked as he sat down, his back upright and rigid.

Her expression instantly became guarded. "I'm fine. Why are you suddenly so interested in my well-being?"

"Why are you always so suspicious?"

"I guess I've always had reason to be." Blythe leaned forward. "Did Mother ask you to come talk to me?"

Justin shook his head. "Nobody had to tell me to come check up on my little sister." He grinned boyishly. "I consider it part of my duty as your big brother."

Blythe didn't blink an eye. "Really now. Aren't you a bit late? About four years too late?"

Justin's mouth went grim. "Blythe, you could have called

me at any time to tell me what was going on between you and Parker. But you didn't.''

"You were in contact with Parker. Why didn't you ever ask him what happened?''

"I did. He said things didn't work out and one day he came home and found you gone. What in hell was I supposed to do? I didn't know he was lying to me. I wasn't in France—I was here.'' Justin raised his hand in despair. "I was the one who tried to talk you out of going, remember?''

"And why is that?'' Blythe sneered. "Why didn't you want me to go? Is it because you knew what would happen? You knew he was nothing more than a gigolo.''

"That's a damn lie!'' Justin rose to his feet. "I'm tired of being the target of your anger. I never wanted to introduce you to the man anyway. But you kept after me about it. This is your own damn fault!''

She rifled him with an unreadable stare. "Get out of my office. And going forward, just stay the hell away from me. I don't need a big brother.'' Her tone was vicious.

A shadow of hurt passed across Justin's face. "Nobody's going to want to be around you, Blythe. Not until you change your attitude. You're much too bitter.''

She pointed to the door. "Leave.''

When he was gone, Blythe crumbled emotionally. How could she have said those things to him? She knew she'd hurt him. At the time, she hadn't cared, but now . . .

Blythe blamed Justin for what happened between her and Parker. She felt like Justin set her up to be hurt. He and Parker had been friends since kindergarten. After all, Justin knew Parker better than anyone.

Chapter 10

"Alda came up with a wonderful idea. What do you all think of Bloodstone's Department Store celebrating Kwanzaa?"

"You're kidding, right?" Nadine sputtered. "You can't be serious."

"Why not?" Harwood asked. "I think it's worth looking into."

Nadine raised her hands in resignation.

"You can continue, Blythe."

"Thanks, Grandfather. Kwanzaa is to remind us of the best that's in us, and to give to ourselves and the world. One of the principles encourages blacks to support black-owned businesses. I think it's only fitting that we participate. We're only talking about one night. I've passed out copies of the events that will be going on simultaneously. Our main event will be the fashion show. That night we will debut Alda's Heritage collection." She eyed her mother, who seemed genuinely interested.

"Where would we hold this fashion show, Blythe?" Nadine asked.

"Why not here? We have that huge banquet room upstairs. We've held private showings there before."

Nadine nodded. "It'll hold at least two hundred and fifty people." She scanned through the sheets once more. "We're going to set up small boutiques on each floor?"

"Yes. I think we should feature all of our goods from Africa. Margaret was able to secure some wonderful African art and handcrafted African masks and figurines. We'll have authentic foods and lots of other merchandise. It's going to be a lot of fun."

"Have you lined up any of the speakers?" Harwood asked.

"Khalil's taking care of that for me. So far, his father, James Sanford, has agreed to be a speaker. We have a dance troop who will perform and a storyteller. I'm hoping to have more for the children."

"When will you have a final itinerary?" Nadine wanted to know. "We don't have a lot of time. Something like this takes about a year to plan."

"In a couple of days. I'm working night and day to arrange everything. We're starting very late but I really believe that we'll be able to pull this off."

"This sounds nice, but maybe we should think about this for next year. I'd rather do things right. When you rush . . ."

"Mother, I can do this. If we wait until next year, who knows if we'll still have customers. We need to do something to salvage our reputation in the black community."

Nadine eyed her father-in-law. "Harwood, I guess you're in agreement with this."

"Yes, I am. I think we should give her a shot. What harm can it do? And Blythe's right. We have to save our reputation. I want to save my store. This is a beginning."

"When do we get to see this new line I've been hearing so much about? This Heritage collection. Is it going to be dashikis and such? What about the other customers?"

Alda stood up. "I'll show you right now."

Blythe took a seat next to her mother, practically holding her breath. Alda went through the line, quickly describing the clothing.

When she was done, Blythe went over and hugged her friend.

"The line is superb. You outdid yourself, and in such a short time."

"I agree," Harwood said. "I like your designs. I especially like the pricing structure."

"I need to go to my office for a moment. I'll be right back." Blythe headed down the long hallway. As she studied her notes, she practically bumped into her brother. "Oh, Justin, I didn't see you."

"Hello, Sis."

"What are you doing here?"

"I just dropped some papers off for Mother and I thought I'd say hello. I see you all were in a meeting." He followed Blythe into her office. "Who's the lady with the dreads?"

"You mean you haven't heard?" When he shook his head, Blythe said, "She's the designer that Mother's been ranting about."

"Oh."

"Why?" she asked as she dropped into her chair.

"She's beautiful—in an exotic way."

Blythe leaned back in her chair. "Really? You really think so?"

"You seem shocked. Why?"

"Well, I guess it's because I've never seen you with anyone who didn't have blonde hair and blue eyes."

Justin's expression was unreadable. "You're exaggerating, Sis."

"No, I really mean it."

"Maybe it's because I've never met a woman like Alda," he countered. "I guess you know I'd like you to introduce me."

Blythe eyed him guardedly. "And why should I do that?"

"Why are you grilling me, Sis? Are you that protective of all of the employees here?"

"She's not just an employee here. She's my best friend."

His eyes registered his surprise. "Your best friend?"

"I met Alda when I first moved to Paris."

"So, is she married or otherwise involved?"

Blythe smiled. "No, she's single."

"Do you think she'd be interested in someone like me?"

"Why do you want to meet her?"

Justin laughed. "Why do most men want to meet women?"

"Well, if that's the reason, you can forget it."

"Blythe, what is wrong with you, girl? Why are you always such a witch?"

"How dare you!" She lashed out in anger. "Justin, you'd better get out of my office right now."

"Look, I'm sorry. I shouldn't have said that. Just introduce me, please."

"Why don't you just go on and introduce yourself?" Blythe twisted in her seat, snapping her fingers, then waving him off. "You don't need me."

"She's your friend."

"Leave her alone, Justin. Alda's not your type."

Justin curled his fist and pursed his lips. "How do you know whether she's my type or not?"

"Take my word for it." Blythe checked her watch. "I've got to get back to work."

"Blythe, there you are. I've been looking for you." Alda rushed over, her dreadlocks flying about her shoulders. Spying Justin, she said, "You're that guy who nearly knocked me down yesterday."

"This is my brother, Justin."

Alda's mouth dropped open. "Oooh no." She put her hand over her mouth. "I didn't know."

Justin stood up and held out his hand. "It's good to see you again, Alda."

"I'm so embarrassed."

Blythe cleared her throat loudly. "You wanted to see *me*, Alda?"

She giggled and turned to face her. "Blythe, I just wanted to let you know that the line will be ready in time. You have a lot on your plate and I don't want you to worry about this, too."

Although Alda was talking to her, she kept her eyes on Justin. Blythe peeped around her to her brother. "Was there something else?"

The caramel in his face flushed up and he managed to stammer, "No . . . no, I guess that was . . . that was all." Justin turned to leave.

"Could you wait just one minute? I want to have a word with you," Alda stated.

Blythe frowned. When Justin stepped outside the office, she asked, "What are you up to?"

"Why didn't you ever tell me about this brother of yours. He's a fine specimen, I will give you that."

She blinked twice, trying to make sense of what Alda was saying. "I think you need to get out more."

Alda and Blythe strolled into the offices of the *Heritage Reporter*, three days later.

"Hello, Caryn," Blythe said. "I want to apologize for my actions the last time I was here."

The receptionist looked surprised. "It's . . . it's okay, Miss Bloodstone. I understand completely." She cleared her throat. "If you'll take a seat, Mr. Sanford will be with you shortly."

"Thanks." Blythe turned to Alda and led her to the chairs nearby.

"I love his choice of art work. This man has good taste."

"They're hand-painted Korhogo wall hangings from the Ivory Coast," Blythe announced. "I have some postcards with similar drawings. They are nice."

"Hmmm, I'm impressed," Alda teased. "But you took a course on African art, didn't you?"

Blythe nodded. "It's one of my dreams to go to Africa and . . ." Her voice died as she spotted Khalil coming their way.

He raked over her body with his eyes and smiled his obvious approval. "Hello, ladies."

"Hi, Khalil," Alda said.

"It's good to see you again," Blythe murmured softly.

Khalil led them to an empty conference room. When they were seated, Caryn came in with coffee and water.

She gave Khalil a quick summary of her plans.

"Blythe, your idea about having boutiques set up on each floor is a good one, I think. Have you already selected your vendors?" Khalil asked.

She nodded. "I want authentic goods, and so some of the vendors are coming from as far as Ghana and Mali thanks to Alda. I've also purchased some fabulous canvas tote bags in beautifully printed African motifs. We're going to give them to every customer who purchases goods from any of the African boutiques."

"What about the fashion show? Will any customer be able to purchase something they've seen modeled?" Khalil shifted in his seat. "I realize the Couture Salon features one-of-a-kind clothing but—"

"We've got that covered," Blythe interjected. "Alda's created a line just for this event. The clothing will be priced from one hundred to one thousand dollars. So, there should be something for everyone." She smiled at her friend. "Khalil, the line is wonderful. I can't wait for you to see the clothes."

"Anything for men?" he asked. "We like to look good, too."

Alda laughed. "Yes, we've got something for you men. In fact, you've just given me a brilliant idea. I think you should model in the fashion show."

Khalil's eyes stretched open. "Me?" He shook his head laughing. "I'm not the model type."

"You'd be perfect. Come on," Alda pleaded. "Do it for our people. We are proud black men and women. Strut your stuff, mon."

Laughing, Blythe nodded. "Khalil, you'd be perfect. You should do it."

There was a knock at the door. A tall slender woman stood there, her eyes filled with curiosity. "What's going on?" she asked.

"Kuiana, come in." Khalil stood up. "Alda, Blythe, this is my sister and partner, Kuiana Sanford."

"It's very nice to meet you," Blythe murmured. The look Khalil's sister gave her made her suddenly uncomfortable. She could tell that Kuiana didn't like her.

Khalil didn't seem to notice. "And this is Alda. She's the designer over at Bloodstone's. She's trying to recruit me as a model for the fashion show."

"For the Kwanzaa celebration?" When he nodded, she said, "I think you should do it."

"What about you, Kuiana?" Alda asked. "I have some things that would look so good on you."

"Me?" Her expression of surprise matched Khalil's look earlier. "Are you kidding?"

"You'd make a good model," Alda continued. "Don't you agree, Blythe?"

She nodded.

"Well, it looks like we've got two more models. Great." Alda checked her notes. "I think we've covered everything. I should get back to the store. I've got a lot of work to do."

Blythe stood up. "I think we're almost ready. I just hope this works." Alda led the way to the door, giving Blythe and Khalil privacy to continue their conversation.

"I don't think you have to worry, Blythe. You should be proud of yourself," he assured her.

"I couldn't have done it without you, Khalil. I don't know how I'll ever repay you." They walked outside.

"How about attending an art show with me later?" he asked as he escorted her to her car. Alda was already seated and buckled in.

"Sure. What time should I be ready."

"I'll pick you up around eight," Khalil said as he opened the door for her.

"I'll be ready." Blythe slid into her car. She waved before driving away. Without looking at Alda, she warned, "Don't you say a word."

"I wasn't going to open my mouth, but since you brought it up, I'm glad to see that you're coming to your senses. Khalil is a good man."

It's just an art show, Alda. I'm not going to marry the man."

"It is a date. That's how it starts, *ma cherie.*"

"Well, I'm going to take it one date at a time. This time

everything that happens will be on my terms. Nothing will happen unless *I* want it to.''

''Good luck, *ma cherie.*''

After Blythe dropped Alda off at the store, she drove home singing at the top of her lungs. She hadn't done that in a long time. She was really excited about her date with Khalil. Turning down the volume on her CD player, she forced herself to be realistic. This was simply a date—two people sharing their love for art.

She reminded herself to be realistic about everything. Khalil's attraction to her was only sexual. She knew that and she didn't care. Because what she felt for him was also physical. This time she would ask for nothing more—expect nothing more. This time she would not allow herself to be hurt. Although Blythe longed to have someone love her, she thought it best to settle for not being lonely.

When she arrived home, Nadine was already there.

''Will you be joining us for dinner?'' she asked.

Blythe stopped near the stairs, her arm on the rail. ''No, Mother. I'm going out. I have a date.''

Adam wheeled himself into the living room. ''Did I just hear you say something about a date?''

She smiled at the astonished expression on his face. He had been after her for weeks now to start dating again. ''Yes, Father. I have a date.''

''Is it anyone we know?'' Nadine asked. ''Are you going out with Percy?''

Blythe turned to face her mother. ''No. It's Khalil Sanford.''

Nadine actually paled. ''Surely you're not going out with *him.*''

Scratching his head, Adam asked, ''Is he the publisher of that paper . . . the *Heritage Reporter?*''

Nodding, Blythe said, ''He's the one.'' She headed up the stairs, ignoring her mother's questioning glance. ''If you both will excuse me, I've got to get ready.''

* * *

Blythe changed clothes several times before deciding on a long black velvet dress and matching shawl. She stepped into a pair of Donald Pliner pumps.

As she stared into the mirror, a twinge of uncertainty crossed her mind. For the first time in her life, she hated the way she looked.

The clanging of the doorbell announced Khalil's arrival. She felt her heart pick up speed. *He was here.* Hearing Nadine call her, Blythe left her room and descended the stairs slowly.

As she glided down, Khalil assessed her from head to toe. "You look beautiful."

She smiled. "Thank you." Those three little words meant the whole world to her. As usual, Khalil was dressed in an Afrocentric fashion.

In the car, Blythe asked, "Where are we going?"

"Mojo Galleries. Ever been there?"

"Yes, of course. It's been years though since I've been there." She felt compelled to add, "I've been so busy with my father and the store . . . I haven't had much time for anything else."

"I understand."

"I remember the first time I went there. It was a visual feast that could rival any good food festival or antique show that I've ever attended. Every inch of their wall space was covered with some of the most beautiful pieces of art work I've ever seen."

Khalil smiled. "It hasn't changed. I've acquired most of my art from them."

As soon as Blythe and Khalil left the house, Nadine turned on her husband. "How could you take her side, Adam? It doesn't look right."

"To whom? Blythe is our daughter. You treat her like she's some stranger."

"I do not." She sat down on the love seat, her shoulders slumped. "I'm so sick of you saying that to me."

"I'm not trying to hurt you, but you need to remember

something. Blythe is a grown woman. She can make decisions for herself.'' Adam began to wheel himself out of the room.

Nadine looked up. ''Where . . . where are you going?''

''To my room.''

''Are you feeling ill?''

''No. Why?''

''I . . . I thought we could talk, Adam.''

He wheeled back toward her. ''Sure. What do you want to talk about?''

''Adam, I . . . I hate it when you call me a bad mother,'' she replied in a low, tormented voice. She stood up and moved to stand before the fireplace.

''I've never said that, Nadine.''

She wouldn't turn around. ''But it's really what you meant.''

''I simply said that you should listen to the children sometimes. When they try to talk to you, you dismiss them like servants.''

Nadine whirled around then. ''Adam, I have no patience for nonsense. All Blythe cares about is her feelings. She wants me to coddle her and I can't do that.''

''Blythe simply wants her mother.''

''See, there you are. You're doing it again. She's my daughter and I—''

''You don't know her at all,'' Adam interjected. ''She craves your love, Nadine.''

''My parents never loved me. My mother died and left me with that sick beast who was supposed to be my father . . . But I survived.'' She put her hand to her mouth as if she'd said too much. ''I didn't mean that I don't love my daughter. I do.'' Tears ran down her cheeks. ''I don't know how to show her. I'm not sure I even know how to love anybody.''

Adam wheeled himself over to where she stood. Pulling her down in his lap, he held Nadine as she cried. ''Honey, you are so full of love, you're just so afraid to open up,'' he whispered. ''These are your children and they love you unconditionally.''

''They hate me, Adam.''

He shook his head. ''No, they don't. They won't reject you like your parents did.''

"I'm not so sure. I think it's much too late. Especially with Blythe." Nadine raised her head, peering at him. "She blames me for your accident, you know."

"I don't think that's true. She knows what happened that night. Blythe knows everything." He stroked her cheek gently.

"Adam . . ." Nadine rose to her feet. She leaned against the built-in entertainment unit, looking unsure of herself.

"Yes," he prompted.

"I need to know something. And I want the truth. Do you still love me?"

"Nadine, I love you more than my own life. I've never stopped loving you."

"Then how could you cheat on me?" she whispered. "Were you going to leave me for her?"

"What I did was wrong, honey. But it had nothing to do with love. We weren't getting along and she made me feel like a man."

"I guess I didn't." His response gnawed away at her confidence.

"Nadine, it was wrong. I was angry with you and the way you were treating me. You made me feel like I was incapable of running my father's company. You . . . you made me feel used. That you'd gotten what you wanted and had no further use for me."

"I never meant to imply anything like that. I simply didn't think you were interested in the business. I love the store, Adam. I realize that it's your father's store—Lord knows, he never lets me forget it."

"I just . . . I guess it was my pride. The truth is that up until Dad gave you the position as General Manager, I hadn't given it much thought. I took it for granted he would give the store to me."

"If you want it, I'll resign, Adam."

He shook his head. "I wouldn't do that to you." He could see her relax visibly.

Nadine studied him. "You look tired. I'll have Winston prepare your bath. And I'll get your bed ready."

"Winston can take care of it."

"No, Adam. I'd like to do it. I really don't mind."

"Are you sure it's no bother?"

"I want to do it." She wheeled him into his bedroom. "Is everything comfortable in here? I tried to make it nice . . ."

"It's fine."

The distance between them seemed to broaden. Nadine chewed her bottom lip. There was so much she wanted to say but couldn't. She was relieved to see Winston. "Adam's tired. Could you give him his bath? I'll have the bed ready when you're done."

"Yes ma'am," was Winston's quiet reply.

Adam gave her a long look before Winston wheeled him into his bathroom.

"I miss you so much," Nadine sighed as she turned down his bed.

"This is beautiful. I love the vibrant colors in it," Blythe was saying as she pointed to an exhibit entitled *A Sunday Afternoon* by Margo Humphrey.

"It is nice. Look at this one." Khalil escorted her over to a Jacob Lawrence painting.

"Magnifique," she murmured softly. "I love this one." She moved closer to examine it.

"I think my favorite is *Harlem Knights* by Allen Stringfellow."

Blythe nodded. "I liked that one too."

After the showing, Khalil drove her to a nearby coffee shop. When they were seated, Blythe allowed herself to get a real good look at Khalil. She thought she would never grow tired of studying him. She drank in his handsome features and sexy smile.

Khalil smiled. "Are you done staring?" His eyes were a beautiful brown, and guarded.

Embarrassed, she took a sip of her mocha mint coffee. "I wasn't staring—just looking."

"Do I pass?"

Blythe put her hand to her mouth and laughed. "Yes, you pass."

He pulled her hand away from her mouth. "You have a beautiful smile. Stop hiding it."

She drank slowly, wanting to drag the evening out. "I'm glad we came here. I can't thank you enough for your help, Khalil. After the way I barged into your office that day, I'm really surprised you've been as helpful as you have."

He laughed. "I knew you weren't a bad person. There's something about you that intrigued me."

"Oh really?"

Khalil leaned back in his chair, this time studying her. "Tell me about yourself."

"What do you want to know?"

"What do you like to do in your spare time?"

"Well, I love to read. I read everything. Romance, mystery, nonfiction—everything. I love to paint and I love to travel. Outside of work, I don't do much else. But then I've only been home four months now."

"What do you paint?"

"Nothing compared to the masterpieces we just saw. Mostly landscapes and I've done a few self-portraits."

"I'd like to see them. As you can see I'm an art lover myself."

"I don't show them to anyone," she said quickly. "They're not very good."

Khalil frowned. "Who told you that?"

"Nobody did. I can see it for myself."

"I'd really like to see them."

"I'll think about it."

They finished up their coffee in silence.

Blythe wiped her mouth daintily with the corner of her napkin. She muttered a curse when she noticed that she'd spilled some on her dress. Finding his eyes on her, she mumbled, "I guess you think I'm a pig or something. It's just—"

"No, I don't," he interrupted. "I was just thinking that you should smile more often."

"Tell me about yourself?" she asked softly. "I'd like to know more about you."

"Well, I'm a lover of black art, a lover of books by black authors and a collector of African-American memorabilia."

"So you won't read books by other writers?"

"I never say never, but my preference is to support my brothers and sisters."

"What type of memorabilia do you have in your collection?"

"I have books, artifacts, documents and photographs. For instance, I have *The History of Alpha Phi Alpha,* a celebration of my fraternity brothers. I have a copy of *The Negro Soldiers in Our War.* It's an important book that documents our contribution to World War I. I have over a hundred books that chronicle our contributions throughout."

"Can't say I've read either of those. What college did you attend—no, wait don't answer that." She laughed. "I bet I already know."

Khalil grinned. "Okay, which one?"

"Morehouse?"

He shook his head. "No, wrong one."

"I know it's a black college. That much I know. Was it Clark?"

Again, he shook his head.

"Florida A & M?" When Khalil shook his head a third time, she broke into more giggles. "Why didn't I think of it before? It's Howard University, right?"

Khalil threw back his head laughing. "Do you give up?"

She loved watching him. When he laughed, he seemed years younger. "No. Was it Grambling?"

"Yes. I attended Grambling. I was even in the band."

"What did you play?"

"Saxophone." Blythe tried to envision him performing with Grambling's talented band.

"I used to work it, girl."

She laughed, hiding her mouth behind her hand. "I'm sure you did."

"So, Miss Bloodstone, let me see if I can guess where you went to college. Probably the University of South California."

"You're right."

"Would you like another coffee?" Khalil asked.

"Yes, thank you."

"A woman after my own heart," he murmured.

Blythe glanced around the coffee shop. "I've really enjoyed myself. I owe it all to you." Grinning, she added, "But then you did say that I needed to lighten up."

"You do. It's not healthy to be so serious all of the time."

She grew solemn. "I don't think I know any other way to be. I've always been this way."

Khalil leaned back in his chair. "You know what? I'm going to teach you to have a good time."

Inclining her head, Blythe asked, "And just how do you intend to do that?"

"You will just have to trust me on this. Think you can do that?"

"Trust doesn't come easy for me, Khalil," Blythe said softly. For a moment, she wished desperately that she were still able to give, to hope, to be loved.

He grinned. "There's always a first time," Khalil said as if in response to her silent musings.

Chapter 11

Blythe dropped her laundry on her bed when the phone rang. Hoping it was Khalil, she rushed to answer it. "Hello."

"Hi, it's me."

She smiled at the sound of Khalil's voice. "How are you doing?"

"I'm fine. What do you have planned for today? I remembered your telling me that you were off."

"Nothing on my schedule. What do you have in mind?" Blythe reasoned that she could do her laundry later.

"Well, I have a surprise for you. I'd like to come by your house, if you don't mind. I thought we could do something later."

"Sounds mysterious. I can't wait." While she talked to Khalil, she kicked off her slippers. Blythe switched the cordless phone from one ear to the other as she strolled into her closet in search of something to wear.

When she hung up, Blythe rushed into the shower.

By the time Khalil arrived, she had dressed in a pair of purple denim jeans and a matching linen shirt.

He assessed her from head to toe, beaming his approval. "I didn't take you for the jeans type of woman. However, do you have a pair of sneakers instead of the expensive leather boots you're wearing?''

She followed his gaze to her shoes. "I do, but why should I change?''

"Because of your surprise. It's outside, by the way."

"Outside?" Blythe eyed him suspiciously. "What are you up to, Khalil?''

"You'll see.'' He pointed upstairs. "Change into your sneakers and I'll show you.''

Blythe went upstairs and changed her shoes. When she returned, she found Khalil was already outside.

All she saw was a brand-new bicycle. "What is this?''

Khalil howled with laughter. "Don't tell me you don't recognize a bike when you see one?''

"I know it's a bike, but what are you going to do with it? And why are there two?''

"I'm going to ride one and you'll ride the other. In other words, we're going to the park and do some bicycling.''

A wave of embarrassment washed over her. "Khalil . . . I don't ride bikes.''

"See, that's what I've been telling you. You need to have some fun.''

"I don't ride because I can't ride," she further explained.

"Huh?" He was clearly astonished.

"I don't know how to ride a bicycle.''

Khalil bit back his laughter. "You're kidding.''

She shook her head. "I've never even owned a bike. Never wanted one.''

"Well, today you're going to learn.''

Blythe eyed the bike. "I don't know about this, Khalil.''

"Come on. Everything will be just fine. You might even have a little bit of fun.''

"Somehow I doubt that," Blythe muttered as she climbed in Khalil's jeep.

They went over to a park in Ladera Heights.

Khalil smiled over Blythe's look of skepticism as she eyed

the bicycle. She didn't look frightened—just wary. Clumsily, she mounted the bike. Blythe looked to Khalil further, as if seeking instructions.

"Now you put your feet on the pedals."

He bit back a smile when she struggled with balancing the bike. Awkwardly, Blythe took off. Khalil started riding his bike behind her.

"How am I doing so far?" she yelled out. She was moving along slowly.

"Just fine," he responded.

Soon she seemed to gain some confidence and picked up speed.

"I think I'm getting the hang of this," she declared with pride.

He stopped riding when he saw her approaching a curve on the trail. "Blythe, turn," he called out. "Look out . . ." Khalil squeezed his eyes shut as she slammed into a palm tree.

He rushed over to her, taking her into his arms. "Sweetheart, are you okay?"

"Couldn't you have said something sooner?" Putting her hands to her face, she said, "I'm so embarrassed. I'm never getting back on that bike." She hurt like hell, but she was amazed at how steady her voice sounded.

"You have to get back on. You can't give up."

"Look at my knees, Khalil." She closed her eyes, unable to hide her pain.

He followed her gaze. Blythe's jeans were ripped and her knees bruised and bleeding. "Ooh baby. I'm so sorry."

She forced a brave smile. "Do you have a first-aid kit in your car by any chance?"

"Actually, I do. I'll go get it."

"Wait, Khalil, I'll go with you." She braced herself on the offending tree. "It'll just take me a moment to get up."

"You stay here with the bikes. After I get you all bandaged up, you're going to get back on it."

She eyed him. *"Are you crazy?* I'm not getting back on that thing."

Khalil moved to within a hair's breadth of her face and said, "You're not going to give up so easily. I won't let you."

Folding her arms across her chest, Blythe turned her head away. She wasn't about to get back on that bike no matter what Khalil Sanford said.

"I know you're not going to let a little old bike get the best of you," he stated before he left to go to his car. She threw daggers at his back with her eyes.

That did it. Blythe wasn't about to let her fear of getting back on the bicycle overtake her. If she had to pull every tree out of the ground by the roots to move them out of her way, she would learn to ride. Standing up slowly and moaning in anguish, Blythe pulled up the bike. Looking it over, she couldn't find any damage. She walked around it, glaring.

When he returned, Khalil found Blythe riding around in a circle. She was still a bit wobbly and unsure of herself, but he admired her determination. When she looked up to find him watching her, Blythe presented him with a bright smile, causing his heart to warm over.

"You're looking good."

"My knees hurt like hell. I think I'd better let you bandage them." She stopped the bike and got off as if she'd been riding for years.

Khalil tenderly cleaned her scratches with an antiseptic. Her skin was soft. Whisper soft.

"You have a gentle touch," Blythe observed. "Maybe you should've become a doctor."

He shook his head. "No, I don't think so. I wouldn't have been a good one. I don't like hospitals or doctor's offices."

"I don't either. I do my best to stay away from them."

When Khalil was done, he pulled her up. Blythe asked, "Are you doing what you've always wanted to do? I mean, is this the way you wanted your life to go?"

"Yes. I've always wanted to have my own newspaper. I realized that when I got my first job. I was a paper boy."

Blythe smiled. "I wanted to be an artist. I even studied art in college."

"What happened?"

She gave a small laugh. "My mother suggested I get a real job."

Placing a Band-Aid on one knee and then the other, Blythe looked up at Khalil and asked, "How could you let me run into that tree like that?"

"I yelled for you to stop." Khalil had to tear his gaze away from her. It was too easy to get lost in the way she looked at him.

"But you didn't tell me how." Groaning, Blythe stood up slowly with his assistance. "Look at me. I've got Band-Aids on both knees and my jeans are torn . . ."

Khalil's dark eyes smoldered as he observed her disheveled appearance. "But didn't you have a good time?"

"Huh?"

"In spite of everything, did you have fun?"

Blythe suddenly burst into laughter. "Yes, I had a wonderful time."

"Good. The next time, we'll go skating."

Her smile disappeared. "Skating? Khalil, I've never been on skates before in my life. Are you trying to kill me?"

"No. Tell me, Blythe, what exactly have you done? Do you swim?"

She shook her head. "No, I don't."

"Play tennis?"

"No. Well I actually took lessons but my instructor gave up. He said I was much too ladylike for tennis."

Khalil threw back his head in laughter.

"Okay, so I'm not an outdoor person. Does that make me strange?" Haughtiness crept into her tone at his laughter.

"No, it simply makes you special." Khalil chuckled. "I've never met anyone like you."

She warmed at his compliment. No one had ever told her that. Parker had always put her down. And her paintings. Blythe smirked. As if he had any room to talk.

In one easy motion, his arm went around her waist. Blythe found herself enclosed in the arms she'd longed for what seemed like forever. It was as if she'd come home.

Savoring the feel of his body against hers, Blythe inhaled

his cologne. She felt as though she couldn't get close enough to Khalil.

Lowering his head, Khalil brushed his lips over hers ever so lightly. "I've been wanting to do this for a while." Reclaiming her mouth, he crushed her to him.

Her kiss shook him to his very soul. It surprised him how delicate and vulnerable she really was. Blythe kissed him with a depth that had both of them swimming in a pool of sexual heat.

Nothing had prepared Blythe for the heat that was generated between them. It was enough to cause a nuclear meltdown. They had a chemistry so potent, she found it hard to believe.

Khalil kissed her once more before he let her go, but not before Blythe felt his reaction to their kiss.

He tried to blank his mind and found he couldn't. Khalil wanted Blythe. He wanted her on his bed, writhing naked beneath his own sex-starved body.

They parted reluctantly and stood in awkward silence.

Blythe cleared her throat. "I'm ready to take a ride around the park. I think I've got the hang of it."

They climbed on their bikes. Khalil let Blythe take off first and then he followed. They were soon riding side by side.

When the sun began to go down, they decided to call it a day. "Let's head to the car. It's starting to get dark."

All during the drive home, she thought about the kisses they'd shared.

"What are you thinking about?" Khalil asked.

"Just about everything that happened today." She peeked over at him. "I had a good time."

"So did I."

"How are your knees feeling?"

"They sting a little, but they will be fine."

They arrived at her house much too quickly for Blythe. The thought of leaving Khalil depressed her. She had thoroughly enjoyed his company.

He turned into her driveway. "Well, I've returned you home the same way I picked you up."

Blythe denied his statement in her mind. She was not the same and she doubted that she would ever be.

Khalil placed a caring hand at her chin. "I would like to see you again."

She couldn't help smiling. "I'd like that."

Leaning over, he took her face in both of his hands and kissed her once more. Tremors of excitement rippled through her and she had to pull away. "I'd better go inside. I still have to do my laundry."

"Care to do mine?" he asked lightly.

Blythe laughed as Khalil got out and walked around the car to open the door for her. They stared at each other for what seemed like an eternity. She couldn't get enough of Khalil.

Nadine was coming downstairs as she stepped into the foyer after Khalil drove away. Taking in her daughter's appearance, she rushed the rest of the way down. "Blythe, what happened to you? Are you okay?"

She burst into laughter, thrilled that her mother was concerned for her. "I'm fine. I went bike riding with Khalil—"

"But you never learned to ride," Nadine interjected.

"That's why I look like this. I learned today."

"I've always assumed you had no interest in learning."

"You're right, Mother. I didn't, but now I wish I had learned. It's a lot of fun."

Her mother smiled "I'll take your word for it."

Blythe's mouth dropped open. "You never learned?"

"No. We couldn't afford a bike. There were too many of us."

"You have siblings?"

Shame crept into her eyes after her confession. Nadine cast her eyes downward. "There were seven of us. I was the oldest. When my mother died, my father tried to put all of us in a home. He didn't want us any more. They took all of them but me."

Blythe could see the pain in her mother's eyes. "I never knew."

"No one did except your father. I've never seen any of my brothers and sisters again. I used to resent them so much for

being able to get away . . ." Her voice broke and she turned
away, walking into the living room.

Blythe followed, feeling that her mother needed to talk about
this. "What happened after they left?" She feared the worst.

Nadine must have sensed this. "He . . . he said that I had to
earn my keep. I couldn't get a job so . . ." She shook her head.
"Then afterward, he would call me a whore. He said he hated
me because it was my fault that he'd had to marry my slut of
a mother." She put her hand to her mouth to keep from crying
out loud.

Blythe wanted desperately to reach out to her mother but
she feared her rejection. "I'm so sorry."

Nadine composed herself. "It's the past. One shouldn't dwell
on the past. You have to move on. Accept what happened and
move on. I know he's a sick bastard and it wasn't my fault."
She moved closer to Blythe and lowered her voice. "I'm going
to ask you to do something for me. Do not ever discuss this
with Moira or Justin."

The distant coldness was back. Blythe nodded.

"After tonight, we must never speak of this again. Understand?"

Again, Blythe nodded.

"Thank you." Nadine moved around her. "I'd better go
check on your father. He went to bed early. I want to make
sure he's feeling okay."

"Well, I'd better head to my room. I've got some laundry
to do."

"Sarah's coming tomorrow. She can do it for you," Nadine
suggested.

Blythe reached for the rail. "I'd rather do it myself. Sarah
has enough to do." Heading upstairs, she kept seeing the pain
and the shame in her mother's eyes. Nadine had opened up to
her, but at the same time, she'd shut herself away from her.
Instead of bonding, the gulf had widened.

Determined to move past what she'd been told, she did her
laundry and cleaned her room. Three hours later, Blythe decided
it was harder to forget than she thought. Dropping down on
the fabric-covered bench at the foot of her bed, she put her

hands to her face and cried until she couldn't cry anymore. Anger seeped in.

Nobody should have to suffer that kind of abuse. Blythe's heart ached for her mother and the kind of childhood she'd been forced to have. If only she could comfort Nadine . . . That wouldn't happen. Her mother wouldn't let her.

Lying in a bathtub full of bubbles, Blythe closed her eyes and dreamed of Khalil. She wanted to take her mind off of her mother's secret anguish. How she wished she were anywhere but home alone right now. Teary-eyed, she sat up slowly. Blythe stood up and reached for a fluffy towel. After drying her still heated body, she dressed in silk pajamas.

She crawled into her waiting bed. Glaring at the luminous numbers on the clock by her bed, she knew that she wouldn't be able to fall asleep for hours. All she could think about was Khalil and how much she wished he were lying next to her.

Blythe stopped into Alda's office. "How did it go with Justin?"

"Oh, we had such a wonderful time. Your brother is divine."

Wanting to change the subject, she asked, "What are you doing for Christmas?"

"Wilma's flying in for the holidays and Justin invited us to spend Christmas with your family. Normally we don't celebrate Christmas—just Kwanzaa—but I think we'll join you all for dinner. He's so thoughtful."

Blythe rolled her eyes. "Good old Justin," she muttered under her breath. "Is Wilma still seeing George?"

"I think they're taking a break from each other right now. What did you do over the weekend?" Alda asked.

"I went bike riding with Khalil."

"Really? I thought you said you couldn't ride?"

In response, Blythe lifted up her boot-length skirt.

Alda laughed. "I take it that all went well."

"With the exception of the battle scars, I think it was kind of fun. I had a good time with Khalil. He's so sweet." Smiling, Blythe fingered a shimmering burgundy and gold fabric with an Egyptian scarab design. "This is nice, Alda. I love the color."

"You know, if I didn't know any better, I would say you were glowing."

Blythe looked up, a distinctly amused twinkle in her medium brown eyes as she caught Alda's smug expression. "What are you talking about?"

"I think you know."

She held up her hand in mock surrender. "Okay, I'll admit that I'm very much attracted to Khalil. I want him so bad, Alda ... " Blythe gave an embarrassed smile. "I sound like a sex maniac, don't I?"

"Non, you sound like a woman who's not been intimate with a man in almost four years. It's only been eight months for me and I'm climbing the walls. *I want sex."*

Blythe closed the door to Alda's office. "I can't believe you yelled that out like that. You're crazy."

"Non, what I am is, what do you say, hor—"

Laughing, Blythe cut her off. "Don't even say it. I've forgotten how blunt you can be sometimes." She sat at the table where Alda was working.

"There is no need to ashamed. We are very sexual beings."

"Let's talk about something else. Like how is everything coming along?"

Alda smiled. "The Heritage collection will be ready and we are going to wow everyone. This is my best work."

"You say that about all of your designs. But you're right— this is your absolute best." Blythe rose slowly. "I'd better get back to my office before Mother comes looking for me. Do you want to do something tonight?"

"Justin and I are going out. Maybe we can do something together this weekend."

"You're seeing my brother again? It's been what? Every night since you two met." Blythe didn't like the thought of Alda seeing Justin. She didn't want to see her friend get hurt.

Without taking her eyes off her work, Alda stated, "We have fun together."

"I just hope you don't let him hurt you. Justin is not exactly the marrying kind."

"Right now, marriage is the last thing on my mind ..."

The expression on Alda's face revealed exactly what was on her friend's mind. Blythe felt the need to caution her once more. "Just be careful."

The phone rang, cutting off any response from Alda. When she answered, she gestured for Blythe. "It's your assistant."

She took the phone. "Yes, Peggy?"

"Mr. Khalil Sanford is here to see you. He says he didn't have an appointment. What would you like for me to do?"

"Tell him I'll be right there." Hanging up, Blythe said, "I've got to go. Khalil's upstairs."

"Have fun, *ma cherie.*"

She rushed back to her office. Khalil was sitting in the outer office. He rose to his feet when he saw her.

"So what do I owe this surprise to?"

"Well, I was in the area, so I thought I'd stop in and say hello." He lowered his voice. "I wanted to see this beautiful face of yours."

Blythe wanted so much to feel his sexy mouth on hers. Determined to keep her passion under control, she glanced away. Catching sight of a figure coming toward them, she opened her mouth to speak but couldn't. Her body trembled and she reached for Khalil. "I've got to call security."

"Honey, what's wrong?" he asked.

"It ... it's that boy. He and another boy tried to steal my car the first day I went to see you."

"What? I don't believe that." Khalil gestured to the youth. "Bobby, can you come here for a moment?"

"What are you doing?" she whispered. "Please don't make a scene."

"I'm not," he whispered back. "Bobby, this is my friend, Blythe Bloodstone."

The young man pulled his hat back. "I remember you. I didn't mean to scare you that day. I was trying to let you know that you left a pad of paper on the trunk of your car."

The sincerity was so clear on his face that she felt compelled to say, "I'm so sorry. I . . ."

"I know you thought we was thugs or something but that's not us at all."

Khalil pulled the boy's cap off. "Looking at the way you're dressed and the way the media portrays blacks on TV, it's no wonder she was afraid."

"Aw man . . . come on, Khalil. This is what everybody's wearing . . . You're always saying that clothing don't make the man."

"Don't try to twist my words around. Go on downstairs. I'll be there in a minute."

"Okay, I found this jamming jacket that I want . . ."

Without taking his eyes off Blythe, he said, "I'll be down in a minute."

"Nice meeting you, Miss Bloodstone. Your family's got a nice store here. Khalil here is buying me something to wear for my winter formal."

She smiled. "I think that's very sweet. We have a wonderful selection of dinner jackets." She was touched by his generosity to the youth. "And it's very nice meeting you, Bobby."

When the boy disappeared, she turned to Khalil, asking, "How do you know him?"

"He and Ralph do little odd jobs for me. They are good kids. Both are from single-parent homes."

"I feel really bad about the way I misjudged them."

"I can see how you would be afraid. But the same thing could happen anywhere. Beverly Hills, Ladera Heights . . . anywhere."

Nodding, Blythe replied, "You're right. Crime is not limited to South Central or Watts."

"Oh, by the way, I have something for you. I was going to leave them for you."

"What is it?"

Khalil strolled over to a nearby chair and picked up two gift-wrapped boxes.

Blythe took a seat. Excited, she tore open the first one. She wasn't sure what to make of the contents. "Knee pads?"

"Yes. Now open the other box."

"Skates. I can't believe you bought me skates, Khalil. I think roses would've been cheaper."

"Try them on. I guessed at your size."

Hesitantly, she put them on. Blythe could hardly believe it. "They are a perfect fit. This is scary."

"Try to stand up on them."

"I don't think so, Khalil. I'm not going to break my butt here in the store."

He grinned. "You'll be fine. It just takes some getting used to."

Blythe raised her eyes to him and pointed to her knees. "That's what you said about the bike."

"I know you're not going to let a pair of skates keep you from—"

"When are we going skating?" she interjected.

"Do you have any plans for this weekend?"

She met his smile with one of her own. "I don't have anything planned. I'm free as a bird." In that moment, Blythe had never been freer. She wanted Khalil in a way that she'd never wanted Parker. Their lovemaking had been okay, at best. But she was sure making love with Khalil would be phenomenal. Blythe was going to have him and it would be on her terms.

Chapter 12

On Friday afternoon, Alda rapped on Blythe's door. "Justin and I are going to play miniature golf this evening. Why don't you and Khalil join us?"

She stood up and walked around her desk. Peering out of her window, Blythe replied, "Oh, I don't know. I don't know if he—"

"If Khalil what?" A deep voice boomed from behind her, causing her to turn around. "Hi Khalil. I didn't expect to see you."

Alda hugged him. "How are you, Khalil?"

"I'm fine. How do you like living in Los Angeles so far?"

"I love it. Your ears must have been burning. I was just asking Blythe if the two of you would like to join Justin and I. We're going to play miniature golf."

Blythe strolled to stand beside Khalil. "Two visits in one week. I'm getting spoiled."

"I came to see if I could kidnap you for a couple of hours." To Alda, he said, "Miniature golf sounds like fun. I haven't done that in a long time."

"You play?" Blythe was surprised.

"Sure, don't you?"

Blythe shook her head. "No. I've never been interested in any kind of golf." She tried to sound intrigued with the idea, but she really wasn't. Why would anyone want to go hit little balls around at an amusement park?

"What time are you planning to leave?" Khalil asked.

"Seven o'clock," Alda replied. She was watching Blythe's face. "What about you, Blythe? Do you want to go?"

Khalil was watching her also. She forced a smile and nodded. "Of course. It should be fun." She took him by the hand. "Give me a minute to grab my things and we're out of here."

"You two have fun. I'll see you later this evening." Alda left the office.

"Okay, out with it. Why don't you want to spend the evening with Alda and your brother?" Khalil asked.

"Huh?" Blythe turned her attention to him. "What did you say?"

"It's obvious that you're not comfortable with the idea of them seeing each other. Why?"

"They don't belong together."

"Who says?"

"I do." Blythe gazed up at Khalil. "Justin will only hurt her."

Khalil rubbed his bearded chin. "How can you say that? Can you read the future or something?"

"No. But I know my brother. He loves women."

"It's their business, Blythe."

Her eyes flashed anger and she stomped out of her office. Khalil followed. They walked to the elevator in silence.

"There's nothing wrong with me worrying about my friend. I assume you would be the same way if it were a friend of yours."

"Maybe, then maybe not."

"Yeah right."

"I didn't come here to spend the day arguing with you."

She stared at him for just a moment before saying, "Let's just forget it."

"Blythe, sweetheart—"

"No, Khalil. I can't take this holier-than-thou attitude of

yours. You're no better than I am, so please stop acting like it.''

"What are you talking about?''

"Think about it, Mr. I Can Do No Wrong Sanford.''

Blythe strode out of the revolving doors, her color high and her heart pounding loudly. Who in the hell did Khalil think he was? Why was she letting herself get so angry? She snatched her keys out of her purse and snagged her nail. Dropping her purse, she put her hand to her mouth to keep from cursing.

Khalil pulled her into his arms. "Calm down, sweetheart. I didn't mean to upset you.''

Blythe reveled in the warmth of his body. "Well, you did. Sometimes you come off sounding like you can do nothing wrong. You're not perfect. Not by any means.''

"I've never claimed to be perfect, baby. I just don't get involved in my friends' business. I stay out of my sister's relationships, too.''

"So you would intentionally let her walk into a bad relationship?'' Blythe asked with her hand on her hips. "I happen to care very much for Alda. When I had no one in Paris, she was there for me. I don't know if I would've survived without her.''

"I understand the depth of your loyalty to Alda, but honey, you've warned her. That's all you can do.'' Khalil brushed back her curls. "I really don't want to argue with you anymore.''

Feeling his fingers on her hair, Blythe made a mental note to call her hairdresser. It was time for a haircut. She grabbed his hand and kissed his fingers. "I don't want to argue either. I'm really sorry. Sometimes, my temper gets the best of me.''

"Get in your car. I'll follow you home. We'll take my car from there.''

"Why don't you at least pretend you're having fun?'' Khalil whispered.

"Look at them. Justin's practically all over her.'' She glared at her brother when she caught his eye.

"I don't know what the problem is between you and your

brother and I really don't care, but I have to be honest with you, I came here to have a good time.''

Blythe eyed the couple a moment longer. She hated the way Justin was kissing and groping Alda. He only wanted to land her into his bed. The way things were going, he wouldn't have to try too hard. She was making it very easy for him.

Khalil placed a hand on her shoulder. ''Are you listening to me?'' he asked.

She looked up into his face. ''I'm listening.'' Grabbing his hand, she added, ''It's your turn, I believe.''

''Loosen up, sweetheart. You might actually enjoy this game.''

''There's something I have to say to you. You don't know me, Khalil, yet you think you do. You know, I really wish someone—just one person—would actually take the time to get to know me before they start criticizing me.'' She forced back her tears of hurt and frustration.

Khalil seemed taken aback by her response. ''I wasn't trying to hurt you. I'm trying to show you how much of life you're missing out on. You shouldn't walk around so unhappy.''

''I'm sorry for putting such a damper on the evening, but I happen to find this game boring. So if you will excuse me, I'll be going home now.'' Blythe headed for the door.

Khalil caught up with her. ''You're looking for a fight. I think that's all you know how to do.''

''Go to hell, Khalil.''

''Oh no you don't. I'm not going to let you get away with that.''

For the longest moment, neither one of them said a word. Finally, he spoke. ''Come on, I'm taking you somewhere. Since you're itching for a fight, I'm going to give you one.'' Khalil grabbed her by the hand and led her over to where Justin and Alda were standing. ''We're going to cut out on you two. Blythe and I need to be alone.''

Smiling, Alda nodded. ''I understand. Justin and I will be leaving soon ourselves.''

Blythe blanched at the pure sexual look she gave Justin. Shaking her head in disapproval, she allowed Khalil to lead her away. As they headed to his car, she asked, "Where are you taking me?"

"Somewhere where we can talk. There are some things we have to straighten out."

He drove to a nearby boxing gym.

Staring blankly, she asked, "Why on earth did you bring me here?" Did he truly mean they were going to fight?

"I told you. I want to talk to you." Khalil hopped out of his car. Blythe had already gotten out by the time he came around. "Look Khalil, this . . . this is weird."

He didn't appear to be listening to her. He unlocked the door and walked across the room briskly to shut off the alarm. Blythe remained standing near the door.

"There's nothing to be afraid of, Blythe. Come here. We can sit over here." Khalil crossed the room and grabbed her by the hand, leading her over to a long wooden bench. "Now tell me. Why do you persist in being unhappy?"

"I'm not trying to make myself unhappy, Khalil."

"Do you want to enjoy your life, or be angry all of the time?"

Blythe struggled with an answer. "I don't like being so unhappy. It just seems that . . . that I'm not meant to be happy. I don't know why."

"I think you depend on others to make you happy and you can't do that. *You* are the only person who can make you truly happy. Baby, stop being mad with the world. Let people be who they are."

"I'm not trying to change anyone."

"Maybe not, but you're also not accepting them for who they are."

"You're wrong, Khalil. If I didn't, I wouldn't have gotten hurt as much."

"You're hurting and so everybody has to pay, is that it?"

Blythe shook her head. "No, how can you say that to me?"

"Holding all of that anger inside is not good. That's why I brought you here." Khalil stood up. "Are you familiar with punching bags?"

She nodded slowly.

"Come here. I want you to hit this one. Give it all you've got. But before you do, put these on."

He handed her a pair of gloves similar to those she'd seen on boxers. "Khalil?"

"Put them on, Blythe."

She did as she was told. She gazed at him hoping he was kidding, but his eyes clearly hinted that he was serious. "Okay, they're on."

"Hit it. Give it your best shot."

Feeling awkward, Blythe swung, tapping the bag lightly. It swayed ever so gently.

"I know you can do better than that. Girl, you have so much anger in you . . . come on, baby. Think of Justin and Alda . . ."

Blythe punched at the bag. It narrowly missed him.

Khalil dodged the weighted bag. "That's much better, baby. Now think about all of those other people. Your mother . . ."

Blythe punched even harder.

"That ex-boyfriend of yours . . ."

Blythe growled and threw her whole body into the bag, punching with all of her might. She started muttering curses and swinging.

Khalil, stepping away from the swinging bag, caught a right hook. "Whoa!" Blindly, he reached for her.

Stopping suddenly, Blythe realized that she'd hit him. "Oh dear. I kind of got carried away. I'm so sorry."

"I'm fine." Khalil looked down into her face and burst into laughter. "How do you feel now?"

Relieved that he was okay, she laughed. "I have to admit, I feel pretty good."

"It's a good way to relieve anger and stress."

"Khalil, how did you happen to have the key?"

"My cousin owns it. I come here maybe twice a week."

"You get angry that much?" she teased. "Mr. Know-it All."

He pulled her to him. "Baby, I don't know everything. I'm just me and I intend to make the most of the life the good Lord saw fit to give me."

"It makes sense." Wrapping her arms around Khalil felt like the right thing to do. It was comforting, holding him, feeling the heat of his body like this. She was caught up in a sexual blaze that kindled and caught so easily between the two of them. When he covered her mouth with his, she surrendered to the fiery sparks of passion that flared between them.

Khalil unbuttoned her shirt and cupped a satin-covered breast in each hand. Her breasts surged at the intimacy of his touch and she moaned softly. Blythe closed her eyes, loving the feel of his touch.

Suddenly, he removed his hands. Closing her shirt, he buttoned her back up, then backed away. Stunned with sensuality, Blythe opened her eyes. "What's wrong?"

"Honey, if we keep this up, you're not going to be able to walk tomorrow, let alone skate. It's been a while since I've had sex and . . ."

Blythe just shook her head and laughed.

"Well, I hope you're satisfied, Khalil," Blythe fussed. "I did a split that I most certainly hadn't intended to do; I didn't know I could do one." She scowled in pain. "I've got a sore behind and an aching back. Worst of it all, I still can't skate."

Khalil's laughter was his response.

Blythe wagged a finger at him. "You think this is funny. Well, let me tell you something. I've made a complete ass of myself and I haven't even received so much as a kiss for my efforts."

Khalil leaned over to kiss her. His tongue sent shivers of desire racing through her. His arms encircled her, one hand in the small of her back, causing her skin to tingle.

Her desire for Khalil making her bolder, she broke off their kiss and asked, "Where exactly do you live?"

His gaze traveled over her face and searched her eyes. "In Inglewood, near the Great Western Forum. Would you like to see my place?"

"Actually, I would. I'd like to see some of the memorabilia you've told me about."

"Are you sure?"

Blythe knew what he was asking her. "I'm very sure." A

quiver surged through her veins and she tried to ignore the sudden heat in her body. From the way Khalil was watching her, he felt the same tumble of emotions.

In silence, they put the skates away and got into the car. When Khalil was on the freeway, he stole a glance at her and asked, "What were you thinking about?"

Blythe couldn't speak. She was too excited.

He reached over and grabbed her hand. "We don't have to go through with it—"

"No, Khalil, I want to. Believe me, I want to do this."

She felt herself start to tremble when they pulled into his garage. They were here. She and Khalil would end up in his bed before this evening was over. Blythe's excitement grew at the thought. When Khalil touched her arm lightly, she realized that he'd been talking to her. "I'm sorry, what did you say?"

He laughed as if he knew what she'd been thinking. "I asked if you wanted a tour of the house."

She nodded. "I'd like that."

Khalil led her through the kitchen and around to the living room, dining room and guest room. "We'll save my bedroom for last." He stroked her face lightly. "Come on, I'll show you my office. Most of my collection is in there."

"How did you get into collecting?" Blythe asked as she studied a photograph of a slave sitting on a stump.

"My passion began when I was a child. My father and grandfather used to tell me about the marches for civil rights they participated in. They both marched with Dr. Martin Luther King. In my family, our history is told orally. Anyway, each summer we would travel to places like Oak Bluffs and Allensworth; we once traveled the route that the slaves would take via the underground railroad."

Blythe was filled with questions. "Really? I can't imagine what that was like."

"One of the first things I acquired was a poster from Coca-Cola commemorating African-American Heritage Week."

She glanced around the room. "Where is it? I'd like to see it."

Khalil led Blythe by the hand to a corner of his office. "It's right here."

She felt a tremendous amount of pride as she stared up at the poster. It was a busy one, with Martin Luther King, Mary McCleod Bethune, George Washington Carver and Whitney M. Young.

He led her over to several other posters in his den. There was one of a buffalo soldier painted by Ernie Barnes, an ex-football player.

". . . I have some things that are not out in the open," Khalil explained. "Would you like to see them?"

"Yes, I would." Blythe sat down on the leather sectional sofa and waited for Khalil to return. He wasn't gone long. In his hand, he carried what appeared to be a scrapbook.

"In here I have a Choctaw slave document that I bought from a dealer in Oklahoma City."

Blythe felt a chill go through her body as she viewed the contents of the aged and yellowed piece of paper. It was a feeling she'd never experienced before. It made everything she'd read or heard regarding slavery real. In her hands was a fragile document of ownership. One human being owning another. Filled with emotion, she handed the paper back to Khalil.

"Black memorabilia is becoming more sought after and now more of the unusual items are getting very expensive. I've invested about seventeen years of my life collecting bits and pieces of our history. I have ancient maps of Africa and even a pair of slave shackles—"

Blythe interrupted, "Why would you want a pair of those?"

"Because I don't want to forget the struggles of our forefathers. I refuse to let the past just vanish from the face of the earth."

"But don't you think that slave shackles will only make you or others angry? It's such a sensitive issue. I think slavery is a time best forgotten."

"I don't agree. It happened, Blythe. Slavery should not be swept under the rug just because it was an ugly time. It is a part of who we are and from whence we came. All of this stuff that I've collected—I hope will awaken curiosity about our history.''

Blythe wasn't comfortable discussing racial issues, so she said, ''You've got an impressive collection, Khalil.''

''Thank you.'' He eyed her. ''Have you ever been to the Museum of African American History?''

She shook her head, somewhat embarrassed. ''I've always meant to go . . . I just never did.''

''Why don't we plan a trip to go?'' he asked.

''After the Christmas holidays, okay?''

Khalil handed her a glass of wine. ''Sure. Are you hungry?''

''Yes, I am actually.'' Blythe sipped slowly.

''Ever had a pepperoni and goat cheese pizza?''

''It's been a while. About three years.''

Khalil reached for the phone. ''I'll call in the order and pick it up.''

Twenty minutes later, Khalil left to pick up the food.

The moment he was gone, Blythe made a visit to the bathroom to freshen up. By now she wasn't surprised to find that it had been decorated in the same cultural theme as the rest of the house. He was indeed very proud of his African heritage. It showed through the way he dressed and the way he lived.

Heading down the hall and back to his office, Blyth walked around the room, admiring alabaster figures from Egypt and the exquisite brass figurines that Khalil told her were from Burkina Faso, West Africa.

She dropped down on the sofa, causing the slave shackles to jingle. Blythe picked them up. Running her hands over the rough metal, she experienced something so powerful—so undefinable—it caused her eyes to fill with water. Just the thought of her ancestors wearing chains and being taken away from their homes, their families . . .

Blythe heard the sound of keys at the front door and knew that Khalil had returned. She blinked away her tears and rose to greet him. She relieved him of some of his burden.

''Did you miss me?'' he asked as he placed the pizza on the counter in the open kitchen.

''Of course.''

Khalil handed her a couple of plates and two glasses. "Put those on the table, please."

When everything was set up, she and Khalil sat down to eat.

Blythe savored the taste of the pepperoni and goat cheese pizza. "This is great."

He nodded. "The simple pleasures in life."

"Khalil, I have to admit that in spite of all of my bruises, I've had such a wonderful time today. I see if I keep hanging out with you, I'm going to need one huge Band-Aid for my whole body."

Laughter bubbled from Khalil's throat.

After dinner, Blythe helped Khalil clean up. She bent over to put the last of the glasses into the dishwasher. He turned around and caught a delicious view of her perfectly shaped body. He felt himself harden.

When Blythe stood up, she caught the lustful expression on his face. Her breath caught and they stood staring at each other. Khalil stood with his legs slightly spread, his arms folded across his chest.

Unconsciously, she wet her lips and Khalil was tempted to take her right there on the kitchen floor. He cleared his throat loudly. "I think we're done." He wrapped his arm around her, saying, "I've saved the best for last." He guided her through double doors to his bedroom.

Blythe expected to see a room decorated in a tiger print or some other safari theme, but instead she found a rich cherry wood king-sized bed draped in a simple black bedspread with a black, white and gold kente trim. In one corner sat an Italian-style chair upholstered in the same kente fabric. The room had been tastefully decorated. "Your room is beautiful."

He eased behind her, standing so close she could feel his breath on her neck and the evidence of his arousal. "Thank you," he whispered in her ear. "I'm glad you like it. I want you to be comfortable here." Khalil wrapped his arms around her, kissing her neck.

Blythe turned in his arms, facing him. Pulling his head down, she kissed him passionately.

Khalil broke the kiss. Stepping back, he gently removed her shirt. When he laid eyes on the lacy bra that hid nothing, he let out a low growl. He wanted her so bad, but he forced himself to slow down. He didn't want to rush her.

Blythe removed her bra. She smiled when Khalil took a deep breath, his eyes never leaving her breasts. She unzipped her pants slowly, enjoying the way his eyes pleaded to view more of her. Blythe removed her pants and thong panties. Khalil dropped on his bed, the expression on his face causing her to laugh. "How long has it been for you, Khalil?"

"E . . . Eight months. Come here." His loins were longing for complete fulfillment. "When I met you, I was fully prepared to dislike you. Now look where we are."

She moved to stand before him. "I think we've both wanted this from the moment we met."

Khalil pulled her to him, putting a swollen breast in his mouth, brushing them softly with his lips. His hand seared a path down her abdomen and between her legs, seeking. Removing his mouth from her breast, he murmured, "I love your body."

Backing away from him, Blythe asked, "Why don't you show me yours?" While he undressed, she turned down the covers and slid into his bed. Her passion burning, she watched him.

Naked, Khalil climbed into bed with her. She reached for him immediately, her need to feel the warmth of his body great. Her mouth was smothered by his ardent kiss, his tongue darting between her lips with such reckless abandon that a small moan of pleasure sounded deep in Blythe's throat.

He moved his lips past her neck and down to her breasts, where he played with one, then the other. When she could bear it no longer, she whispered, "Love me, Khalil. I want you to make love to me."

After insuring their safety, he rose over her and entered her gently. Khalil was overwhelmed with glorious sensations as Blythe arched rapidly against his fiery strokes.

Engulfed in mindless rapture, the two lovers quickly reached a powerful climax.

Khalil kissed her softly before stretching out at her side. "I'm sorry, baby. It's been a long time and I couldn't wait—"

Blythe placed a trembling hand to his mouth. "Sssh, it's okay. It's been a long time for both of us. The next time," she whispered, her tone seductive, "it won't happen as fast."

"I love having you here with me. I've wanted this to happen for a while but I didn't want to rush you."

"I was more than ready. You didn't have to rush me." She cuddled against him and rested her head on his shoulder. They fell asleep in that position.

Blythe awakened an hour later to Khalil's gentle kiss. "I love you," he whispered huskily.

It thrilled her to hear those words, however hollow. Blythe knew better than to believe them. He was only saying them because it's what he assumed she wanted to hear.

This time she would keep her emotions under control. As long as she did, nobody would get hurt. After tonight, she would not see him again.

Chapter 13

"Blythe, you wanted to talk to me?" Justin stood in her doorway. "What's up?"

She glanced up briefly. "Yes. Come on in and close the door behind you."

"Ooh, sounds serious. What have I done?" Justin teased.

Blythe went straight to the point. "I think you should back off where Alda's concerned."

"What?" He ground out the word between his teeth.

"Leave Alda alone," she demanded.

Justin's mouth tightened in anger. "Who in hell do you think you are? But this isn't about Alda at all. It's about Parker."

"Alda is my best friend. I don't want to see her hurt."

"You think I'd hurt her?"

"Why not?" she sneered. "You're a man."

"Look, Blythe. I'm real sorry about the way Parker treated you—"

"You don't know the half of what he did to me," Blythe interrupted.

"Then tell me."

Shaking her head no, she said, "I don't want to talk about your best friend, Justin. This is strictly about my best friend."

"I'm not some little boy with something to prove to my friends. I'm a man, Blythe."

"What is that supposed to mean? Are you saying that you're in love?"

"No, that's not what I'm saying. I *am* interested in Alda. Very interested, and I want to see what happens between us."

"I don't like it, Justin."

"It doesn't matter whether you like it or not. You don't have anything to do with it," he stated, spacing the words evenly.

"What does Mother have to say about your relationship? I'm sure she's not thrilled about it."

"You're right, she isn't, but it's none of her business either." Justin stood up, straightening his suit. "I need to get back to my office. I have to meet with a client."

"If you hurt her . . ." Blythe let the threat hang.

"Goodbye." Justin was gone.

Blythe was so angry, she snapped her pencil in two. Why wouldn't Justin listen to her? He could have any woman he wanted. Why did it have to be her best friend? Well, she wasn't going to give up. If she couldn't get through to him, she would try to talk to Alda.

"*Ma cherie,* what a pleasant surprise. Come on in." Alda stepped aside to let Blythe enter. "I called you last night." She grinned. "Where were you?"

Blythe sat down on the edge of the sectional sofa in Alda's living room. "I spent the night with Khalil."

"It was magnifique, *non?*"

"It was wonderful. He's a very passionate man."

Blythe surveyed the mid-sized apartment. "Alda, I love your place. You've done a lot with it."

Following her gaze, Alda asked, "You think so? It's not quite there yet. She gestured toward the kitchen. "Would you like something to drink?"

Shaking her head, Blythe said, "No thanks. I'm not planning to stay long." Laying her purse beside her, she stated, "I want to talk to you about my brother."

"What about Justin?"

"Alda, I care about you. I love you dearly and I don't want to see you get hurt. Justin is . . . well, he's a ladies' man."

"We're just going out, Blythe. I'm not looking to marry the man." Alda burst into laughter.

"I never thought in a million years that you'd hook up with my brother." Shaking her head, Blythe added. "This is really strange."

"Girl, what's really bothering you? I've known you for three years and I know there's something more going on here."

"I'm just concerned about you. That's all."

"*Non,* I don't think so. I think you're lumping Justin in the same boat as Parker."

Blythe gave a short laugh. "You're crazy. I'm not doing that at all. Parker doesn't even enter into this equation," she lied. "My concern is strictly for you."

It was clear Alda didn't believe her.

Blythe answered the phone on the third ring. "Hello."

"I've been trying to reach you for a couple of days. You're too busy to return phone calls?"

It was Khalil. She bit her trembling lip. After their night of passion, Blythe had avoided him. They had both gotten what they wanted.

"Blythe?"

"I'm here. I haven't called because I've been extremely busy," she lied. "How are you?"

"I'm good. I was hoping to see you tonight."

She wasn't sure she could face him or if she even wanted to. "Can we make it another night? I brought some work home with me and I'm still working on it."

"Honey, why are you avoiding me?"

"I'm not."

"Yes, you are. We made love, Blythe. It was the most passionate night of my life. I won't ever forget it and I hope it's not the last."

"Khalil, I never expected to feel . . . I can't find the words to clearly describe what I'm feeling. It defies description."

"I know what you're saying. I feel it myself. Baby, I don't want you to run away. You've got to stop running sometime. Why not do it with me? I'm not going to hurt you."

Blythe believed he meant it, but there were some things that even Khalil could not control.

"Tell me something. Do you view every aspect of your life with such intensity?"

"Yes, I guess I do," she replied quietly.

She stretched out on her bed, her thoughts in turmoil. She had to find a way to rein in her emotions where Khalil was concerned.

"I want you to be my date for the Hale Foundation dinner," he was saying.

"Is it formal?"

"Street dress is appropriate. Does that mean you're going with me?"

"Yes, I'll go." When they hung up, Blythe could have kicked herself. Why on earth did she agree to see him again. Blythe was falling in love with him and she cautioned herself to be wise.

Khalil took her around the room, introducing her to some of his friends. "Blythe, this is Xavier Johnson."

She smiled. "It's very nice to meet you."

He stroked his chin. "You look very familiar . . ."

"I work at Bloodstone's Department Store. Perhaps it was there. Actually, I've been there about four months now."

Xavier shook his head emphatically. "No I know it wasn't there." He shook his head. "I haven't been in that store in what? About a year now."

She was curious. "Really? May I ask why?"

Khalil grasped her hand and said, "Harwood Bloodstone is Blythe's grandfather."

Xavier nodded. "I see." He shook Khalil's hand once more

before saying, "It's good to see you again, my brother." To Blythe, he said, "Nice to meet you, Miss Bloodstone."

When they returned to their table, Blythe asked, "Khalil, why did you do that? Were you afraid of what he was going to say?"

"What are you talking about?"

"You told him that I was a Bloodstone. I wanted to find out why he stopped coming to the store."

"No, you didn't," he responded.

Now he had her really curious. "Khalil?"

Covering her hand with his, he said, "We're supposed to be enjoying ourselves. Let's just have a good time."

They were seated at the table with six other guests and Khalil seemed to know all of them. Flustered, Blythe stabbed at her salad. How was she supposed to have a good time sitting around a table when the topic of conversation was the African-American diaspora. Feeling she had nothing to contribute, Blythe remained silent.

"Why are you so quiet?" he whispered.

"Just listening to what everyone's saying, that's all."

Two hours later, Blythe was relieved when Khalil announced that they were leaving.

During the drive home, Blythe decided to bring up what had been on her mind all evening. "Khalil, can I ask you something?"

"Sure. What do you want to know?"

"Do you always dress like this . . . I mean, don't you ever wear regular clothes? Even when you had on the tux, you wore an Afrocentric scarf, bow tie and cummerbund."

"What do you mean by regular?"

"You know. A pair of jeans or a suit even. You're always dressed in clothes like this."

"What's wrong with them? These are the clothes of my people."

"You don't know that for sure."

"Excuse me?"

"How do you know your ancestors came from Africa, Khalil?" Blythe challenged.

"My aunt Maida traced our family all the way back to a slave named Ezra. His father came from Africa."

"I see."

Khalil asked suddenly, "Does the way I dress bother you?"

"I never said that. I was just curious though."

"The clothes I wear are simply an extension of me. They do not define who I am as a person."

Blythe could tell they were nearing her house. "I know that. I didn't mean to offend you."

"You didn't."

In her driveway, Khalil turned off the car. Turning to Blythe, he asked, "Is that why were you so quiet back there?"

"I really didn't have anything to add."

"What's wrong, Blythe? You can be honest with me."

"This is really going to sound snobby, Khalil, but I didn't feel comfortable around your friends. All they talked about is how the white man keeps them down. I don't happen to agree with a lot of what they were saying."

"That's not exactly what Xavier was saying. What do you think is wrong with the world, Blythe? I'm curious."

"Well . . . I think that a lot of the problem is that people focus on the issue of color far too much. If something goes wrong, it's blamed on skin color. That's not going to get us anywhere. There are far too many black people in power for that to continue to be true."

Khalil rubbed his beard thoughtfully. "Where have you been?"

"Excuse me?"

"Blythe, skin color is still very much an issue. I wish it weren't the case—"

"Okay, I take that back," she interjected. "You have a point, but I have to disagree to a point. Some people are so pro black, they can't see anything else. Nothing's wrong with that, I guess, except that they have a certain idea of how you're supposed to act if you're black."

"I don't think I'm following you."

"Well, if you don't talk a certain way then you're perceived as not being black enough. If you don't wear your hair in an

Afro or in braids, you're not being true to your race. They accuse you of being an Uncle Tom."

"I think you're exaggerating. It's more than that, Blythe."

"I disagree. I mean, look at practically everyone that was there tonight. How were they dressed? *Like you.* I don't dress that way, nor do I go around shouting the injustices done to the black race. I don't just read black books or support black businesses. Does that make me less black than you or any of them?"

Taking her hand in his, Khalil shook his head. "That's not what it's about. It's about having pride in your race, where you've come from. It's about having something of your own and giving back to your community. Yes, I read books by black authors. If there is a choice between a mystery by a black author and a white one, my first choice is to read the mystery written by a black author. I want to support my black people."

"So do I, Khalil. What I don't want is to feel that I'm being a traitor if I don't live in an all-black community, spend my money in black-owned stores or wear clothes made of kente cloth. And I don't want to be criticized if I happen to like Danielle Steele as much as Bebe Moore Campbell."

"Nobody is making you feel that way. It's up to you to live as you choose. If you feel guilty about it, then maybe you should examine the real reason why," Khalil pointed out.

"What are you saying? Do you think I feel guilty because I'm not running around trying to prove how black I am?"

"I didn't say that."

"You know, you accused my family of forgetting where they came from, Khalil. Do you remember that?"

He nodded.

"Do you still feel that way?" Blythe wanted to know.

Without so much as a flinch, he nodded again. "Yes, I do."

She sighed. "Well, you're wrong. We've never forgotten. We just choose not to live in the past. What good is constantly calling the ugliness of our past to mind. All it does is make people angry."

"That's where you're wrong. I think it gives us perspective

on what's really important. I think it shows our children so much of what they take for granted. Even you, Blythe.''

"What are you talking about?''

"There was a time when blacks couldn't own land, own businesses or even vote. We worked long hours for no pay. Do you think you could survive something like that?''

"No," she had to admit. "I don't know how they did it.''

"Our ancestors had no choice. The law was for the white man. But there were a few who knew slavery was wrong and they were willing to die to right that wrong. Did you know that some of those very same people were turned in by other slaves? Thinking they would get their freedom, they sold out their black brothers.''

"I gather they didn't get what was promised to them.''

Khalil shook his head sadly. "No, they didn't. Some were even killed to insure that they wouldn't turn on their master in vengeance.''

"It's hard not to get angry over the events of the past. That's why I don't like to think about it.''

Khalil wrapped his arm around her. "It's okay to feel anger, but you have to let it go. When you think of our ancestors, it shouldn't be with pity or shame, but with pride. They carried a heavy load without complaint. Today, we can't get out of bed without complaining about something.'' He laughed. "It's because of the tragedies of the past that we are who we are today. *We must not forget that.*''

"Why can't we just be people, Khalil? Why do we have to be separate?''

"Because there are still people in this world who would love for things to go back to the way it used to be. Prejudice is still very much alive. And it's not just about black and white. Some of our own people are prejudiced against us.''

"That's what I've been saying, Khalil. If you don't fit in a certain mold, then other blacks accuse you of turning your back on your race.''

"I still say it's more than that.''

"Well, as far as I'm concerned, it shouldn't be. We should have the freedom to make our own choices.''

"Nobody is telling you where to live, Blythe, or where to put your store. All they want is to be treated like any other customer when they walk through those doors."

"And we do." She wished desperately to make him understand.

Khalil opened his car door and stepped out. He strolled around to the passenger side and helped her out of the car. "Let's table this discussion until another time." Walking her to the door, he said, "I hope you had a good time tonight."

"I did. Actually, I think I learned that I didn't know much about my own race. I'm really ashamed of that."

"There's still much of our history to be uncovered." Stepping inside the dimly lit house, Khalil leaned over and kissed her. "I wish you would've come home with me tonight. My bed is going to be so lonely without you."

Blythe grinned. "Not tonight. I've got a lot to do tomorrow at work. Keep it warm for me, okay?"

Kissing her again, Khalil pulled away slowly. "I will. You sleep well." He left, closing the door behind him.

She watched him drive away before going upstairs. "I'm not going to get any sleep as long as I think about you," she whispered.

An hour later, Blythe still wasn't asleep. She sat up, punched her pillow, then lay back down. She tossed and turned in bed, silently cursing Khalil, his fine body and herself for not going home with him. She eyed the clock on her bedside table. Midnight and all she could think about was Khalil and the warmth of his bed. Her own felt cold and lonely.

She suddenly had a thought. Blythe jumped out of bed and went straight for her lingerie chest. She searched through for just the right teddy. Nothing. Turning around with her hands folded across her chest, Blythe strolled into her closet. Spotting a black leather skirt and jacket, she smiled as she remembered a tiger print teddy that she'd bought on a whim but never wore. There was never an opportunity.

Blythe walked softly across the hall to the bathroom to freshen up. She perfumed her body and brushed her teeth. Back in her room, Blythe dressed quickly. From the back of her closet, she retrieved a pair of black leather pumps with spike heels. She pulled out an overnight bag and double-checked to see if her spare toothbrush and toiletries were there. Moving quickly and quietly, she packed a pair of jeans, a T-shirt and a pair of shoes.

Downstairs, Blythe penned a note and stuck it on the refrigerator. She took a deep breath as she unlocked her car and slid in.

Blythe drove to Khalil's house, praying that he was still up. The closer she got to his street, the more insecure she began to feel. What if he didn't like surprises? She kept reassuring herself that he would like what she had in mind.

She pulled up in front of Khalil's house and turned off her lights. The house was dark and Blythe felt the thread of disappointment seeping through her body. Khalil had gone to bed. She was about to drive away when a light came on.

Khalil couldn't believe his eyes. His heart lurched in his chest. Blythe's Mercedes was parked outside. Having heard a car outside, he took a peek out of his bedroom window. He quickly turned on a light when it looked like she was about to drive away.

He navigated to the front door, opening it and gesturing for her to park her car in the garage. Blythe backed up and turned in the driveway just as Khalil opened the garage door.

He was there to assist her after she parked the car. Blythe stepped out and into his arms. Holding him tight, she murmured, "I couldn't sleep. You were on my mind."

Khalil grinned. "I think I wished you over here. I'd just cut off the lights right before you pulled up. When I looked out the window, I couldn't believe it was you." He led her into the house.

Seated on the sofa, Blythe removed her leather jacket. Khalil was about to offer her a glass of wine, but when he saw the tight, ankle-length leather skirt with the thigh-high split and the tiger print top, he could only stare.

Blythe laughed huskily. "I take it you approve."

He could only nod, causing her to burst into laughter again.

She stood up slowly and moved to join him in the kitchen. Blythe took a glass from him and poured herself some wine. Looking up at him playfully, she said, "My goodness, Khalil. I don't think I've ever known you to be speechless."

Slowly and seductively, his gaze slid downward. "You are so sexy, Blythe."

Sipping her wine, she eyed him. When she put her glass down, she said, "I'm glad you think so. I'd hate for all of this to be in vain." Blythe took him by the hand. "I'm sleepy—let's go to bed."

Khalil grabbed the wine and the glasses and followed her to the bedroom. Blythe sank down on the bed and asked, "How about some music? Something soft and romantic."

"Your wish is my command." He pressed a key on the remote control and music filled the room, surrounding them with the sultry sounds of jazz.

When he turned around, Blythe was lying down on the bed with her eyes closed. He moved forward, removing his shirt as he walked. She opened her eyes and gazed up invitingly into his face.

Khalil lay down on the bed beside her, drawing her into his arms. He bent his head and captured her lips in a demanding kiss. Locking her hands behind his neck, Blythe returned his kiss fervently.

His passion soaring, Khalil stopped his kiss and started to take her skirt off. He pulled the skirt past her hips and his breath caught. The sexy tiger print was a teddy—not a shirt like he'd first thought. And she looked damn good in it. "Ooh, baby . . ." he groaned.

When he had removed her skirt, Khalil started to undress himself. He soon joined her on the bed. His mouth covered hers hungrily.

Blythe kissed him with a hunger that belied her outward calm. When Khalil's hand found her breast, she moaned loudly. She drew herself closer to him as his hands explored her body.

Wanting to kiss her breasts, Khalil eased the straps of her teddy off her shoulders. When her breasts were bare, he touched them, his fingers quivering and tentative. "You have beautiful breasts, sweetheart."

She lay panting, her chest heaving. As his hands lightly traced a path over her skin, she wanted to explode into a million pieces. She wanted Khalil right now. Another thought scurried across her mind. She wanted Khalil forever. Blythe shut her eyes to block out the truth. All she and Khalil could ever have was a physical relationship. No matter how much she was falling for him. His hand slipped between her legs, demanding all of her attention. Tonight. She would live just for tonight in Khalil's arms. Dealing with her out-of-control emotions would have to wait until tomorrow.

Determined to remain emotionally uninvolved, Blythe abandoned herself to their physical intimacy, while Khalil made love with deep emotion.

Chapter 14

"I saw your note this morning. I suppose you spent the night with that Khalil person," Nadine said when Blythe entered the kitchen.

She turned to face her mother. "Yes, I did."

"I hope you're using . . . well you are an adult. You know how to protect yourself." Nadine looked uncomfortable.

Blythe smiled. "I'm very careful, Mother." She poured herself a cup of black coffee.

Nadine nodded. "I'm relieved to hear that." She took a sip of her own coffee before asking abruptly, "Does he love you?"

Blythe did not respond. Instead she put a cube of sugar into her cup. "We need more sugar. And maybe cream, too."

"Well, do you love him?"

She turned around to face Nadine. Blythe wasn't ready to acknowledge her feelings yet. "Why are you asking me this, Mother?"

"Because I'm concerned for you and your happiness. You give your whole soul . . . well, you thought Parker loved you. So much so that you followed him to Paris. Look what he did to you."

She turned away to stare out of the patio doors. "Khalil's not going to hurt me," she said quietly.

"How can you be so sure?" Nadine wanted to know. "You haven't known him that long."

"I won't let him, Mother. I'm a big girl now and I've learned some hard lessons. I know where I stand with Khalil and I accept that. I'm not asking the impossible. Not anymore."

"Blythe dear ... please understand that you don't have to settle or accept anything less than you deserve."

"Mother, everything is fine. I know what I'm doing. I'm not going to get hurt. You don't have to worry." Even as she said those words, Blythe didn't believe for a moment that her mother was worried for her. It wasn't Nadine's way. "If you will excuse me, I need to get ready for work."

"Blythe ..."

She turned around slowly. "Yes, Mother?"

"Just be careful."

Blythe kept her outward calm until she reached the confines of her room. This whole thing was getting out of control. "I'm not supposed to care about you, Khalil," she whispered. "I can't let you hurt me."

Beneath the running water, Blythe cried in the shower. She thought she'd been in control. She wasn't supposed to fall for Khalil or his soft whisperings of love. He would soon realize that it was only lust talking. After the way Parker and the others had treated her, Blythe didn't have the energy to go through all of it again. Her chin went up and she felt the familiar surge of determination and sheer will. She could get through this. Blythe knew she would survive—she would simply do what she had to do.

Khalil wondered if he was losing his mind. Was he really in love with Blythe? He'd told her so, but ... Shaking his head, he almost had to laugh. He'd never been one for falling in love fast, but somehow Blythe had gotten under his skin. Little by little, he was successfully tearing down Blythe's wall. She'd built up blocks to cut herself off from the world as a way to protect herself. She spent so much of her time mourning the love of her mother that she somehow had stopped living.

She was now enjoying her life as it was meant to be, and Khalil was happy to be a part of the reason. He loved her and had confessed it to her. Blythe, on the other hand, had said nothing so far. He didn't have a problem with it because he knew it was part of her cautious nature.

He was not going to rush her. Khalil wanted Blythe to take her time and get to know him. He was not Parker or any of the others that had hurt her. He would show her how it felt to be truly loved by a man. Khalil vowed to one day give her the family she craved so much. He wanted to make her the happiest woman in the world.

"Why is traffic so backed up at this time of day?" Blythe questioned aloud. They had been sitting on the freeway much too long.

"I think there must have been an accident or something. Turn to the twenty-four-hour news station."

Blythe did as she was told. "There is an accident. We should be coming up on it pretty soon."

"It's over on your side."

As they neared the crash site, Blythe suddenly put her hands to her mouth. "Oooh my," she moaned. There were two bodies lying on the ground covered from head to toe. She began to cry.

Khalil reached for her. "Honey, what's the matter? Did you know them?"

Filled with a sense of deep loss, Blythe shook her head sadly. "No." She brushed away her tears. "It's so sad. That was a child lying back there." Her eyes filled with tears once more. "Life is filled with so much pain."

He took her hand in his. "You going to be okay?"

She nodded. "I'm sorry I broke down like this. It's just when I look at the news—it's all bad. On the freeway, fatalities. Death's everywhere. It really tears me apart when it's a small child. I always wonder if they were loved. Really loved. I mourn for them. I mourn for the ones who lose a parent or both parents. It's so scary to feel alone when you're that young . . ."

Khalil took the next exit off the freeway, prompting her to ask, "Where are you going?"

He pulled into a park. "Right here." After finding a parking space near a lake, Khalil cut the car off. Opening the door, he said, "Let's take a walk."

They strolled along the edge of the lake hand in hand. "You have so much love to give . . . You are a very caring person, Blythe. It's one of the things that attracted me to you. But, baby I have to tell you—you can't carry the weight of the world on your shoulders."

"I'm not trying to, Khalil. There is still so much about me that you don't know. I wish I could just take all of the lonely people—the ones who are heartbroken, lost and feeling rejected . . . I wish I could make their pain go away. I wish I could tell them that someone cares." She looked up at him with tear-bright eyes. "You don't know what I'm talking about because you've never gone through it." Blythe asked suddenly, "Have you ever had your heart broken?"

"No, I can't say that I have." Wrapping his arm around her, he whispered into her ear, "You have me, sweetheart. You have me. I'm so sorry you were hurt."

Was it pity she heard in his voice? Blythe pulled away from him suddenly. "I don't want you feeling sorry for me. I'm fine. We weren't even talking about me." She didn't want Khalil to delve that deep into her soul. "We should go. I need to get home." It was a weak excuse at best, but the only one she could come up with right now.

"Don't shut me out," he began. "I can see the pain in your eyes. I'm not blind."

"I'm not shutting you out. Can we leave now?"

Resigned, he nodded. "Let's go." They headed back to the car in silence.

What was it going to take for Blythe to trust him? Khalil wondered. Stealing a glance in her direction, he found her lying back with her eyes closed. Pretending to be asleep, he surmised. One day she was going to have to stop running.

"Sweetheart, I care for you. I love you—"

Blythe shifted in her seat. "Please don't say that. You don't have to. I know you care something for me but I think love is too strong a word."

Khalil chided himself for opening his mouth. It was still too soon. He decided to try another approach. "What are you doing tomorrow night?

"Nothing, why?"

"I want to take you somewhere special," was all he would say.

She studied him with a curious intensity. "Where?"

He looked over at her and smiled. "It's a surprise."

They could still feel the air of tension that swirled around them.

Blythe asked, "So do I need a bulletproof vest or a helmet, perhaps?"

Khalil broke into laughter. "It's nothing like that. What I'm planning will be totally harmless but a lot of fun."

She looked skeptical, causing him to burst into laughter once more. Khalil pulled into the driveway of her home. He scanned her face. Blythe looked tired. "Go and take a nap, sweetheart. You look exhausted."

"I am," she admitted. "This store project is wearing me out. I'll be glad when it's all over." She leaned over to kiss him before getting out of the car. "I'll call you later."

Khalil waited until she entered the house before he drove away. He made a mental note of everything he needed. If he was going to pull off what he planned, he was going to have to work fast.

"Wilma's plane should arrive in a couple of hours," Alda announced as she made adjustments to the garment the model was wearing. "Would you like to join us for dinner?"

Blythe picked up a pen and twirled it around in her fingers.

"Ooh, I'd forgotten she was flying in today. I've already made plans."

"You can take this one off. Try on the gold catsuit and the white caftan with the gold brocade trim." When the model left the room, Alda turned to Blythe. "Romantic evening with your lover?"

Blythe smiled and shrugged as she dropped down into a chair. "I'm not sure what Khalil has planned. Who knows, I may end up boxing Mike Tyson or something."

Alda's expression made her laugh.

"Why would you box Mike Tyson?"

"Khalil took me to a boxing gym the night we all went out together."

"That's why you left?" Alda lapsed into a string of French.

Laughing, Blythe shook her head. "Actually, it's not what you're thinking. We didn't box each other although I did hit him. It was quite by accident," she assured Alda.

"He wanted me to take out my frustrations on a punching bag.

"You two have such interesting dates."

"I've had a lot of fun. We have a good time together." She put the pen down on Alda's desk. "How are you and Justin doing?" she asked quietly.

"Do you really want to know?" Alda replied just as the model strolled into the room.

Rising to her feet, Blythe smiled blandly. "I have a meeting with the buyers. Give Wilma a hug for me, okay?"

Chapter 15

Her appointment at the hair salon had run late and had Blythe rushing. She didn't want Khalil arriving before she was dressed. He'd called her office and left a message regarding how to dress for this evening.

She put on a shimmering platinum slip dress. Blythe stepped into a pair of silver strappy heels and surveyed her appearance in the full-length mirror. Not happy with the lip color she'd chosen, Blythe took a tissue and wiped. She selected another color and reapplied her lipstick.

Nadine rapped on her door. "Khalil Sanford is downstairs."

Blythe turned to face her mother. "I didn't hear the doorbell." She hadn't known Nadine was home either.

"He pulled in right after I did." She assessed her daughter. "You look very nice. He must be taking you somewhere special."

Shrugging, she said, "I guess. I really don't know."

Nadine seemed alarmed. "You don't know where he's taking you?"

"It's a surprise."

"I checked your father's room. He's not here."

"He had a physical therapy appointment. He should be home

any time now." She saw a hint of disappointment in her mother's face but she didn't have time to contemplate the reason why. "I've got to go. I don't want to keep Khalil waiting." She reached into her closet and pulled out a black velvet swing coat.

"Have a good evening, Blythe."

"Thanks, Mother." She headed to the door.

"Should I . . . will you be coming home tonight?"

They eyed one another for a moment. Finally, Blythe nodded. "I'll be back."

Nadine smiled, then looked away.

Khalil let out a low whistle as Blythe glided down the stairs. He'd never seen her look so beautiful and told her so.

"Thank you," she replied softly.

Offering her his arm, he led her to the door. "An evening you'll never forget awaits . . ."

A shiny, black limousine sat outside. Blythe looked up at him, puzzled.

"Trust me," he whispered.

She stepped into the car, moving over to make room for Khalil.

He couldn't take his eyes off her. "Would you like a glass of champagne?"

"No, thank you. I'm too excited. Would you please tell me what you have planned?"

"You'll see real soon."

Blythe looked out the window and saw that they were driving downtown. When they neared the bus station on Alameda, she asked, "Why are we down here? It's nothing but abandoned old buildings and homeless people."

"I know. I want you to get a good look out there and tell me what you see."

She looked at him as if he'd lost him mind. "Is this your idea of a date?" Blythe suddenly grew angry. "Take me home, Khalil."

"Baby, trust me. You've got to trust somebody. Just trust me this once."

"I don't have to look out there. I . . . if you're trying to get me to see the ugliness—I see it, I can smell it. I can smell the hopelessness . . . all of it." Her eyes filled with tears. "I can't look at those people."

"Why not, sweetheart?"

"Because I can't do anything for them and I feel ashamed."

He reached for her, wanting to comfort her. "Come here, baby." When she drew close, he held her tightly in his arms. "Do you think you can bear with me? I want to show you something else."

Blythe wiped her tears. "What?"

He pointed out of the window. "That building." Khalil asked the driver to stop. "This should be ready in the next few months. These are rent control apartments and you'll soon see them throughout Los Angeles. It's a project my family and I have been involved with for a while now. This is the first but not the last." His voice filled with pride. "Do you see the large room downstairs?"

She nodded. "What is it?"

"It's a training center where volunteers will teach people to read, hold classes for computer and other skills. We're going to try to train and retrain people, giving them the necessities to compete in the job market.

"Tenants will be allowed to stay here rent free while they are taking classes. However, they will have to pay utilities. After the training is completed, they have to find a job. Once employment is secured, they can stay on for one full year, but they have to pay rent."

"Will the amount be based on their income?"

"Yes."

"What happens to them after the year is over, Khalil?"

"We'll help them find a permanent place to live. That way we can take in more families."

Her eyes brightened. "What a wonderful idea."

"It's a beginning." Khalil gestured to the driver to leave. "Ready for our next stop?"

Her reply was an enthusiastic "Yes."

They drove cross town to the Jefferson Park area. Amidst the Christmas decorations, one street was lined with murals and children of all ethnic groups were painting a fence that stretched the length of the block. Blythe glanced over at him and smiled. "It's beautiful."

"We call this our street of hope. Look at the children— they're playing together and holding hands."

"I can see the happiness in their expressions. I can feel the warmth of the artist's touch as he worked on this." She turned to Khalil. "Who painted it?"

"Some children from the local high school."

Blythe looked surprised. "Extraordinary talent."

"We all feel helpless when we're faced with crime, homelessness and things like cancer and AIDS, but we must never give up hope. These kids donated their time to clean up the graffiti. They erased the ugliness by painting what you see instead." Khalil hoped he was getting through to her. The words weren't coming out the way he wanted them to.

She smiled and reached for a chocolate-covered strawberry. "They gave of themselves the only way they could. It's not about what you can do monetarily."

Khalil nodded.

Blythe took another look out of the window. "You are a wonderful, caring man. Thank you for showing me all of this."

"Our evening isn't over. This was just the first part."

Smiling seductively, she said, "I can hardly wait for the next part."

He laughed. "I promise it'll be a lot of fun."

Blythe leaned into him, offering him her mouth. Her kiss was slow, thoughtful and driving Khalil to distraction. He took her mouth with savage intensity. He was tempted to forget the rest of the evening and take her home to his bed.

Khalil's passion was now raging, and his mouth went to her neck, trailing hot kisses down to the hollow of her throat. "Blythe," he murmured huskily.

"Khalil, we'd better quit. We don't want to give the driver a peep show, do we?" she whispered shakily.

He could tell desire was flowing as rampantly through her as it was through him, spreading like wildfire. He straightened up reluctantly. Her hand in his, he asked, "What do you say we move forward to the grand finale. Skip the expensive dinner?"

Blythe traced his lips with her finger lovingly. "Don't you think we need to eat?" Lowering her voice, she added, "We're going to need our strength."

"We can have something delivered," he countered.

She seemed to be thinking it over. "Well, I did tell Mother that I would be home tonight." She smiled. "Have the driver take us back to your house."

When Khalil opened the door to his house, Blythe felt like she'd stepped into another world. There were flowers and candles everywhere. She spun around. "This is incredible."

"I'm glad you like it." He embraced her. "This is all for you. Dinner should be arriving any moment."

Her eyes widened. "You had this planned all along."

"Guilty. Right now I want you to make yourself comfortable. I'll get you something to drink."

There was a knock on the door and Khalil left to answer it. He returned carrying two containers. "Dinner's here."

Sitting at the table together eating, Khalil asked, "Where do you see yourself in the next five years, Blythe?"

She gave his question some thought. "I don't know . . . I guess I haven't really thought about it much."

"I'm sure you have something in mind." He stuck a fork full of salad in his mouth.

"Well, I've always wanted to pursue my painting, so I guess that's one thing I'd like to do. I would also like to think that I'll be happily married and a mother of at least one child. How about you?"

"I see myself married to a beautiful woman and with two point five children."

His eyes seemed to delve into her soul, and Blythe felt her body react to his heated gaze. She refused to let herself even hope that she would be the woman Khalil married. It was too much to ask.

* * *

When they were done with the dishes, Khalil said, "I'm going to put this stuff away. Why don't you do me a favor and take off your clothes?"

"Excuse me?"

"Trust me." He grinned at the look she gave him.

She left the room while he finished cleaning the kitchen. When he returned from taking out the trash, Khalil found her wearing his robe. He couldn't remember that robe ever looking so good. He tried to keep his desire under control. Tonight belonged to Blythe.

When Blythe opened her arms, Khalil went into them, and they surrendered blissfully to the feelings drawing them together. He kissed her over and over, courting her senses with sweet and fiery sensations. Opening her robe, his hands roamed over her breasts.

She matched him kiss for kiss. Her hands moved down to his belt, unbuckling it. Blythe unzipped his pants and pulled them down. Khalil helped her. He removed the rest of his clothing quickly. She let the robe fall off her shoulders, down her arms and to the floor, pooling around them both.

His love-filled gaze traveled over her curvaceous thighs and her long, shapely legs. Blythe was so seductive that he shivered with desire. His lips seared hers aggressively as he pulled her down to the floor. After giving her the most sensual massage Blythe had ever experienced, they made love in front of the burning embers in the brick fireplace.

Blythe clutched him tightly, never wanting to let him go. They rode the waves of passion together, finally crying out their pleasure in unison.

Chapter 16

"I don't know why I let you talk me into this. This is going to be a dreadful day," Blythe fumed. She wished she'd just stayed over at Khalil's.

"Will you just give it a chance!" Moira snapped. "We haven't even left the house and you're already predicting doom."

"Why did you have to go and invite Mother?"

"Because we're going Christmas shopping and I thought we could turn it into a special day for the three of us. I also thought it would be a good time to discuss the wedding."

"Are you really going to go through with—" Blythe began.

"Well, I'm ready," Nadine announced as she climbed down the stairs. She stopped short. "Blythe . . . I didn't know you were joining us."

That remark did it. She wasn't going. Blythe began to take off her coat. "Actually, I won't be. I've changed my mind."

Moira stopped her. "NO, Blythe. You *are* going with us. Now it's time you start acting like a member of this family."

"Please, Blythe. If it's me—"

Nadine looked hurt and Blythe felt guilty. "I'm sorry. It's

not you, Mother," she lied. "I just don't want to ruin the day for you and Moira."

"You won't. Unless you decide not to go with us." Embracing her, Moira pleaded, "Please come with us."

Against her better judgment, Blythe nodded. "Okay."

Nadine smiled. "I'm glad."

She was afraid to trust her mother's smile. Nadine would turn on her at a moment's notice, so Blythe chose to remain guarded. They drove to Century City mall.

Going from store to store, Blythe walked behind Moira and Nadine, unshed tears burning her eyes as she watched her sister embrace her mother.

Nadine abruptly stopped dead in her tracks, causing Blythe to run smack into her.

"What is it, Mother?" Moira asked.

Her eyes conveyed the fury within her. "Blythe, that's exactly why I told you to guard your heart. That man is no good. I knew it."

Blythe and Moira exchanged puzzled glances. Blythe finally asked, "Mother, what are you talking about?"

"Your friend, Mr. Khalil Sanford." Nadine gestured with her hand. "Isn't that him over there? With the woman?"

Blythe followed her mother's gaze. "Yes, that's him." She started to laugh. "And the woman with him is his sister. Her name is Kuiana."

Nadine was silent, her face flushing bright red.

Moira whispered to Blythe. "Mother had no way of knowing. She was simply trying to protect your heart."

Blythe said nothing. She wasn't as convinced that Nadine had been looking out for her best interests. To her, it was a way of gloating.

"I didn't know she was his sister."

"Mother, it's okay. Just forget it." Blythe pretended to be interested in a dress on display in one of the store windows.

Laden with shopping bags, Moira asked, "Why don't you go over and say hello, Blythe?"

"He's with his sister. This is their time. And this is ours."

They found a bench and sat down.

Moira announced, "Now that all of the Christmas shopping is done, we can concentrate on my wedding."

"Moira, why don't you think this out a little more? I don't think you should marry William."

"Blythe, it's not your decision. Your sister knows what she wants to do."

"Mother's right. I want to marry William. You don't like him because you think he's too old for me," she accused.

"It's not that, Moira, and you know it," Blythe argued. "You want children and you don't know if he does. You're planning to get pregnant without his knowledge. I don't agree with that."

Moira glared at her. "I want children."

Blythe tried to reason with her sister. "Then talk to William. See if he wants them, too. Are you afraid to find out?"

Nadine spoke up. "I'm afraid I agree with Blythe. Moira, you can't just get pregnant without informing him. It's not right."

Shaking her head in disbelief, Moira declared, "Whoever thought you two would actually agree on something?"

Blythe tried to climb out of bed but Khalil pulled her back, drawing her close to him.

"You're not playing fair, Khalil. If you keep this up, I won't be going anywhere."

He grinned. "That's my plan exactly. When I play, I play for keeps."

"I've got an early meeting tomorrow regarding the Kwanzaa celebration. I need to do some last-minute notes on the presentation."

"Okay, I'll let you off the hook this time." Khalil released her. "Just remember, it won't be so easy to get away from me the next time. I guess I'm feeling generous tonight."

"Well, thank you." Blythe rushed out before he could change her mind. She showered and dressed quickly. When she came out of the bathroom, Khalil had fallen asleep. Blythe kissed him goodbye. He didn't stir. She left quietly, locking the door behind her.

When she arrived home, the house was dark. Blythe bumped into someone. Stifling a scream, she peered for a closer look. "Mother! You scared me. Why are you roaming around the house with the lights off?"

Nadine looked a bit shaken herself. "I was checking on your father, if you must know."

"Is something wrong?" Blythe was instantly concerned.

"No. I just came down to get something to drink and I thought I heard your father, so I went to see if he was up."

"Was he?"

"No. He was asleep, so I didn't disturb him. I wasn't sure you'd be coming home, so I turned out all of the lights." She moved toward the kitchen. "I'm going to have some herbal tea. Would you like some?"

Blythe was tempted but she refused. "I'm kind of tired. I think I'll just go straight to bed."

"Sure. I understand." Nadine looked at her hands. "Well, good night."

"Sleep well, Mother." Blythe watched Nadine leave for the kitchen and wondered why she felt so guilty.

At the meeting the next day, Nadine asked, "Is everything in place for the Kwanzaa celebration? Are the booths ordered?"

Blythe nodded. "Yes. They should arrive by the end of the week. The display department will assemble them. Some of the merchandise has already arrived and more will arrive by Friday."

"What about the food?" Harwood asked.

She nodded again. "Everything will be ready. I promise."

Clearing his throat, Harwood said, "I've been giving this some more thought and I really think this is good for the store's image. I'm proud of you, Blythe."

"It wasn't really my idea. It was Alda's. She deserves the praise."

"Speaking of Alda, is everything ready on her end?"

"Yes. She's even hired another seamstress. Mother, everything has been taken care of." Blythe stood up. "If that's all, then I really need to get back to my office. I've got a few calls to make."

"That's all for now, darling." Harwood stood up slowly. "Have a good day. Our meeting is over."

Nadine followed Blythe to her office. "I spoke to Alda this morning and she's designing a new dress for me to wear for the celebration."

Blythe struggled to hide her surprise. "That's wonderful. I was thinking of having her make something for me, too."

"I have to admit that her designs are divine."

Blythe caught sight of Harwood and called out to him. "There's something else I need to discuss with you both. Could you come in for a few minutes?"

Harwood ambled into Blythe's office. "Sure."

"What is it, dear?" Nadine asked.

She took a deep breath. "Well, I think we should all attend the Kwanzaa celebration at Khalil's parents' house. We're asking them to support us—we should support them as well."

"You're right. I'll probably make it every night but one," Harwood stated.

"I'm sure that's fine." Blythe turned to her mother expectantly. "What about you? Will you be able to attend?" She prayed her mother wouldn't let her down.

"I'm going to try to make it a couple of nights. I can't promise any more than that right now."

"I've asked Father to join us at the store."

Nadine perked up. "What did he say? Is he going to come?"

Blythe heard the excitement in her mother's voice. "I don't know. I think you should ask him again."

"I will. I'll talk to him tonight." Nadine moved toward the door. "I need to get back to my office. Have we covered everything this time?"

Harwood nodded. "I think so."

When Nadine left, he turned to Blythe. "What's going on with Nadine and Adam? Are things any better?"

"I'm not really sure but I think so. They seem to be getting closer."

"I'm sure glad to hear that."

Nodding, Blythe agreed. "I was worried for a while."

"Your father loves that mother of yours. I hope she knows it. He loves her to death."

Wilma Forrester spread cream cheese on a cinnamon raisin bagel. "Justin is so handsome. I didn't even know Blythe had a brother. Did you?"

Alda shook her head. *"Non,* but she didn't talk much about her family. I think she blames Justin for the way things went with Parker."

"Why would she do a silly thing like that?"

Stirring her coffee, Alda replied, "Neither one of them will talk about it, but I think Justin's known Parker a long time. They were best friends. I guess Blythe feels that Justin should have warned her somehow."

"Maybe she felt he should've protected her," Wilma suggested. "That's really sad though. They are brother and sister."

"I know. I've been trying to stay out of it, but I can tell it really bothers Justin. I hate seeing him so sad."

Wilma chewed thoughtfully. "What about Blythe? How do you think she's taking it?"

"You know her. She keeps so much bottled inside. She's just mad with the world."

"Who's mad with the world?" Blythe asked. When Alda and Wilma burst into giggles, she put her hands on her hips, glaring at them both. "I know you two weren't talking about me."

The two women exploded into more laughter.

Blythe sank down into a chair at the small table upstairs in the cafeteria of Bloodstone's. "I'm not mad with the world. How could you say this about me?" She was genuinely hurt by Alda's comment. "Is this what you really think of me?"

Alda reached over to hug her. "You know I love you, girl, but you have a chip on your shoulder the size of Europe."

"I do not. I just don't care for a lot of foolishness."

"And when someone hurts you, that's it for them. You simply cut them out of your life."

Khalil had said the same thing to her. "What am I supposed to do? Just let them continue hurting me," Blythe argued.

"Well, I'm not. I've been hurt. I think more times than I truly deserve. I'm not inclined to let it continue."

"We've all been hurt at one time or another," Wilma stated. "It's a part of life."

Anger coursed through her. *"I know that.* I just think I've had much more than my share. I don't know what it's liked to be loved by a man. You know why? Because I've never experienced it." Blythe stood up then. "So if I appear to be a little rough around the edges then I damn well deserved to be." She turned to walk away.

Alda grabbed her arm. "Come on, Blythe. You don't have to leave. That's exactly what I'm talking about. It's what I've tried to tell you for years. Just because you've had some rough times—you can't just quit."

"Yes, I can. Don't you get it, Alda? I'm tired of trying. I'm so tired." She put a hand to her heart. "I have so much love in here. But there's no one for me to give it to. Nobody wants it."

"Honey, that's not true. Come here and sit down. I want to talk to you." Alda patted the seat beside her. "I'm not saying it's fair that you've been treated the way you have. But you have to remember that one day you're going to find that wonderful man. He's going to love you so much . . ."

Blythe was shaking her head as she sat down. "I don't believe that anymore."

"What about Khalil?"

"I care a lot for him, but I already know it's not going to last long. As soon as he gets to know me, he'll be on his way."

"Do you really believe that?" Alda asked.

Blythe waved her hand in resignation. "I'm not really sure of anything right now."

"Well, I believe that Khalil really cares for you. And if you step from behind that self-imposed wall, you'll see the same for yourself. If you don't, you're going to lose him.''

She eyed Alda. ''Do you really think Khalil is different from the others?''

''Yes, I do. Deep down, Blythe, you know what went wrong in all of your relationships. Once you face that, you'll be ready to move on with your life.''

''What are you saying?''

''I'm saying that you've lived your whole life around your version of the events of your past. Think about it.'' Alda stood up and reached for her coffee. ''I've got to get downstairs. Would you like to join Wilma and me for lunch?''

''I'll give you a call.'' Blythe glanced over at Wilma. ''What are you doing today?''

''I think I'm going to visit the Museum of African-American History.''

Hugging Wilma, Blythe uttered, ''Have fun. I need to get upstairs.'' Alda's words were still on her mind as she ventured to her office. Was there any truth in what she'd said?

Chapter 17

That evening when Blythe arrived home, she froze at the sound of someone crying. Letting her eyes adjust to the darkness of her surroundings, she just could make out the slender figure of a woman curled up on the sofa. Moving closer, she said, "Moira, is that you?"

"It's me."

"What's wrong? Why are you sitting alone in the dark like this?"

She sniffed loudly. "I just needed some time to think."

Blythe was tempted to ask why she hadn't gone to her room, but she decided to remain silent.

Patting the space beside her, Moira asked, "Do you have a minute? I need to talk to someone."

"Sure." Blythe sank down on the sofa. "Do you mind if we turn on the lights? At least one."

"That's fine."

Blythe could tell from Moira's face that she'd been crying for a while. Her eyes were swollen and she had red blotches on her cheeks. "What's wrong?" she asked again.

"You were right. William doesn't want any more children." She burst into fresh tears.

Reaching for Moira, Blythe held her close. "I'm so sorry. I wish that I'd been wrong, but it's best that you know this up front. Now you can decide if you still want to get married."

"There's more to it, Blythe. I'm already pregnant."

She stared wordlessly at her sister.

Looking down at her hands, Moira admitted, "I didn't tell you everything before. I'd already stopped taking the pills the moment William asked me to marry him. I was so sure that he'd want to have children with me. I was so sure." She wiped away her tears. "What am I going to do now?"

"Does William know about the baby?"

Moira shook her head. "I was trying to think of a way to tell him, so I brought up the subject of children. After he told me that his child-rearing days were over, I lost my nerve."

"You need to let William know that he's going to be a father again whether he likes it or not."

Moira shook her head. "It's not like he's going to change his mind, Blythe. I got myself into this mess and I'll have to figure out what I'm going to do."

"Are you thinking about getting rid of this baby?" Blythe asked quietly.

"Oh no. Not ever. I want my baby, Blythe. I just never anticipated single parenthood."

"I'm so sorry, Moira. I really am. But I'm going to make a promise to you. You won't be by yourself. You have me, little sister."

"Blythe, I'm so scared. I wanted so much to have a husband and a family . . ." Tears streamed down her face.

"What have I done to my little innocent baby? I wanted the best for him or her."

"Your baby will be loved so much. By all of us."

"What do you think Mother will say?"

"Who knows? Moira, this is your life."

"I know. I just wish I'd listened to you and Mother. You both tried to warn me."

"I can't believe that William would abandon you or this baby. I think you should tell him."

Moira shook her head. "I can't."

"Listen to me. Tell him and tell him soon. If he doesn't want to be a part of the child's life then so be it. Even so, he still has a financial obligation to this baby."

"I don't want his money! If he doesn't want to be a father to this baby then I don't want any ties to him whatsoever."

"Have you eaten?"

Moira shook her head. "I'm not hungry. I think my morning sickness comes at night."

Blythe smiled. "Come on. I'll help you get upstairs. You need to take a nice long bubble bath and get a good night's sleep."

Moira gazed into her eyes. "I'm so glad you're my sister, Blythe. I missed you so much while you were in France."

"Really? You hardly ever wrote or called."

"I didn't think you liked me very much."

"That's not true. I was going through a lot, but it's no excuse. I'm sorry I made you feel this way."

"I love you, Blythe." Moira reached over and hugged her tight.

"I love you, too." Blythe's eyes filled with tears.

After seeing to her sister's comfort, Blythe made her way to her bed, falling asleep instantly.

The next day, Blythe answered the phone minutes after she arrived home from the store. It was William.

"Blythe, is Moira there?"

"William, she's not here right now. She should be home in about an hour."

"Is something wrong?"

"Excuse me?" she asked, stalling for time.

"I was wondering if you knew what was bothering your sister. She's not been taking my calls for the past couple of days."

"I think you'll have to ask her that yourself, William."

"So then you do know?" he pressed on.

"I've got to go. Call back in about an hour." Blythe hung up quickly. Hearing the doorbell, she rushed to answer it. She was expecting Khalil.

Greeting him with a kiss, she pulled Khalil into the house. "I'm so glad to see you."

He laughed. "Well, I'm glad to see you, too."

The phone rang again, but Blythe made no move to answer it.

Khalil glanced over at her. "Aren't you going to get it?"

Shaking her head no, Blythe replied, "It's probably William calling back. He's looking for Moira."

"Are you ready to leave?"

"Yes. Just let me get my purse." Blythe ran upstairs. She was back a few minutes later with a black leather handbag and suede jacket. "I'm ready."

Moira arrived home just as they were leaving.

Blythe stopped to talk to her. "William called again. He wants to know what's going on with you."

"Did you tell him anything?" When Blythe said no, she sighed and stated, "I guess it's time I talk to him."

Nodding, Blythe agreed.

"Well, I'll tell him tonight. Wish me luck."

Blythe hugged her tightly. "I'll be home around nine o'clock. We'll talk then." She stopped. "If you need me before then, call me over at Khalil's. The number is in my phone book."

"Thanks." Moira embraced her and kissed her cheek.

This time Blythe didn't wipe it off.

In the car, Khalil commented, "Looks like you and your sister are closer. I'm glad to see that."

Nodding, Blythe said, "She's going through something right now."

"I kind of figured that out." Khalil covered her hands with his own. "Family should always stick together. Especially in the rough times."

"Sometimes that's not possible. Not all families are like the one on the Cosby show."

"I know that, Blythe. I'm not trying to make it sound that way. But it takes effort from all concerned. One person can't do it alone."

"If you're talking about me, then come right out and say it. Khalil, you don't know how hard I've tried to fit in—to be a part of my family, but it's no use. My mother doesn't want me there."

"I know you don't want to hear this but I'm going to say it anyway. You've let your anger and your hurt consume you. You don't know how to just let go and relax."

Blythe pulled her hand away. "You're right, I don't want to hear this. I don't because you don't know anything about me or the hell that I've been through." Her eyes filled with tears. "I just wish someone could see my side of it. Just once."

"Baby, I'm trying. I can look at you and tell that something is just eating you up inside. I wish I could make it go away. I really wish I could."

She wanted so much to believe him. Blythe needed someone. She needed someone to hold her and tell her that it would be all right. That the worst was over. "I wish I could make you understand."

Khalil kissed her forehead. "I'm not going to hurt you, sweetheart."

Blythe prayed he was telling the truth. Although she'd prepared herself for the inevitable, she didn't think she would survive another blow to her heart. She was in love with Khalil Sanford.

The next day Blythe found Khalil sitting outside her office. She welcomed him with a smile. "Hi there. I didn't know you were here."

A small frown creased his brow. "I was supposed to meet you here, right?"

"Yes. Just let me grab my purse and my attache case, and I'll be ready to go."

He rose slowly. "Do you need to go by your house?"

Blythe nodded. "Do you mind?"

Kissing her quickly, he said, "No, I don't mind, sweetheart." He took her attache case from her. "Have everything?"

"I'm ready." They left her office. While waiting for the elevator to arrive, Blythe leaned into Khalil saying, "I'm so glad this day is over."

He gently massaged her back and asked, "Hard day?"

"Grueling."

"Well, it's almost over. The Christmas holidays and Kwanzaa will soon be here and gone."

They took the elevator downstairs. After dropping her safely at her car, Khalil followed her home in his car.

Blythe pulled into the driveway and parked. She waited for him by the front door.

"How many speeding tickets have you gotten?" Khalil asked as he followed her into the house.

"Only three. But that was before I moved away to Paris. I haven't had any since I moved back home."

He laughed. "Give it time. You drive like you're out on a race track somewhere."

"I do not." Blythe unlocked her door and entered with Khalil on her heel. "I'm going to say hello to my father."

"Give him my best."

After checking on her father, Blythe ran upstairs and packed an overnight bag. She wanted to be long gone before her mother arrived home. On her way out, Blythe and Khalil ran into Justin.

"Where are you going?" he asked.

She glared at him a moment before replying, "Out."

"Looks like you plan to be away for a while," he teased.

"It's none of your business," she snapped.

Justin's mouth tightened but he said nothing. He strode in the house, shutting the door.

"Do you think that was really necessary?" Khalil asked.

"I don't need him in my business. He has no right."

"Justin was only kidding, Blythe. I don't think he meant any harm by it."

"Whatever." She didn't care what Justin meant. He had no right.

When they were en route to his house, Khalil brought it up once more. "I really think you need to be nicer to your brother."

"Khalil, stay out of it. This doesn't concern you."

"Maybe not, but family is all you have in this world."

"For some. There are people who are better off without family. Ask a child who has been molested by her father."

"Dammit, Blythe. Why do we have to always take opposite sides?"

He was angry. She could hear it in his voice. "I'm sorry, Khalil. I don't want to get into a debate with you. Not today."

His expression was a mask of stone.

Although she tried to make small talk, Khalil wouldn't say more than a word or two. She had never seen him so distant.

They arrived at his place and Blythe got out of the car. She followed him into the house. "Khalil, are you still upset with me?"

He simply looked at her and headed to the kitchen. Blythe followed, saying, "I've already apologized."

Leaning against his kitchen counter, he said, "I know. So where do you think that leaves us?"

She was irked by his cool, aloof manner. "I think I'll call Moira and have her pick me up."

"Do what you want. Look Blythe, you seem intent on making yourself miserable. I'm not going to be a part of that."

She was silent and defeated.

They stood listening to the silent room. When Blythe looked up at him, her eyes were wet with tears. "You ask that I accept people for who they are. Why c-can't you accept me? This is the only way I know how to be."

Khalil reached for her. "This is not you. I've seen the real you, sweetheart. It's not you when you're full of anger and bitterness. That's not the real you—I won't believe that."

Blythe peered up at him. How did Khalil really see her? He made her sound like this woman who was loved and gave love in return. That wasn't her. He was wrong.

He seemed to read her thoughts. "I think you need to take some time and get to know Blythe."

"All I need right now is you, Khalil." Blythe wrapped her arms around him. "I need you to make love to me. I need you to hold me tight. Please, no more talking."

His expression was sad. "You're running again. One day you're going to have to face reality."

Chapter 18

"So who was that man with Blythe last night at the rehearsal?" Wilma asked her sister. "He's handsome."

"Why are you so interested? What about George? You two have been going back and forth for what? Six years. Why don't you just marry the man?"

Wilma frowned. "Our timing is off. When I'm ready, he isn't. I don't think we belong together."

"So are you looking to stay in America?" Alda wanted to know.

Wilma's eyes slid over Khalil. "Well, if he wants me to, I might. That man is gorgeous."

Alda nodded. "He is nice-looking. But he's also taken. He's dating Blythe."

"Are they serious?"

"I don't know. I know that Blythe likes him a lot."

"Hmmmm. I wonder if he feels the same way."

"Wilma! I can't believe you. Blythe is a close friend of ours. How could you even consider—"

Wilma burst into laughter. I'm only teasing, Alda. I would never go after Blythe's man. Never."

"I hope you're telling me the truth, dear sister. If not, I'll put you on a plane myself and send you back to Paris."

* * *

"Father, it's your turn. Come on and let's keep the game moving."

"I'm thinking," Adam mumbled as he concentrated on the cards in his hand.

"I don't cotton to spending the rest of my life playing this card game, Son." Harwood winked at Blythe.

Nobody heard Nadine slip into the room until she asked, "What are you all playing?"

"Gin rummy," Adam replied. "Would you like to join us?"

Blythe and Harwood exchanged a look of surprise.

"Sure, if nobody minds." She sat down on the sofa, next to Blythe. "I think I remember how to play."

"You know how to play gin rummy?" Blythe asked.

"I haven't played in a long time. But your father and I used to play when we were first married."

"You did?" It was Harwood's turn to look surprised.

Nadine smiled. "Don't you two look so shocked. I even play old maid and go fish."

Blythe burst into laughter.

"What's so funny, Blythe?"

"I can't imagine you playing cards. Especially old maid."

"It helped to pass the time." Nadine positioned herself at the table. "Deal me a hand, please?"

Adam, Harwood and Blythe exchanged amused glances.

Two hours later, Adam and Nadine were winning their fourth hand. Harwood looked fit to be tied and Blythe found the whole matter funny.

After winning one game, Harwood decided to call it a night. Sensing that her parents wanted to spend some time alone, Blythe bid them good night. It thrilled her to see them happy like that. If only for one night.

Adam and Nadine played another hand. "Did you hear Blythe's laughter earlier tonight? She hasn't laughed like that in a long time."

"I was thinking the same thing. It was good to see her so happy." Nadine peered over at her husband. "I think she's in love."

"I agree. Khalil Sanford has been good for her."

"I suppose. I wish I could be happy for her but I'm just not sold on him."

Adam laughed. "Honey, you're still angry over the article he printed in his newspaper."

Nadine was quiet.

"He's a good man, sweetheart."

"I hope you're right."

Adam yawned.

Nadine took the cards from him, laying them down on the table. "You're tired. Let's call it a night."

Adam grinned. "I was winning."

Nadine stood up and wheeled Adam to his bedroom. Winston was turning down the bed.

She spoke up. "I'll leave you with Winston."

He touched her hand. "Would you like to sleep in here tonight?"

"I don't want to disturb you. You need your rest."

"You won't be disturbing me. I think I'd sleep better knowing you were lying beside me."

Nadine stared speechless.

Adam smiled. "Is it so strange to want to sleep with my wife?"

"I guess I thought . . ." She shook her head. "This is so unexpected." She gazed at the handsome face of her husband and a sudden unfamiliar warmth spread through Nadine. She struggled to maintain her composure.

A strange expression came over Adam's face. "I'm sorry, I guess I assumed . . ."

"No, you didn't. I miss sleeping with you, too. After Winston has you settled in bed, call me and I'll come join you." She was actually excited over the prospect of lying in Adam's arms once more. Her smile saddened. She also missed their lovemaking.

Upstairs, Nadine sat down at her vanity, staring into the

mirror. Adam was in that wheelchair because of her. If it hadn't been for her being so self-absorbed, he wouldn't have turned to another woman. She brushed at a lone tear that slid down her cheek.

"How am I ever going to make up for the pain I've caused you?" she whispered.

Blythe left the bathroom after her shower and headed to her sister's room. She knocked on the door before entering. "Moira, are you asleep?"

"No, come on in." Moira propped up her pillows and sat up. "What's wrong? You can't sleep?" she asked.

"I heard you come in earlier. I was worried about you." Blythe sat down on the edge of the bed. "How are you doing?"

"I'm okay. I told William about the baby."

"How did it go?" Blythe held her breath.

"Well, he was shocked. I thought he was about to pass out at one point."

"Is he going to be a father to this child?"

Moira's voice sounded distant. "He doesn't know. He needs time to think. *His words.*"

Blythe was angry. "I don't believe that! How can he be so heartless."

"I became pregnant without telling him. He has a right to feel the way he does."

She shook her head. "No, I don't agree. You could've become pregnant without intending to. Birth control often fails."

"Maybe William would feel different if that were the case." Moira sighed heavily. "I don't care anymore. At least I have you."

"When are you going to tell Mother and Father?" she asked quietly.

"How about tomorrow at breakfast?" She embraced Blythe. "Will you hang around long enough to be my support system?"

"I'll be here," Blythe assured her. "I still can't believe you're going to have a baby."

"I know." Moira hugged her middle. "I can hardly believe it myself."

"You will be a good mother. I know you will. You love children."

"Don't you want a baby, Blythe?"

She nodded. "Maybe one day. Right now I have to find a man."

Moira smiled. "I think you've already found him."

Back in her room, Blythe climbed into bed. She closed her eyes, dreaming of Khalil. She hadn't heard from him at all today and she missed being with him. Wondering if he was feeling the same way, she reached for the phone.

"Hello."

He sounded as if he'd been sleeping. "Khalil, this is Blythe. I missed you and so I thought I'd call. Did I wake you up?"

"No, baby. Actually I was lying here and thinking about you."

She smiled. "What about me? Was it some sex-filled dream?"

Khalil's laughter was his response.

"You're terrible."

"It wasn't all sex. I've been going over in my head how to get you to trust me. I want inside of that wall you've built around yourself."

"You have a one-track mind, Khalil."

"No, I'm just not one for giving up without a fight. I thought we were similar in that respect."

Blythe had heard it all before. "What would you say if I were to drive over there with nothing on?" She hoped it would take his mind off of her self-imposed prison, as he called it.

"I'd say I don't have a problem with it, but the police might."

They talked through most of the night. Blythe eyed the clock and murmured sleepily, "I think we'd better say goodbye. We have both got to get up in a few short hours and get ready for the workday." They made plans to get together the next day and ended the call. As much as she hated ending the call, she was tired and needed some sleep.

Chapter 19

"Everyone, I have an announcement to make," Moira said as she seated herself next to Blythe at the dining room table.

Nadine and Adam exchanged glances.

"I'm going to have a baby."

"You're what?" Nadine asked.

Gazing into her mother's eyes, Moira stated, "I'm pregnant, Mother."

Adam cleared his throat. "I guess congratulations are in order."

"What does William have to say about this? I suppose the wedding will take place sooner than you planned."

"Mother, this baby is mine. I'm going to be the best mother possible."

Blythe could read the distress in Moira's expression. So she reiterated, "I think you'll be a wonderful mommy."

"I think so, too," Adam declared. He covered Nadine's hand with his. "Don't you agree, dear?"

"Yes, of course you will. And you have your family. We will all support you. My first grandchild will want for nothing."

Moira's eyes filled with tears. "Thank you all for saying that. I'm going to need all the support I can get."

"See that wasn't so bad," Blythe leaned over and whispered to her. "They took it better than I thought they would."

"You're very quiet tonight. Is something wrong?" Khalil asked. She seemed in a strange mood.

Blythe smiled. "Nothing's wrong. I was thinking about relationships and how strange they can turn out."

He gave her a narrowed glinting glance. "I'm not sure I'm following you."

"I think people should be honest with each other. It would alleviate some of the hurt."

Lifting her chin so that she gazed into his eyes, Khalil asked, "Do you think I haven't been honest with you, Blythe?"

"I'm not talking about us. My sister is going through something right now. If she'd been honest and up front, I think it may have turned out differently for her. I want us to be very honest with each other."

"I'd like to think that we have." He leaned closer to her. "You know that I care a great deal for you, don't you?"

"I know that you enjoy my company. I love being with you, too."

"But . . ."

She held up her hand. "There's no buts. I enjoy the time that we have together. It means a lot to me."

Khalil wasn't positive he was following her. What was it Blythe wasn't telling him? "I sense that you're trying to tell me something. What is it?"

She seemed to take tiny deep breaths as if summoning courage. "I want you to know that I have no expectations. Whatever time we spend together is precious to me and I'll cherish the memories always."

"You make it sound as if I'm only here temporarily." Khalil grabbed her by the shoulders. "Do you think I'm going to just up and disappear on you?"

Shrugging, Blythe said, "I don't know but if you did—then it's time to move on."

What she said stung. "You could just move on like that?"

"Yes."

"It wouldn't bother you?" he wanted to know. Was she really this cold? Khalil had to know.

"I wouldn't be happy about it, but I'd do what I had to do. Life's too short to dwell on things like that."

Khalil was quiet. He wasn't sure he liked this conversation they were having. "I hope we never have to worry about it. I plan to be around a long time."

Shrugging, Blythe replied, "We'll see."

Khalil wrapped his arms around her. "I don't want to lose you."

"As long as you want me, you'll have me."

He pulled away from her. "Why do you talk like that?"

"Like what?"

"The things you say, Blythe. Do you really feel that way? If you do, then why are you with me?"

Blythe detected a hint of censure in his tone. "I enjoy your company. Khalil, I'm not going to delude myself into thinking that we have more going on between us than we do. I've done that in the past and it's very hard on the heart. I walked into our relationship with my eyes open and you know what? It feels good."

"I'm not with you because of your body," he said flatly.

She remained quiet this time. He could tell that she wasn't convinced. Khalil reached for her, pulling her into his arms. "Blythe, I care for you. I really do."

"I know you care for me. But I also know that you don't love me." Khalil was about to respond that she was wrong, but she held up a hand, stopping him.

"It's okay. I'm not looking for love. What we have is fine."

When he tried once again to speak—to declare his love for her, Blythe covered his mouth with her hand. "Let's not talk anymore. Take me to bed." Removing her hand, she kissed him passionately. "I want you so much."

Determined to show her how much he loved her, Khalil pushed her away gently. "Not yet. I want to talk to you about something."

"Khalil . . ."

"I want you to meet my parents," he threw in quickly, startling them both.

"Why?"

"Well they've heard so much about you—they want to meet you."

"You've told your parents about me?" She took a quick breath of utter astonishment. "I can't believe it."

"Should I have kept you hidden?"

Blythe shook her head. "No. I just thought you were the kind of man who will only bring home the girl he plans to marry."

"Well, I don't take everybody over there."

"Khalil, I consider it an honor and I would love to meet your parents. You make them sound so sweet."

"We're having a big dinner on Sunday. Will you be able to join us?"

"I should be able to. What should I bring?"

"Just yourself. Your beautiful smile and that sexy body."

She laughed. Khalil noticed she didn't hide behind her hand anymore. Each day she was loosening up. Now he had to just convince her of his love. He knew she'd been hurt, but he never comprehended the extent of that pain. It was a deep-rooted angst that had her convinced love was simply not in the cards for her. Khalil vowed silently to prove otherwise.

"Grandfather! I didn't know you were here." Blythe climbed off her bed to greet Harwood.

"I wanted to check on Adam. See how his doctor's appointment went."

"Sit down." She pointed to a nearby chair. "Father said that he's feeling stronger each day. Just no feeling in his legs. I keep praying for a miracle."

Harwood nodded. "We all are. But I'm thankful that the good Lord spared my only son. Parents shouldn't outlive their children."

He seemed deep in thought. "You're thinking about Aunt June, are you?"

He nodded sadly. "I miss my little girl."

Blythe was touched by his statement. Her aunt had died a couple of years ago at the tender age of fifty. But to her grandfather, June Bloodstone-Davis would always be his little girl.

"Aunt June was a character. I loved her stories. I still have her Pee Wee Plane series. I'm saving them for my children."

"I have everything June ever wrote. Do you know she wrote her first story when she was six years old?"

"You still have it?"

Harwood nodded. "I sure do. I have all of her stories."

"I bet Mother threw away all of my papers. My stories, my drawings . . . everything. I used to draw a lot. I think I was drawn to Parker because he was living my dream. I wanted to be an artist. I actually thought I was kind of good."

"You were very good. I have all of the drawings you gave to me. I keep everything."

Blythe laughed. "I guess you do." Deep within she was touched by her grandfather's sentimental side. It was a quality she wished her mother possessed.

"You and I never finished our conversation about you thinking that your mother hates you."

"She does. Grandfather, I can see it in her eyes."

Harwood shook his head. "Nadine doesn't hate you, child. The problem with the two of you is that you're too much alike."

"I'm not like her!"

"Don't get all riled up. Nadine is a little self-absorbed but she's not a terrible person, Blythe."

Clasping Iris's hand, Blythe felt a nurturing kind of warmth. It was something she'd never experienced with Nadine. She liked Khalil's mother immediately.

"Come in here and sit down, dear. Khalil's in the kitchen talking with his dad. That's all they do when they get together."

"He seems very close to his father," Blythe observed. "I think that's nice."

Iris nodded. "They share a special bond. It's always been that way."

They reminded Blythe of the Huxtables. Blythe sat silent, wishing her family was more like Khalil's. When he entered the room, her mood brightened.

"What are you and my mom talking about?" he asked.

"You. What else?" She moved over to let him sit down.

He was about to respond when Kuiana strolled into the room. Khalil stood up and greeted her. Blythe smiled but inside she felt uncomfortable. "Hello."

"Hi, Blythe. Good to see you."

Kuiana's smile never reached her eyes.

"You, too," Blythe replied.

They stood in uncomfortable silence. Finally Khalil spoke up. "Why are we all just standing? Let's sit down."

Blythe followed him back to the sofa and sat down. Kuiana took a seat across from them.

"How are things at the store, Blythe?" she asked.

"Things are fine. We're having great sales figures for Christmas thus far. I'm hoping it continues."

"I'm sure," Kuiana murmured.

"Where's Danny?" Khalil asked. "I thought he was coming with you."

"He'll be here shortly. He had to work late."

Khalil stood up. "Dad's calling me. I'll be right back."

Inside, Blythe panicked. She didn't want to be left alone with Kuiana. And it was obvious Khalil's sister felt the exact same way. She sat staring into her hands.

When Khalil didn't return promptly, Kuiana spoke up. "I'm kind of surprised to see you here."

Blythe looked up, her expression guarded. "And why is that?"

"Well, this being South Central and all. I would've thought that you'd be afraid to venture this far."

Kuiana was baiting her. She smiled and replied, "I'm not afraid of coming to South Central. But contrary to what you may want to believe, there are some bad areas around here."

"There are bad areas everywhere. Including Beverly Hills," Kuiana pointed out.

"You don't know me. Nor have you tried to get to know me. Tell me something? Why do you dislike me?"

Kuiana seemed caught off guard for a moment.

"You don't even have to answer. I just think that you should wait until you have a valid reason for not liking me."

Before Kuiana could respond, Khalil had come back into the room.

His parents soon joined them in the living room. Blythe sat back, enjoying the teasing and the conversation between the Sanford family members. Every now and then she caught Kuiana watching her.

Danny arrived and Kuiana seemed wrapped up with him. Blythe was able to relax and fully enjoy herself. Dinner was announced and they gathered into the dining room.

"What do you think of my parents?" Khalil whispered.

She smiled up at him. "They are very nice. I like them."

He kissed her on the forehead. "They like you too."

That pleased Blythe.

The teasing continued around the dinner table. Blythe had never laughed so much in her entire life. After the dessert was served, she wasn't sure she would be able to get up.

"Blythe, after dinner we usually take a walk around the block. Would you like to join us?" Iris asked.

"Yes, ma'am. I would love to." She pushed away from the table.

Khalil put an arm around her. "We don't have to go, sweetheart, if you don't feel up to it."

"I'm fine. I think the walk will do me good." She rubbed her belly for emphasis.

He threw back his head and chuckled. She followed him outside. Hand in hand, they walked behind his parents. Blythe felt like a part of his family. She wanted a family like this. They seemed to really love each other.

No family is without flaws.

Khalil had told her that early on in their dealings with each other. Somehow, she couldn't imagine this family as flawed.

After their walk, Blythe helped Iris and Kuiana clean the kitchen. She'd surprised them by offering to help and then insisting when they turned her down. She wanted to be a part of this fantasy for as long as she could.

They stayed for a couple of hours more before Khalil drove her back home. As they neared the house, Blythe caught sight of a familiar car. She turned around in her seat.

"Somebody you know?"

"I think that was William. He must have been over to see Moira."

Khalil pulled into the driveway and parked. "Isn't that her boyfriend?" he asked.

"He was. Maybe he's come to his senses now. Write down your parents' address for me, please."

Khalil nodded. He reached for a pen as Blythe handed him her address book. He wrote quickly.

"Here it is."

She kissed him passionately. "I miss you, Khalil." She wanted him, but right now with the project so close to coming together, they didn't have much time for pleasure.

He knew what she meant. "I miss you, too."

Blythe got out of the car and headed up to the door. Moira opened it before she could retrieve her key out of her purse. Turning around, she waved to Khalil. He blew her a kiss, then backed out into the street.

"Was that William I just saw leaving here?" Blythe asked her sister.

Moira smiled. "It was. He came by to see how I was doing."

"Really?"

"We talked. He wants to be a part of the baby's life. He wants to marry me and be a father to our child."

"What do you want?"

"Blythe, I want that to. I didn't know how much I loved him until I thought I'd lost him. I love him, Blythe."

"Then I'm very happy for you. Moira, how are you feeling? I've been so busy with Khalil and the store . . . I didn't mean to abandon you."

"I understand. Sometimes, I wished I'd worked at the store."

Blythe was surprised. "Why? Don't you like what you do?"

She nodded. "Being a computer analyst is okay. I'm good

at it, but I feel like I'm missing something not being with you all at the store.''

"Will you continue to work after the baby's born?"

Moira shrugged. "I don't know. William doesn't want me to work. He's ready for me to quit my job now. Enough about me. I've been noticing that you have a glow yourself. I think Khalil has been wonderful for you. You seem happy for the first time in a long time."

"I am happy, Moira. Very happy. Khalil is wonderful. So much so that I'm scared it's going to end. He taught me how to live."

"Take each day and live it as if it's your last, Blythe. Celebrate each moment spent with the man you love."

She smiled. "You're very wise, little sister."

"Not really. Grandfather said those exact words to me last night."

"I gather you told him about the baby, then?"

Moira nodded. "Would you believe that he offered to take a shotgun and force William to marry me?"

Laughing, Blythe nodded. "That unequivocally sounds like Grandfather."

Chapter 20

"How did you know about this place? I've never even heard of it."

"The Hideaway is one of Los Angeles's best-kept secrets. My parents used to come here a lot," Khalil explained.

Blythe appraised the room as they walked around, looking for an empty table. "It's very cozy in here. And with the soft lighting—it's very romantic." She glanced around, discovering that the club catered to a mixed clientele. There were couples who looked to be in their seventies, men and women around the mid-fifties, and there were couples under thirty.

They found a table. Khalil pulled out a chair for her. When she was seated, he sat down across from her.

"Would you like to dance?" he asked.

"No thanks."

"You know this is the second time you've turned me down."

"It's because I can't dance," Blythe confessed.

"Come on. I'm not that great a dancer either. We'll just go out there and have a good time." Khalil rose to his feet. He reached out to her.

"You really want to make me look like a clown. I'm telling you that I have no rhythm."

"Baby, we all have rhythm."

"No, Khalil. I'm one of the few who don't."

He pointed to the floor. "Nobody out there is going to win any dance contests. We're here to have a good time. It doesn't matter what these people think. It's just you and me, baby."

A lady who looked to be well into her sixties paused at their table. "Come on, darling. Show us your stuff. You don't want to leave that handsome fella standing alone too long. If you don't take him to the dance floor, I will."

Blythe burst into laughter. "Yes, ma'am. I'm on my way."

The elder woman winked at Khalil. "Now you owe me a dance, sweet stuff."

He leaned over and kissed her cheek. "Will that do instead?"

"Girl, you got yourself one fine fella. Take care of him."

Laughing, they wandered to the center of the dance floor.

"You're doing well, sweetheart. I thought you said you couldn't dance."

"Hush, I can't talk and keep the beat at the same time. I have to concentrate."

Khalil bit back his laughter.

Escorting Blythe back to their table, he whispered, "I thought you said you couldn't dance. You could've fooled me."

"I wasn't doing much—just rocking back and forth. Is that what people are doing these days?"

"Pretty much it's freestyle. The whole point is to have a good time."

"Well, I have to admit that you were right once again. I had a lot of fun tonight. We should come to the Hideaway more often. I like it here."

They danced the evening away.

On the way home, Khalil asked, "When are you going to show me your paintings?"

She scanned his face. "You're really serious, aren't you?"

"Yes, I am. I would really like to see them."

"Well, there's no time like the present. I'm going to forewarn you, they're nothing special."

"I'll be the judge of that," Khalil stated matter-of-factly.

Blythe had Khalil wait in the family room while she went

to retrieve her paintings. She returned carrying a huge black portfolio.

They sat side by side viewing her work in silence. Blythe's stomach was in knots as she awaited a response from Khalil. "Well, what do you think?" she whispered. "I told you that they weren't any good."

"I want you to stop putting your art down, Blythe. I think you show great talent. These are good. Real good."

"You really think so? I mean you're not just saying it, right?"

Khalil broke into a grin. "I mean it. They're great." There was a tenderness in his voice that she'd never heard before. His hand curved gently along the softness of her face. "I don't think you should give up this dream of yours. Whoever it was that said you had no talent, lied."

Blythe smiled back. Somehow she managed to hold back her tears of happiness. "I'm glad you like them."

He flipped back to one in particular. "This one reminds me of you. Would you mind giving it to me?"

Shock coursed through her body. "Wha . . . what? You really want this picture?"

"I'd like to have it."

"I'll get it framed for you, okay?" She could not believe Khalil wanted one of her paintings. Blythe was touched beyond words.

After one cup of coffee, Khalil stood up and announced, "Honey, it's getting late. I'd better be on my way."

Rising to her feet, Blythe nodded her understanding. "I'll walk you out."

Blythe made the introductions. "This is Alda's sister, Wilma. I think you've seen her at the rehearsals for the fashion show."

Khalil held out his hand to Wilma. "It's nice to meet you."

"You, too. I have to tell you, my sister made a good choice in selecting you as a model."

Blythe didn't like the way Wilma was eyeing Khalil. Or the

way she seemed to be throwing her full breasts in his face. She spotted Justin coming their way and frowned.

"Hello, everybody," he announced.

While Alda and Wilma made a fuss over her brother, Blythe went over her notes with Khalil. ". . . Your father will speak at this time. I wasn't able to get Dr. Mason but I think we'll still be okay."

Khalil nodded. "I don't think we'll need him either."

Blythe glanced over at him. Khalil was watching Wilma. She clenched her hand into a fist. "Am I keeping you?"

He looked at her strangely. "What?"

"Would you like to go over and talk to Wilma? You can't seem to take your eyes off of her."

"She was mouthing something to me."

"What? Alda's phone number?"

Khalil shrugged. "I don't know. I couldn't make out what she was saying."

"I see."

He grinned. "You're jealous."

She stood up. "If you will excuse me . . ." Blythe stormed off to the ladies' room. She needed to clear her head. Massaging her temple, she closed her eyes and prayed for strength. Blythe knew this day would come.

She vowed that she would not let herself get upset over Khalil wanting another woman, but Blythe never expected to hurt like she did. She stayed in the bathroom for a few minutes just breathing in and out. Deep, calming breaths.

When she returned to the cafeteria, they were all seated around a table, drinking coffee and talking. Rehearsal wouldn't start for another thirty minutes.

". . . It's a holiday that intertwines African traditions with American customs. It was created by a man named Dr. Maulana Karenga," Khalil explained. "My family and I also celebrate Kwanzaa."

Blythe wondered for whose benefit he was saying that.

"Well, I've never understood why we needed a man-made holiday like that," Justin stated.

"All holidays are man-made, but the way I see it is that

historically, we as blacks needed faith, determination, courage and an abiding hope in the future.''

Sitting next to Khalil, Wilma agreed. "Khalil's right. Society has changed very little in that regard. With the desire for ties to our African past, Kwanzaa is an ideal forum to explore our cultural roots. Kwanzaa also helps us apply the universal principles—grow and change, live and love, create and build, honor and respect—to our everyday lives, using our own creative energy.''

"It's a way we must live in order to begin to rescue and reconstruct our history as well as our lives,'' Alda added.

"So this is what Kwanzaa is about.'' Justin shook his head. "I never knew that.'' He leaned forward. "If that's the case, then what is the significance of the candles? And why are there seven? Why not three or six or even eight?''

Khalil downed the last of his coffee. "The number seven has always been considered sacred. God made the world in six days and rested on the seventh. Our bodies replace cells and completely renew themselves every seven years and so on.''

Clearing his throat, Justin asked, "How did this all come about? Did this Dr. Karenga just wake up one morning with this idea?''

"No,'' Khalil replied. "The word Kwanzaa means 'the first fruits of the harvest.' The calendars of African countries have always been filled with festivals that celebrate important events such as the first fruits of the harvest. Harvest festivals usually began in late December and continued on for seven or eight days.''

"And each day had a special meaning attached to it,'' Alda supplied. "The Zulu celebrated Umkhosi, the Sudanese observed the millet festival and the Yoruba commemorated the New Yam Festival.''

Wilma leaned forward, saying, "And regardless of the location, all first fruit festivals had five things in common—gathering, reverence, commemoration, recommitment and celebration.''

Justin was shaking his head. "I had . . . I never knew. I mean I knew something about seven principles . . .''

Blythe cleared her throat loudly. "Looks like everybody's here. I think you all should get started."

Justin followed Blythe home. Before she could open her door, he was there. "Did you feel as stupid as I did during the rehearsal earlier?" Justin asked.

"I did at first but not now. I've been doing a lot of research on the subject."

"Can you imagine Mother celebrating Kwanzaa?" Justin burst into laughter. "I can't believe she agreed to this plan of yours."

"She still thinks of it as being somewhat primitive, but Mother had no choice. Grandfather put his foot down."

"I had a feeling that's what happened."

Justin and Blythe both burst into laughter. He closed the door and locked it behind them. "Grandfather is a force to be reckoned with."

While Justin settled on a couch in the family room, Blythe headed to the kitchen. Looking back, she asked, "Would you like something to drink?"

"Some juice if you have it."

"I think we have apple. Is that still your favorite?"

"Yeah."

Blythe returned with a chilled glass of apple juice which she handed to Justin.

"Thanks." He drank greedily, causing her to smile.

"This is almost like old times. I've missed that."

Blythe said nothing.

"Will you please talk to me? What did I do to you that was so bad?"

"Let's not get into this right now. We've had a good day—I don't want to ruin it."

Blythe started to get up. Justin grabbed her by the arm. "Don't run away. Talk to me, dammit. If you're angry with me then at least tell me why."

"You know what you did, Justin."

"You badgered me into setting you up with Parker."

"And so you paid me back, didn't you? You knew what he would do."

"Hell, I tried to warn you, Blythe, but you wouldn't listen. I'm so damn sick and tired of this sh—"

"Justin!" Adam wheeled himself into the room. "What's going on here?"

"I'm sorry, Father. We didn't mean to disturb you, did we, Justin?" She glared at him angrily. "We were just having a tiny disagreement."

"Didn't sound that way to me."

"Blythe's right. It was nothing."

"Look, you two. I may not be able to get up out of this chair, but my hearing still works. Life is much too short to be carrying around a grudge, Blythe."

She opened her mouth to speak, but Adam's expression stopped her.

"You're brother and sister. You both should start acting like it. Family is very important." Adam started to wheel away. "Justin, I have some papers I want you to take a look at, if you have a moment."

"There's no time like the present." He stood up and moved to assist his father.

Blythe sat alone in the family room, trembling with hurt and anger. She'd thought her father understood but it was clear he didn't.

She must have fallen asleep because Adam was nudging her gently. "Why don't you go upstairs, dear?"

"I'm okay." She glanced around. "Is Justin still here?"

"No. He's been gone almost two hours. You can call him if you want to talk to him. He was going straight home."

"I don't want to talk to him. I just wanted to make sure he wouldn't be hounding me for the rest of the evening."

Adam frowned. "Trying to get his sister to talk to him is hounding?"

"I don't feel like talking, Father."

"Blythe, why are you so bitter?"

Her eyes filled with tears. "Why does everyone keep saying

that about me? I don't bother anybody. All I want to do is live my life in peace.''

"Why can't you?"

"Because nobody will let me. I'm so tired of being the one who forgives ... the one who has to apologize ... I'm tired of it, Father. *I'm tired of everything.* I just wish people would leave me alone.''

"No you don't, baby. I know you, Blythe. You're a very loving person. You love so deeply that it nearly tears you apart when that love is not returned. That's just the way you are.''

"Why can't someone love me, Father? Why can't I just skip all of the heartbreak and go on with my life. I'm tired of being hurt.''

"You are not the first person to get hurt and you won't be the last. Blythe, you have to learn from it and move on.''

"Shouldn't you practice what you preach?''

"What are you talking about?''

"Since your accident, you won't leave the house. We went to Barbados and you refused to leave the cottage. Why?''

Adam grew quiet.

Blythe was ashamed. "Father, I'm sorry. I shouldn't have said that.''

"No, honey. It's okay." He looked down at his legs. "You know all these years, I took my hands, legs, my body for granted. I never thought that I'd end up like this." Adam stared off into space. "Some mornings I wake up—I forget until . . .''

Blythe covered his hand in hers.

"I thank the good Lord for my life. I do. But there are days, I'm so angry." He turned to face her. "This is my punishment. Blythe, before the accident, I was a very bitter man. Nadine and I weren't getting along. Dad and I were at odds over the store ... When he told me that he'd made your mother the general manager, I snapped.''

"I didn't know. I never knew you felt that strongly about the store.''

"I was very angry. But it wasn't at your mother or my father—I was angry with myself. I didn't want the store. I just wasn't happy because I wouldn't let myself be happy. Are you understanding what I'm saying to you?''

"I understand." She understood, but Blythe didn't believe that it pertained to her. "I think I'll go on upstairs to bed. I'm tired."

"Think about what I've said, Blythe."

"I will. Good night." She kissed him on the forehead before heading up the stairs. Blythe could hardly see her way through the tears blurring her eyes. Why was she always the one in the wrong?

Chapter 21

Moira peeked in Blythe's room and found her sitting in the middle of her bed. "Khalil's called a couple of times for you. Have you called him back yet?"

"It's not like he's sitting by the phone. I'm sure he's too busy for that."

Coming into the room, Moira eased down on the bench at the foot of the bed. "Why are you talking like that?"

"I think Khalil is attracted to Wilma." Blythe said it a little too abruptly. She instantly regretted it.

Moira looked surprised. "Why would you think that?"

"Well, whenever she's around, they seem to have so much in common, I always feel like I'm an outsider. Besides that, the woman is gorgeous. Big boobs and all."

Moira laughed. "She could walk around naked in front of him and I don't think he would notice one bit. Khalil only has eyes for you, Blythe."

"I'm not so sure."

"Then why don't you ask him?"

Blythe frowned at the question. "Because he's not going to admit it. I've been there, done that."

"What are you talking about?"

"Parker."

"What happened between you two? You never seem to want to talk about him."

"He treated me like dirt. Nothing more to say."

"I never liked him, you know. I don't know why Justin ever introduced you to Parker."

"Sometimes I ask myself that same question. Justin had to know what kind of person he was. He had to."

Moira scanned her sister's face. "You're mad with him, aren't you?"

Blythe nodded. "Every time I see Justin, I get angry all over again. I just don't know why he'd introduce me to someone like Parker. It was as if he were trying to hurt me."

"I don't think Justin would deliberately set you up for something like that. I can't believe that."

"I don't know."

"Blythe, he wouldn't do it. He's our brother."

"And you honestly think that matters to him?" she asked. "Do you really think he cared?"

Moira took Blythe's chin in her hand. "When are you going to get it in your thick skull that we're not shutting you out—it's you who's shutting us out. We love you, Blythe. All of us." She stood up. "Call Khalil. You love him—tell him."

She sat staring at the phone after Moira left her room. Better to get this over with, she decided as she picked up the phone.

Khalil greeted Blythe at the door. When he bent to kiss her, she avoided him. "What's wrong with you?" he asked.

"Nothing," she mumbled. She waited for Khalil to lead the way to his den.

He was shaking his head. "Something's wrong, Blythe. I can see it on your face."

She stood in front of the fireplace, remembering—remembering a different time. The time they made love in front of a roaring fire. Without turning to face him, she said, "I've been wondering if you have something you need to tell me."

"Like what?"

She turned then. Blythe needed to see his face when he gave his answer. "Are you interested in Wilma Forrester?"

Khalil threw his head back and laughed loudly. "No, Blythe. I'm not interested in Wilma. Why would you ask me something like that?"

"Well, she's up in your face every chance she gets."

He sobered up. "And so you're getting an attitude with me because of it? I can't control what that woman does."

"Well I wouldn't feel this way if you'd get her out of your face. Every time I look around, she's right there with you—grinning."

"What do you want me to do? I'm not going to be rude."

With her hands on her hips, she asked, "Instead, you'll just disrespect me, right?"

Khalil held up his hands. "No. Look, Blythe. You need to get over this insecurity of yours. Not every person is the same."

She folded her hands across her chest. "I know that. I don't need you to lecture me, Khalil."

"Then stop acting like a child!"

Sudden anger lit through her. "How dare you talk to me like this." Moving quickly, she threw her purse strap over her shoulder and headed to the door. "I think it's time for me to go."

He blocked her path. "Why do you always take off running? If you're going to make accusations, then you need to stay and take the heat."

She shook her head. "I'm not going to stay here and argue with you, Khalil." Blythe had to get out of there right now. She had promised herself that she would accept his response without question. As much as she loved him, she didn't trust him. "Move out of my way, Khalil."

He did as she asked. "If you leave, don't bother to come back. I can't take any more of this, Blythe. You've got to stop all of this damn running away."

Blythe ran out of the house and to her car.

When she arrived home, she went straight to her room. Blythe threw herself down on the bed, sobbing. It was over between her and Khalil. She'd expected it, but why did it hurt so much?

She loved him so much but she was so afraid to trust.

She finally overcame her pride and called Khalil. Blythe was stunned when no one answered. She tried again He wasn't home. Her insecurities resurfaced and she imagined all sorts of places he could be and whom he could be with. She reached for the phone, fully intending to call Alda's apartment. Blythe chided herself for even thinking about checking up on Khalil and Wilma.

After a sleepless night, Blythe climbed out of bed and headed to the shower. After getting dressed, she reached for the phone but changed her mind.

At the office, Blythe tried to concentrate on her work but couldn't. Each time the phone rang, she hoped it would be Khalil, but she was disappointed.

After her work was completed, Blythe left work early. Unable to take the loneliness anymore, Blythe decided to take the bike out. Chewing her bottom lip, she struggled with the bike as she pulled it out of her trunk. "I don't know why I'm trying to ride this darn thing . . ."

Bike on the ground, Blythe climbed on. Slowly at first, she took off. She tested a few turns until she felt more secure.

"You're doing great," a voice boomed from behind her.

She turned, falling to the ground. "Khalil! Every time you're around, I make an idiot of myself."

Laughing, he helped her up. "Are you okay?"

"I'm fine." Brushing the dirt off of her jeans, Blythe asked, "How did you know I was here?"

"I didn't. I was driving by and at the spur of the moment, I decided to stop."

She hid her disappointment. "I called you last night."

"I know," was his reply.

"Well, where were you?"

"I needed some fresh air and so I went out."

"In other words, it's none of my business." Blythe tried to control her anxiety. "Apparently you have something to hide."

"No, I don't have anything to hide." Khalil held up his

hands. "Look, Blythe, I'm not about to play your little game. If you can't trust me, then why are we trying to have a relationship?"

"I've told you before that trust is hard for me."

"I'm sorry for your pain, Blythe. But you need to know something—I'm not going to allow you to make me pay. I've tried to make you happy."

"You have, Khalil. I'm very happy with you. I've never felt the way you make me feel."

He wrapped his arms around her. "Honey, you have to learn to make yourself happy. I don't want you to depend on me for happiness."

Blythe gazed up at him. "Why not? Is it because you don't plan to be around?"

Placing both hands on her shoulders, Khalil said, "Listen to me. I care for you. Hell, I'm crazy about you. I'm not going anywhere—unless you want me to."

"I need to know something, Khalil. Do you love me?"

He smiled. "What do you think?"

"I don't know. That's why I asked."

Khalil removed his hands. "Are you serious? You really don't know how I feel about you?"

She shook her head no. "You said it the first time we made love. I thought maybe you might have said it just to . . ." Blythe stopped short.

To her surprise, Khalil looked angry. "You think I said it just to get you into bed?"

Holding her chin up, Blythe squared her shoulders, saying, "Well, it's not like it hasn't been done before. Why are you mad?"

He was genuinely hurt. "I thought you knew me better than that. You must really have a low opinion of me."

"Khalil, I've been played by some of the best," she explained. "I'm simply trying to keep my eyes open."

He moved around her. "Well, I'll tell you what. I won't touch you again until you know without a doubt how I feel about you." Khalil started to leave.

Blythe was stunned. Walking briskly, she tried to block his

path. She could see the hurt in his eyes. "I'm sorry. I didn't mean to—" She clawed at his arm.

Khalil removed her hand. "Don't worry about it. I'm glad it happened. I know how you see me."

"You're not being fair."

"Tell me something, Blythe. Why did you make love with me? Were you just feeling a little horny?" he sneered.

"No. No, you know that wasn't it at all, Khalil."

He shook his head. "Then what's going on in that head of yours, Blythe? Hell, you sure don't trust me." Khalil sighed. "I think it's best if we don't see each other for a while. We need some time apart to re-evaluate our relationship."

Blythe grabbed at his arm once more. "No! I don't want to do that." She hated the desperation in her voice.

"Then what do you want?"

"I want you to make love to me. Khalil, I want you to be my friend. My best friend. I want to be your best friend." Her voice became a hushed whisper. "I need you."

"Blythe, take a few days and just think this over. I'll be here, but I want you to be sure about us. I'm not looking for anything temporary—do you understand what I'm saying? I'm not looking for a body."

Blythe wanted to reach out to him, but she didn't. Instead, she just watched him walk out of her life.

Chapter 22

Tossing the book on the floor, Blythe was furious with herself. How could she doubt Khalil's love? He'd shown her in so many ways how much he cared for her.

It had been two days since she'd seen him that evening and she missed him terribly. Blythe decided she would do something about it. She changed into a long, calf-length dress and grabbed her purse.

She drove over to Khalil's house. She needed to see him. Blythe bit her trembling lip while she waited for him to answer the door. When he did, she said, "I know I should have called but I really wanted to see you. I hope you don't mind."

Khalil's smile was warm and friendly. "Come on in. I was in here just listening to some music."

She followed him into the den. "Are you sure you don't mind my coming by like this?"

"I missed you. I'm glad you're here."

When she took off her coat, Khalil whistled.

She moved toward him, swaying to the music. Blythe unbuttoned his shirt. "I've missed you so much, Khalil. I want you—"

He gently pushed her away and shook his head. "We can't."

Her mouth opened in her surprise. "Why not?"

"I don't think it's a good idea for us to make love. I meant what I said the other day."

His rejection stung and her eyes became tear bright. Blythe composed herself. "I think I'd better leave." She searched around for her purse. "I'm sorry I bothered you."

Khalil reached for her. "Sweetheart, I'm not rejecting you. The next time we make love, I want you to know that it's not just sex, but that we are truly making love. I want you to believe it with your body, your mind and your soul. Blythe, I want you to know it like you know your own name." He stroked her cheek. "I want you, baby. My body wants to be next to yours, believe me." He walked her over to the sofa and they sat down. "We don't have to make love to enjoy each other's company."

"You're right. I'm sorry about the way I reacted." When he nodded, she said, "So what should we do?"

"You pick out a movie and I'll go make us some popcorn."

Scanning his video collection, Blythe pulled one out. "Would you believe that I've never seen *Shaft?*"

"Never?"

"I've never seen *The Mack* or any of those." She selected another video. "*Blacula?* Is this the black version of *Dracula?*"

Khalil laughed. "Yes."

Blythe spent the rest of the evening in Khalil's arms watching various black movies, one right behind the other. In the middle of *Cabin in the Sky,* she fell asleep. Khalil cut off the television and nudged her. "Come on, sweetheart. Let's go to bed."

Yawning, Blythe stood up slowly. She followed him into his bedroom. Khalil handed her a shirt to sleep in. While she dressed in his room, he changed in the bathroom. She was already in bed when he came out.

Khalil wrapped his arms around her, pulling her close. "I love you, baby," he whispered.

Blythe snuggled up next to him, fast asleep.

*   *   *

"You didn't last long," Khalil commented.

"I'm sorry I fell asleep on you. I was exhausted," Blythe said over breakfast.

"It's okay. I wasn't far behind you." Khalil poured two glasses of orange juice and handed one to her.

"Khalil, I still feel like there's some tension between us. How do we get past this?"

His eyes opened as they delved into hers with a fierce intensity. "I really don't know, Blythe. I wish I did. I thought we wanted the same things, but I guess I was wrong."

Blythe stared into her plate of scrambled eggs and toast. When she finally raised her eyes to meet his, she said, "I just want to take it one day at a time. We shouldn't rush into anything, Khalil."

Her response reminded him of days gone past. Days when he struggled to avoid entanglements and it shamed him. It gave him insight into what those various women may have been feeling. Khalil was certain he didn't like the vibes he was experiencing. He felt used. Used to satisfy her lust. He felt a thread of resentment flow through his body.

"Khalil, what's wrong?"

He shook his head. "It's nothing. I'm just thinking about something."

Pushing her plate away, Blythe leaned back in her chair and folded her arms across her chest. "I don't like all this tension in the air."

"We want different things from this relationship, Blythe. I don't think it's going to work."

"I see." She looked away. "So, what is it you want to do?" she asked softly.

"I think we should just be friends." There, he'd said it, but Khalil didn't know how he was going to deal with just being her friend. He was in love with her, but it was clear to him that she didn't feel the same way. He'd known from the beginning that she was going to be trouble. He just never thought she'd break his heart.

* * *

Blythe couldn't concentrate. All day long, she pictured her conversation with Khalil, mulling it over and over, but it was never the way she wanted it to be. She was in love with Khalil but couldn't tell him so.

He just wanted to be her friend. At least that's what he'd said this morning. Anxiety built to a roiling turmoil and Blythe felt sick. She kept telling herself that it was for the best, but her heart wouldn't listen.

Peggy came in with some reports she needed to review and Blythe pushed away her thoughts. She couldn't let anything distract her now.

Throughout the rest of the day, Blythe worked steadily, trying to stay busy in an effort to keep her mind off of her troubles.

Around five thirty, Nadine stopped by her office. "I'm on my way home. How much longer will you be here?"

"I'm not sure." Blythe massaged her temples. "Maybe another hour or so."

"I hope you're coming straight home tonight."

"I'm thinking about going to see a movie after I leave here."

"Blythe, it's Christmas Eve. Please consider coming straight home."

"I'll think about it," Blythe murmured softly. She wondered why it was so important to her mother that she come straight home.

When she decided to call it a day, Blythe locked her office and headed to her car. She debated whether to head home or catch a movie. Not wanting to face her lonely bed, Blythe opted to have dinner at the Cheesecake Factory and then head to the theater.

All the lights in the house had been turned off. She fumbled around for the light switch. Blythe choked back her scream upon hearing her name called softly.

"I didn't mean to frighten you, darling."

She turned around slowly. *"Parker.* What are you doing here? How did you get in?"

He laughed. "Your mother let me in, silly. And you know I'm here to see you."

Backing away from him, Blythe hissed, "Why?"

"Another silly question. I love you."

She held up her hand to stop his kiss. "I don't want you to touch me and I certainly don't want to hear how much you love me."

"Blythe, don't act like this. I made a mistake."

"I really don't care."

"I've never known you to be so cold."

"It's late, Parker. You should leave."

He reached for her once more. "Why are you acting so distant? I know you still care for me."

"Let me go. I don't care anything about you. Now I want you to leave."

"I can't," he replied smugly. "Your mother invited me to stay here."

Blythe couldn't believe what she was hearing. "You've got to be kidding. She couldn't . . ."

"Go ask her."

Taking the stairs, Blythe rushed to her mother's room. Without knocking, she entered. *"How could you do this to me?"*

Nadine closed the book she had been reading. "What on earth is your problem?"

"You told Parker he could stay here."

"What's wrong with that? I didn't mean he was sleeping in your room. He's in the guest room."

"But how could you even think of letting him stay here after all he's done to me."

Nadine climbed out of bed. "Blythe, please calm down. Parker came all the way here just to spend Christmas with you. What should I have done?"

She glared at her mother. "For starters you could've told him to stay at a hotel."

"He was going to do that but I felt that it would be rude of us to have him do so."

"Why do you care about his feelings?" Especially since you don't care about mine, she added silently.

"Blythe, it's almost Christmas. We can afford to be kind—"

"Mother, he hurt me. Can you understand why I'm not feeling generous toward Parker?"

"Let him stay tonight," Nadine pleaded. "I'll tell him tomorrow that he has to move to a hotel."

"Good night, Mother." Blythe walked briskly out of Nadine's room. Taking a deep breath, she headed back downstairs. Parker was standing before the marble fireplace.

He grinned. "I wasn't sure you'd come back downstairs."

"I only came to see if you needed anything. If not, I'm going to bed."

Lowering his voice to a husky whisper, he said, "I'd like to join you. We used to have some good times . . ."

She rolled her eyes. "You've lost your mind."

"Blythe, calm down. Look, I made a mistake. I married Jessica because—"

"She was rich," Blythe finished for him. "You fell in love with the fact that I was a Bloodstone—it was never me."

He looked offended. "That's not true."

"Yes, it is. You wanted me to support you while you painted pretty pictures and had affairs. But when you found out I didn't come with as big a checking account as you'd thought . . ." She paused. "You dumped me so fast."

"I was wrong for that."

"You trashed my paintings. Made me feel as if I had absolutely no talent." She laughed bitterly. "You're the one with no talent."

"Honey, I love you," he pleaded. "As far as the paintings. I thought you would rather I be honest with you. I guess I should've lied about your talent, or lack thereof."

Infuriated, Blythe held up her hands. "Parker, I've had enough. I'm going to bed."

He grabbed her arm. "Don't. We need to talk. I'm thinking of moving back here."

"And?"

"And I thought maybe we could start over."

Blythe shook her head. "I don't think so."

"Is there someone else?"

"Yes."

"Do you love him?"

"Yes, I do."

Parker shook his head as he gazed at her. "I don't think so. You see, I know how much you loved me. This guy—he's just someone you met on the rebound."

Blythe gave a small laugh. "We haven't been together in over three years. You don't know what you're talking about."

Chapter 23

Blythe was surprised to see Khalil standing at her door on Christmas morning.

"You look shocked to see me. Did you forget that you invited me over?"

"I didn't forget. I just didn't think you would come after everything that happened."

Khalil leaned over, kissing her chastely on the cheek. "Merry Christmas, Blythe."

"Everybody's in here." Khalil followed her into the living room where everyone was gathered.

"Mr. Bloodstone, Moira. Merry Christmas to you both."

"It's very nice to see you again, Khalil. Merry Christmas," Adam said.

Blythe kept glancing over at the stairs.

"What's wrong?" Moira whispered. "You don't look too happy to see Khalil. You actually look nervous about something."

"It's not him," Blythe whispered back. "Everything is fine between us, but Justin's bringing Alda and Wilma here for dinner."

"What's wrong with that?"

Blythe stole a glance in Khalil's direction. He was still engaged in conversation with her father. "Wilma has the hots for Khalil, that's what's wrong. And then on top of that, Parker's here."

Moira's mouth dropped open.

"He's here. At this house."

"When—"

"Merry Christmas everyone," Parker announced as he came down the stairs.

Blythe rose to her feet. Before she could say anything, he wrapped his arms around Blythe, kissing her fully on the lips.

"Oh my Lord!" Moira declared.

She pushed away from him. "Don't you ever do that again," she hissed under her breath. Khalil was watching her, his face a mask of confusion. Blythe immediately made her way over to him.

"Who is he?" Khalil asked, his eyes never leaving hers.

"Parker Stratton. He's my ex-boyfriend."

"What's he doing here?"

She shrugged. "Who really knows."

Parker navigated toward them. "You must be the love of Blythe's life. She told me all about you."

Khalil nodded. "She's told me something of you, also."

The two men eyed each other until Parker shrugged and grinned. Holding out his hand to Khalil, he said, "Merry Christmas."

"Same to you." When Parker was out of earshot, he asked Blythe, "Are you okay?"

"Everything is just *perfect.*"

Khalil stared at her.

She regretted her comment instantly. "I'm sorry. I didn't mean to snap at you like that."

He led her over to the couch. "If you need to talk about this, I'm here."

Blythe stroked his cheek. "I know and I really appreciate it."

Nadine entered the living room, looking from one person to the other. She approached them. "Khalil, it's nice you could join us for dinner. I would've thought you would be with your family.''

"Mother . . ." Blythe warned.

"Actually, I spent yesterday and all morning with them. It's a tradition in our family to have a big dinner on Christmas Eve, then go to church together. We open our gifts Christmas morning and then we have a huge brunch.''

"Sounds wonderfully sentimental," Wilma cooed as she sashayed into the room. "Merry Christmas, everyone.''

Justin and Alda went around the room greeting and hugging each person.

". . . Christmas is a very special time for our family," Khalil was saying. "They mean a lot to me.''

"That's very admirable of you," Nadine commented. "Unfortunately, Blythe doesn't have a family-oriented bone in her body. She only came home because of her father's accident. If it hadn't been for that she never would have come home at all.''

"Nadine!"

She turned to face her husband. "Why on earth are you yelling at me, Adam. It's the truth.''

Blythe stood up. "I don't think I'm hungry. And I'm certainly not in the mood to be insulted.''

"That's not what I'm doing.''

Khalil grabbed her hand. "Sweetheart, sit down please.''

"I didn't mean anything by it, Blythe.''

Blythe saw the look in Khalil's eyes and sat down.

"Our little Blythe has always had such a hot temper," Parker announced. "It's one of the things I've always loved about her.''

"Nobody asked you anything," Blythe snapped. Standing up, she confronted her mother. "You know, Mother, you are one to talk about family loyalty. After the way this man has treated me, you still invite him to share our home. You knew I was bringing Khalil." She shook her head sadly. "I've made a decision. I'm moving out of here as soon as I can find a place. If you want to invite every man who's ever dogged me— then you can do it. Only I won't be around to have my nose rubbed in it.''

In the tension-filled room, Khalil rose up suddenly. He reached for her. "Come on, Blythe. We're taking a walk."

"I don't—"

"If I have to pick you up, I will," he threatened. Blythe followed him outside, fuming.

"Honey, what just happened?" Khalil asked.

Blythe leaned into Khalil. "I can't believe she let him stay here. After everything he did to me. She's supposed to be my mother."

Holding her close, Khalil kissed her forehead. "Today is Christmas. You shouldn't let her upset you. This is your mother's house and she's free to invite whomever she pleases to stay here."

"You're right. That's why I need to move out. It's time I got my own place anyway." She glanced up at him. "I'm not thinking about moving in with you, so you can relax."

He grinned. "Now you're trying to read my thoughts. If you want to come and stay with me, that's fine."

Blythe shook her head. "Thank you but no thanks. I'd rather find my own place. I need to live on my own."

They watched a little boy test his brand-new bike. When he fell, Khalil glanced over at her. Blythe laughed.

As they walked along the driveway, he said, "I think your ex-boyfriend's out to win you back."

Looking up at him, she whispered, "Khalil, he could never do that."

"I'm not worried about him." Pulling her into his arms, he asked, "Was Parker telling the truth?"

"About what?"

"About me being the love of your life."

She gazed into his eyes. "What do you think, Mr. Sanford? You know men will say anything."

His hand curved around her jaw and Blythe was rising up to meet him even as he was bending down. Their kiss was slow, thoughtful, suggestive of what they couldn't share.

Khalil straightened. "Are you ready to go in and face your family and this Parker?"

Blythe looked away and nodded. "I'm as ready as I'll ever be."

"Parker, what are you doing here?"

"Justin, it's good to see you again. What have you been up to?"

"Why are you here?" he asked again.

"I made a mistake. I came home to set things right."

"Blythe doesn't seem to be interested in anything you have to say."

"She's still angry but I'm going to do everything in my power to make things right between us."

Justin and Alda exchanged glances.

"I will win her back," Parker vowed. "Deep down, Blythe still loves me."

"Do yourself a favor and leave her alone. My sister has moved on."

Alda touched Parker's elbow gently. "Justin's right, Parker. Just leave Blythe alone. She's met someone else and she's very happy. Don't try to ruin that for her."

"She's not in love with him. She's just trying to get over me."

Justin muttered a curse. "I don't believe you, man. I regret the day I ever introduced you to my sister. If I had known that you'd break her heart . . ." His hand curled into a fist. "I could break your neck—"

Parker blinked twice. "Justin, I didn't mean to hurt Blythe. We broke up and I met someone else. That's how that came about."

"You're lying!" Alda practically shouted. "You left Blythe stranded in a flat with no money. You stole all of her money."

"I did no such thing."

"What's going on here?" Blythe asked. She and Khalil were standing in the doorway. When no one responded, she said, "Well?"

"Parker was just saying his goodbyes."

"Now look, Justin. We're friends—"

"No. We used to be friends. Our friendship ended when you hurt my sister."

Blythe gasped.

"You took my sister all the way to France and you treated her like crap. I introduced her to you because you were my best friend and I thought you would do right by her. You damn near destroyed her and you almost caused her to hate me."

"Justin, I don't hate you."

He turned around to face her. "Sis, I know that you blamed me, too. I could see it in your eyes each time you looked at me. I'm sorry. I'm so sorry he hurt you."

Blythe rushed over and wrapped her arms around Justin. "It wasn't your fault. I was wrong to blame you. I guess I just felt like you were supposed to protect me . . ."

He nodded. "And I didn't. If I'd known what happened, I would've come and gotten you myself."

Parker crossed the room to join them. "Hey, I'm not going to stand here and take all of the blame."

"Why don't you just leave? It doesn't matter anymore. You're out of my life."

Khalil moved to wrap his arms around Blythe. "You heard her, Parker. She wants you to leave."

He looked Khalil up and down and laughed. "Man, you'd better get out of my face. You don't know her like I do."

Justin grabbed Parker. "That's my sister you're talking about. Do all of us a favor and get the hell out of here."

Jerking out of Justin's clutches, Parker straightened his clothing. "Let go of me."

"Is everything all right in here?" Harwood asked. He stood behind Blythe. "Everything is fine, Grandfather. Parker was just leaving."

"Yes, I'm leaving." He moved close to Blythe and whispered, "You can pretend all you want but I know you still love me." Parker kissed her cheek.

"Keep your lips to yourself," Khalil warned. "If you care as much for Blythe as you say you do, then leave her alone."

Standing in the doorway, Parker laughed. "Not on your life." He shut the door quickly and was gone.

* * *

"Why do you want to destroy your own daughter?"

"What on earth are you talking about, Adam?" Nadine asked.

"Blythe is our daughter, honey. She needs your love. Our love."

"The two of you have a special relationship, Adam. She and I have never had that. I love her so much . . ."

"Why don't you tell her?"

"I don't know."

"I do. And I think you do also, honey."

Nadine stiffened. "What are you talking about?"

"What your father did to you. You have always been afraid to touch your children, to let them get close to you because of what he did."

Huge tears rolled down her cheek. "I've been so afraid that I-I would be l-like him. I didn't want to do that to my own children. He was a horribly sick man. The things he made me do in the name of love."

"You're not like him, baby. Nothing like him. It's okay to hug your children—to tell them that you love them."

"It's too late now." She crawled in a fetal position on his bed, sobbing.

Adam shook his head. "It's never too late." He reached for Nadine, trying to console her. "You will have to forgive him, baby. And you have to forgive yourself."

She nodded. After a while the crying stopped. Nadine sat up slowly. "Perhaps in time. Right now I've got to find a way to keep from losing Blythe."

"Love her."

She sniffed into a tissue that Adam handed her. "Adam, I need to know something. Blythe talked you into coming home, didn't she? I know you were planning to move in with your father."

"Yes," Adam admitted. "I'm glad she did. My question to you, Nadine, is do you want me to stay?"

"I don't want you to leave. Please stay with me."

"Nadine, this house is filled with so much tension. I can't continue to live like this."

"I can't bear it any longer myself. I admit that I've not been a perfect wife. I've even taken you for granted, but I've never once stopped loving you."

"Can you love me like this?"

Nadine smiled. "Yes. Adam, you are still very much the man I married."

"Before you leave, Khalil, I have something for you." Blythe handed him a large, brightly wrapped gift. "Merry Christmas."

He sat down and tore off the paper. Smiling, he admired the framed painting he'd asked Blythe for a few weeks back. Khalil glanced up at her. "Thank you."

"Do you like the frame? I tried to match it with the other frames in your house."

"It's perfect. Blythe . . ."

"We're just friends, Khalil."

That statement was a hot sear, as hot as the frustration burning his heart. Why in hell wouldn't this woman give an inch? Khalil loved her and when he looked in her eyes, it was love he saw. He rubbed his bearded chin. Maybe it was all his imagination. Khalil had to find out. "Blythe, I'm going crazy here. I need to know something and I want the truth. Do you love me?"

Blythe swallowed the lump in her throat, but she didn't reply.

Khalil sighed heavily. "I love you, Blythe Bloodstone. I wish you'd believe me. Hell, I plan to marry you one day."

Blythe remained quiet. Instead, she let her fingertips stroke his cheek. "Do you mean it, Khalil? Do you really mean what you're saying to me?"

"I mean it with all of my heart."

She accepted that. "I don't want to rush—"

His kiss cut off the rest. It wasn't the response he wanted, but it was enough for now. Khalil kissed her over and over until Blythe thought she might faint.

The two of them walked to the door, neither wanting to say good night.

Chapter 24

Blythe called out to Justin as he was passing her office. "Could you come here for a minute?" She could read the distrust in his eyes. Smiling, she said, "I wanted to say thanks for last night."

Justin relaxed visibly. "It's nothing. I'm really sorry, Blythe."

"Will you please stop saying that. It's not your fault. I was wrong for blaming you for what happened. I was hurting . . ." She stopped. "Let's not rehash it. I just want to forget about Parker and what happened." She stood up and turned to stare out of her window. "It's time to move on."

Gripping both of her shoulders, Justin turned Blythe to face him. "Sis, I really care about you. I want you to know that."

She nodded. "I care about you, too. You used to be my best friend. I kind of miss that."

"I do, too," Justin replied. "Maybe we can work on recapturing our friendship."

Blythe smiled again. "I'd really like that, Justin."

They embraced and Blythe walked Justin to the door. He had to rush off to meet with a client.

Blythe had barely sat down when her assistant breezed in. "This card arrived by messenger for you."

"Hmmmm. I wonder who it's from." Blythe reached for the envelope. Opening it, she found a handmade card from Khalil. In it he'd written in his neat handwriting:

Umoja

> *We are one, our cause is one and we must*
> *help each other if we are to succeed.*
>   *Frederick Douglass*

"Is it a love letter?" her assistant teased.

"No. Something more." Khalil was right. Without unity, you can't get anywhere. Whether it was family, friend or stranger. Blythe put the card away. "I'm going to run downstairs to see how things are going."

"I just got back from lunch and it's still a madhouse. Lines are practically out the door. I thought Christmas was bad but this seems worse."

"Did you happen to notice if the lines were moving?"

"They were. I think it was a good idea to designate one register out of each department for returns or exchanges."

"Thanks, Peggy." Blythe stood up. "I'll be back in about an hour. I want to do a walk-through."

"Okay. I'll page you if anything comes up."

Downstairs, Blythe caught sight of her mother standing across the room. She eased out of the men's department and headed to children's, taking the escalator upstairs. She didn't want to talk to her mother right now.

The words on the card Khalil sent to her reverberated in her mind. She and her family had to find a way to unite. Not for public appearances but in reality. Blythe reasoned, sadly, that once she moved out, things might change for the better.

She avoided her mother for most of the day. It wasn't hard because Nadine seemed to be avoiding her as well. Blythe left work an hour early and headed over to the apartment building where Alda lived.

*   *   *

Nadine seemed surprised to see Blythe moving around the room, putting her possessions in cardboard boxes. She rapped lightly on the open door. "If you have a minute, I think we should talk."

Without looking up from her packing, she asked, "About what, Mother? The way I see it, there's nothing more to say." Pausing, Blythe added, "Well, except that I'm moving out. I've found a place in the same building Alda lives in. I'm moving in after the first of the year."

Nadine walked in, wringing her hands in despair. "There is no reason for you to do that. I'm sorry about the other morning. I never should have said anything like that."

"No, you shouldn't have."

She put a trembling hand on Blythe's arm. "Please don't leave, Blythe. Your father would be devastated and he'd blame me, of course."

Eyeing her mother, she said, "I assure you, he'll understand."

"Blythe, please. I . . . I don't want you to leave. There, I've said it."

She dropped the shirt she was holding on the bed. Blythe folded her arms across her chest. "Can't you understand, Mother, that it hurts me to be here. You know what's strange? I really thought I'd accepted the fact that you didn't love me." Her eyes filled with tears. "It still hurts."

Nadine's mouth dropped open in complete shock. "I was under the impression that you didn't love me."

It was Blythe's turn to be surprised. "You can't be serious."

"I know I'm not the most affectionate person in the world, but each time I would reach out to you, your body would literally tense up." Nadine's eyes filled with water. "You never reacted that way with your father or your grandparents."

"I'm sorry. I never knew you felt this way."

"Blythe, you don't have any idea of what it's like to be hated by your parents. Neither one of my parents wanted me. Everything wrong in their life was my fault. They made my life a living hell. When Mama died, well I've already told you of my shame. I was so afraid that I would be like him."

"Mother—"

"Please let me finish. I think you need to hear this. My father used me in horrible ways. I shut down to stay sane. All of the love I had—I kept buried." Nadine wiped her tears. "He hurt me so bad that I felt nothing but relief over his death. Then I fell in love . . ." She shook her head sadly. "Every man I met hurt me just as deeply. It seemed no one could love me." Nadine smiled. "And then I started working at Bloodstone's and I met your father. Adam was so good to me." Observing her daughter's face, she added, "I know you always assumed it was for money, but it's not true. Your father was the only person who ever loved me. He always treated me like I was someone special, even after I told him about my past."

Blythe averted her eyes.

"It's okay. Money wasn't the reason, but I'd be lying if I said it didn't have an effect on me, as well. I grew up dirt poor. I didn't know what it was like to have brand-new shoes or a new dress . . ." Nadine seemed caught up in memories. Snapping out of it, she continued, "Anyway, back to what we were talking about. Adam and I got married and everything was so wonderful. Then I found out I was pregnant."

The tone of Nadine's voice prompted her to ask, "Were you upset?"

"In truth, yes. I didn't know what to do with a baby. I was scared I would be like my parents—my father mostly, but Adam was so happy. We had Justin, and then I found myself pregnant again."

"With me?"

"Yes, and it was much too soon. But again, Adam was ecstatic and what could I do?"

Blythe's heart felt like it would break. "So, you didn't want me?" She turned away from her mother. Blythe moved to the window in her bedroom and stared out. "I want to hear the truth. I need to know whether you wanted me or not. I need to know."

"Of course I wanted you, dear. I was afraid, Blythe. I loved you—I loved all of you, but I was afraid that I wouldn't be a good mother. I was afraid of my own children."

Blythe didn't know what to say, so she remained silent.

Nadine joined her at the window. "After Moira, I had my tubes tied against your father's wishes. He wanted another child, you see."

"I didn't know that."

"Oh, yes. Adam was furious with me. After that, he seemed to draw away from me and simply focused on the three of you. It was as if he had no room for me in his life anymore. So, I locked up my heart and dove into my work. When your grandfather made me general manager, the gap widened even more. The night I found him in his office with that woman . . ."

Blythe reached for her mother's hand. "I wish I could take your pain away."

Nadine smiled and stroked Blythe's face. "I should be saying that to you. I'm so sorry, my little girl. I love you so much and I'm going to be honest with you. After numerous rejections, I admit I quit trying. I was wrong."

"I've always felt like an outsider. I'm as guilty as you."

"Blythe, please give us another chance. I don't want you to move out. I know I can't take back the pain, but I'd like the chance to be a better mother to you. I hope it's not too late."

"It's not. No matter how old I am, I will always need my mother." Blythe wrapped her arms around her mother, holding on for dear life. "I love you so much."

"Then please don't move out. We need this time to get to know one another. I missed you so much while you were in France."

Blythe was touched beyond words. "Mother, we can still get to know one another, but I think moving out will be best. You and Father need time alone." She smiled through her tears. "I promise I'll visit often and we can . . . we can do a girls' night out or something."

"That would be wonderful, dear." Nadine wiped at her eyes. "I've wanted this for a long time. This is the best Christmas present I've ever received."

"Me, too," Blythe agreed. Her eyes strayed to the clock on the table. "Oh, goodness, I need to get ready for tonight." She gazed at Nadine. "Are you coming tonight?"

"Yes, I'll be there."

Blythe could read the fear in her mother's eyes. Nadine wasn't comfortable with the idea of traveling to South Central at night. "If you'd like, you can ride with me."

Nadine relaxed visibly. "I would love it."

Nadine eyed the homes with interest. "You know, there are some really beautiful homes over here. You don't see this on the news. They always show you the worst of everything."

"Ugliness sells, I guess," Blythe murmured. "People who are determined to harm come from all walks of life. All colors." She parked in front of a green and white house. "This is it."

The first person Blythe saw when she entered the Sanford home was Wilma. She took a deep breath to calm her temper and made her way over to stand beside Khalil. He leaned over, greeting her with a kiss. "Hello, sweetness." He hugged her mother, surprising them both. "I'm glad you could make it, Mrs. Bloodstone."

Nadine smiled. "I'm looking forward to learning about Kwanzaa. Thank you for including me."

"Come with me, I'd like to introduce you to my parents." He excused himself from Blythe and Wilma.

"I'm surprised to see you here so early. Where's Alda?" she asked Wilma.

"Oh, she's coming with Justin." She smiled and gestured to Kuiana, who was standing a few feet away. "Kuiana and I spent the day together."

"I see." Blythe rewarded Khalil's sister with a cool stare. "How are you, Kuiana?" she asked as Khalil rejoined them.

She smiled. "I'm fine. And you?"

"Couldn't be better." Grabbing Khalil by the hand, Blythe led him away. "It looks like they're about to get started. Where's my mother?"

"She's with Aunt Maida." Khalil exchanged a puzzled glance with Kuiana, who only shrugged.

Iris called everyone together. As they gathered around a table that had been set up for the celebration, Blythe nudged Khalil and asked, "What is your mother doing?"

"She's going to light the black candle."

"Isn't she going to light the rest of them?"

He shook his head no.

Blythe listened in awe as Khalil's grandfather, James Sr., welcomed everyone and talked about the importance of Kwanzaa.

Alda leaned over and whispered, "Well, what do you think so far?"

"It's interesting," she whispered back. She observed the whole ceremony in awe.

Later that evening, while everyone was eating, Khalil asked, "Did you enjoy yourself, Blythe?"

She smiled at him. "I did. I've learned so much tonight. Your grandfather is a very interesting man. So is your father."

He nodded in agreement. "Dad's seen a lot in his lifetime. From registering blacks to vote in Mississippi to marching with Dr. King—he's seen the worst of it."

"Your family has been a part of the fight for civil rights a long time. Your grandfather told me that he went to Birmingham, Alabama, right after they bombed that church and killed those four little girls. Your grandfather said that your aunt Maida is the family historian."

Khalil leaned back into his chair. "She is. Tell me about your family."

"Well, my great great grandfather and his family had been settled on the Kennedy farmland since before the Civil War. They lived in a small town called Kenville in North Carolina. After the war they stayed on and worked the land. My great great grandfather and his brother bought the ten acres of land off of the last surviving Kennedy in the early 1900s. Eventually, they bought another four acres. Over the years, there were several other land deals up until 1940. When his brother died, my great great grandfather sold the land to some big corporation.

I don't really know much about my mother's side of the family."

Khalil sat up then. "Really?"

"You make that sound unusual."

"Well, to me it is. Knowing your history is so important."

Blythe was quiet. Khalil was making sense. She didn't know hardly anything about her family. What could she tell her children or her grandchildren?

"Blythe?"

"I'm sorry. I was just thinking about what you were saying. You're right, I need to find out more about my family. That's what impressed me so much about yours. You all are so close and your past is rich with some important events of history."

"Yours may be as well. You don't really know," Khalil pointed out.

"I guess I'll make that one of my resolutions for the new year. I'm going to find out more about my family and our history." She leaned into Khalil. "You know, I have so much to thank you for."

"What are you talking about?"

"You taught me how to laugh at myself and how to live, but mostly, you taught me how to love again."

Khalil grinned. "I'm glad I could be of help."

She saw Nadine sitting alone, eating. "I'm going to check on Mother. She looks lonely."

"While you're doing that, I'm going to get rid of these plates. Want anything else?"

Blythe shook her head as she headed in Nadine's direction.

Khalil found Kuiana in the kitchen when he went to throw away their paper plates. "Are you hiding out?"

"Aunt Maida's trying to talk me into telling a story one night this week."

"I think you should."

"Maybe. I'll think about it."

"One more thing. I need to know something. What's going on with you and Blythe?"

She bit into a stick of celery and chewed slowly. When she finished it, Kuiana asked, "What do you mean, big brother?"

"You know what I'm talking about. I know you don't like Blythe—"

"You're right, I don't like her. She's so fake it's not even funny."

"You don't know anything about her. But you know what? It really doesn't matter. I happen to be in love with her and I'm thinking about marrying her."

Kuiana's mouth dropped open. "You can't be serious. You haven't known her that long."

"The point is that I love her and you need to respect that."

She was quiet for a moment. "What about Wilma?"

"What about her?" Khalil asked.

"She's interested in you. The way I see it, Wilma is more of your type. Not Miss Bloodstone. She's just a white girl dipped in chocolate."

"I want to be with Blythe, Kuiana."

She gazed into her brother's eyes. "You really mean it. You're in love with her. You really are."

Khalil nodded. "Give her a chance, Kuiana. She's not a bad person."

"Where is Khalil?" Wilma asked. "I haven't had a chance to talk to him at all."

"He's out there somewhere with Blythe." Kuiana lowered her voice. "Wilma, he told me tonight that he's in love with her."

Wilma's smile disappeared. "Oh."

"Are you okay? I'm sorry. I had no idea he was that involved with her."

"He hasn't known her that long, right?"

"No, he hasn't," Kuiana agreed. "But he says he loves her and Khalil doesn't take something like that for granted."

"Well, I hope Blythe realizes just how lucky she is . . ." Wilma sighed wistfully.

"She'd better. Miss Thang had better not do anything to hurt my brother."

"She won't, Kuiana. Blythe is a very caring person. I know

that much about her. I used to tease her about caring too much. Underneath that cold facade is a very gentle spirit. She's been through a lot."

"I think she's stuck-up."

"No, she really isn't. Blythe is very selective about her friends. She keeps to herself mostly. I've always suspected that she wasn't doing it because she wanted to, but because she was terribly afraid of being rejected."

"How long have you known her?" Kuiana asked.

"Let's see . . . hmmmm, I guess it's been about four years. I met her shortly after she moved to France. She was at a very low point in her life."

"I don't know . . ." Kuiana mused.

"You really have to get to know her. Blythe is pretty up-front, which I can respect. She's the way she is because she's been hurt a lot."

Chapter 25

Someone tapped her on her shoulder. Turning around, she found Parker standing there. "What are you doing here?"

He gazed at her, his eyes full of lust. "I'm shopping. This is a department store, isn't it?"

"Whatever." Blythe turned to walk away.

"Hey, don't walk away angry." Parker reached for her. "Come here, baby."

Blythe snatched her hand away. "Don't you baby me. And keep your hands off me."

"Why are you treating me like this? I said I was wrong about the way I treated you."

"And you think that's supposed to make things right? You treated me badly, Parker."

"You're not going to let me forget it, are you? I know what I did, Blythe. Now I'm sorry, but my head was in the wrong place back then. I've come to my senses and I want to be with you."

"Why?"

"What do you mean why?"

"Why do you want to be with me now, Parker? Nothing's changed. I'm not rich. I work for a living."

Something flashed in his eyes that Blythe didn't recognize. She stood with her arms folded across her chest. "Well?"

Parker shook his head. "I can't believe you said something like that to me."

"I don't know why not. You dumped me for a woman with a bigger checkbook than mine." Blythe wagged her finger at him as she continued to speak. "But that wasn't all you did to me. You took every cent I had to my name and left me stranded."

"I didn't steal your money."

She could tell he was angry now, but she didn't care. This confrontation was a long time in coming. "Yes, you did, Parker. I am many things but I'm not stupid. You left me in a flat with no money. If it hadn't been for Alda . . ."

"I love you, Blythe. I want you to be my wife. See, you've got me proposing to you already."

She gave a bitter laugh. "I don't think so. I've moved on." Blythe started to walk away but turned around. "You know, Parker, I suppose I really should thank you. Leaving me was the best thing you could've done for me."

"What do you mean by that?"

"I finally have someone in my life who treats me the way I deserve to be treated. He loves me."

"I guess you're talking about Khalil."

"Yes, I am."

He burst out into laughter. "The way I see it, he's got his eyes on Wilma. The two of them were pretty cozy."

"You don't know what you're talking about," Blythe snapped. "There's nothing going on between them."

"Not that you'd know." Parker gave a nasty laugh. "You're cold. Cold like a fish. You only think about everything that's gone wrong in your life. Screw everybody else."

Blythe blinked back her hurt. "I've got to go."

"What's wrong? Can't take the truth?"

She whirled around to face him. "As if you'd know the truth. You're nothing more than a gigolo and a thief. Matter of fact I think I'll alert security to keep an eye on you." Blythe enjoyed seeing him flinch. "Now I want you to stay as far away from me as possible."

"You little . . ." His eyes filled with disgust. "I can see why your own mother hates you. If nobody's kissing your butt, then you're not happy. I've always tried to be honest with you. You don't want that."

"Be honest with yourself, Parker. You're looking for a meal ticket, that's all. You have no talent and you insult anybody who makes you feel threatened. Instead of trying to analyze me—take a real long look in the mirror. Work on yourself." She turned away, walking as fast as she could. Her eyes filled with hurt. Blythe wanted to die right on the spot when she spied her mother nearby. From the expression on Nadine's face, she knew that her mother had overheard their conversation.

When she arrived to the safety of her office, Peggy handed her an envelope. "Here's another card for you. It just arrived a few minutes ago."

"Really?" She ripped the envelope off and smiled as she gazed at the card from Khalil.

Kujichagulia

> *We can't rely on anyone but ourselves*
> *to define our existence, to shape*
> *the image of ourselves.*

Spike Lee

Khalil's card couldn't have come at a better time. Blythe knew enough about Kwanzaa to know that he was sending her cards he'd made himself and had chosen quotes from people he felt exemplified the seven principles. She also knew that each quote had been chosen with care. Each one echoed a private message to her in regards to her own life.

Her assistant came to the door. "Wilma Forrester is here to see you."

Putting the card away, Blythe nodded. "Send her in." She wondered what in the world Wilma wanted to talk to her about.

When she walked in, Blythe motioned for her to close the door. When Wilma took a seat, Blythe asked, "What did you want to speak to me about?" Deep within she knew. It was about Khalil.

"I felt we needed to talk."

"About what?"

"About Khalil. It was nothing but harmless flirting. I'm sorry if I upset you."

"I thought you were my friend, Wilma. How could you do this to me?"

"I really don't know. I saw him and . . ." She shrugged. "I never would've acted on it. I just wanted to have some fun."

"At my expense."

"No, Blythe. I'm sorry it went as far as it did. I wouldn't have done anything to hurt you, but I thought you two were just friends. At least that's what Kuiana led me to believe."

"Even so, it gave you no right to do what you did."

"You're right. I'm really sorry, Blythe." She stood up. "I want you to know that I'm going home after the new year. George called and said that he misses me like crazy. I miss him, too. Most of all, I love him. We're getting married as soon as I get back."

Blythe rose to her feet. "Congratulations. George is a real nice guy and he adores you."

"I hope you're not mad with me."

"I'm not. Actually, I guess I should thank you. I tried to deny my feelings for Khalil. You forced me to deal with them."

"I hope you'll invite me to the wedding."

Blythe laughed. "Get out of here, Wilma. I've got work to do."

Nadine knocked on the door of Blythe's office. "Hi, I thought we could have lunch together."

Blythe stared at her mother. "Sure." She pushed away from her desk and stood up. She collected her purse and they were on their way.

"We'll take my car, if that's all right with you?"

Nodding, Blythe replied, "That's fine."

They drove to an Italian restaurant nearby. Once they were seated, Nadine said, "I want to talk to you about Parker."

"I don't want to talk about him."

"I think we should. Parker is wrong."

Blythe looked away. "It doesn't matter."

"Yes, it does. I saw the way you looked when he said those horrible things. Please don't let that bum get to you. Blythe, you're my daughter and I love you."

"I know that now."

"I'm so sorry about everything. I handled—"

Blythe covered her mother's hand with her own. "Let's not dwell on Parker. He's not worth it. In a way though, I guess I should thank him."

Nadine frowned. "Thank him? For what?"

"Well, if it wasn't for Parker dumping me, I never would've met Khalil and I wouldn't have you."

They ordered their food. When it arrived, they discussed the store and the upcoming Kwanzaa event while they ate.

After Nadine paid the bill, she and Blythe headed to the car. Before they got in, they stood staring at each other. Finally Nadine spoke. "I love you, Blythe and I'm very proud of you. In spite of my not being there for you, you've grown into a beautiful young lady. You're the kind of woman I wanted to be. In a way, I think I envied you."

Blythe warmed all over as she listened to her mother say the things she'd longed to hear over the years. She reached out to embrace her mother, then pulled back.

Nadine saw her and smiled. "Come here, sweetheart. I won't reject you." She held Blythe close to her heart. "I won't ever reject you again. I love you. I do. I love you."

Nadine nudged her. "Isn't that Khalil's sister over there? In the junior department?"

Blythe was surprised to see Kuiana in the store "Yes, it's

her. I guess I should go over and say hello. Wearing a smile, she moved forward to greet Kiuana.

"Hello, Blythe."

"I saw you over here so I thought I'd say hello. I hope you'll enjoy shopping at Bloodstone's." Not having anything else to say, she turned to walk away.

"Blythe, wait!"

She turned around. "Yes."

"I didn't come to shop. I came to see you. I want to talk to you about my brother."

"Do we have to do this now? I've got a busy day today and I don't feel like fighting with you."

"I didn't come to fight. I simply came to talk."

Blythe checked her watch. "Let's get this over with. We can talk in my office."

"Thank you." Kuiana followed Blythe to the elevator.

Once they were in her office, Blythe sat down behind her desk. "Well?"

"As I said earlier, I'm not here to fight with you. Khalil can take care of himself. He doesn't need me to fight—"

"Then why are you here?" Blythe interjected. "I know you don't like me. So, what would we have to discuss?"

"You're right, I didn't like you. Right this minute, I'm not sure how I feel about you. That's why I'm here. Khalil is my brother and I love him very much. He told me that he's in love with you."

"And I love him, too."

Kuiana relaxed. "I'm relieved to hear that. I want him to be happy. He thinks his happiness is with you. I pray he's right."

"Kuiana, I love him so much. He's my best friend. I don't know what I'd do without him."

"Well, I feel I have to be honest with you, Blythe. I'm not sure about you."

"Since we're being so up-front with each other, it's not your business what happens between your brother and me. Kuiana, I know you love Khalil and you don't want him with me, but there's nothing you can do about it."

"I respect my brother and for his sake I will try to get along with you."

"I appreciate your candor. I hope that we will be able to become friends."

Kuiana smiled. "Maybe in time ..." She stood up and grabbed her purse. "I guess I'll see you tonight."

"I'll be there."

She stopped in the doorway. "One more thing. Kwanzaa is not something we take lightly. It's not a way to get back into the good graces of the black community either."

"I admit that maybe it started out that way, Kuiana, but in the last few weeks, I've learned so much about Kwanzaa. I'm learning not only about others but about myself as well. Khalil has been a great teacher."

Kuiana opened the door and left.

"How was your day?" Khalil asked.

"It was fine." Blythe didn't feel it was necessary to tell him about Kuiana's visit. "How about yours?"

"I had a good one. Just couldn't keep you out of my thoughts."

Blythe grinned. "That's encouraging."

"Are you two lovebirds going to join us?" Iris asked. We're about to start."

Khalil wrapped his arms around Blythe. "We're coming, Mom." Just as Iris turned the corner, he pulled Blythe closer to him, kissing her passionately.

Hand in hand, they walked into the living room to join the others.

Khalil's aunt Maida lit a red candle. Blythe had been told by Khalil that the red candles represented the struggle by blacks for justice.

Maida was saying, "The second principle of Kwanzaa, Kujichagulia speaks to the issue of self-definition. It means to define ourselves, name ourselves, create for ourselves and speak for ourselves, instead of being defined, named, created for and spoken for by others."

Kuiana walked up to the podium.

"While doing some research on the Internet, I came across this information on the slave revolt of 1811, and I thought it fitting to include since we're talking about self-determination. I won't read the entire piece but those of you who want to learn more about this struggle, should get the book *On to New Orleans* by Albert Thrasher."

She began to read, "When one mentions slave revolts, the names Gabriel Prosser, Denmark Vesey and Nat Turner come to mind. But tonight I'm going to tell you about Charles Deslondes. He has the distinction of having organized and led the largest slave revolt in U.S. history."

Blythe leaned over to whisper to Khalil. "I'm so embarrassed. I've never heard of Charles Deslondes."

"A lot of people haven't heard of him."

". . . On January 8, 1811, Charles Deslondes and his comrades began the revolt on the plantation of Manual Andry in Southern Louisiana. Armed with cane knives, clubs and a few guns, they marched in columns of four and gained in numbers as they moved from plantation to plantation along the east bank of the Mississippi River.

"Charles Deslondes and his compatriots liberated twenty-five miles before they were intercepted on January 10th by U.S. troops from New Orleans. Some of the leaders were captured and executed. Their heads were cut off and placed on poles along the River Road in order to frighten and intimidate the other slaves.

"The sacrifices of these brave men and women were not in vain. The 1811 revolt weakened the system of chattel slavery and stimulated more revolts in the following years, setting the stage for the final battle, the Civil War, that put an end to this horrible system.

"It is only fitting that we show our appreciation to these men and women who represented the best quality of our people. These were people of exceptional self-determination, valor and dedication. People who understood that we should not be defined by others but by ourselves. The names of the heroes and heroines of the 1811 antislavery struggle shall forever be honored.''

Blythe was moved to tears. She was vaguely aware of Khalil handing her a tissue. When she chanced a look at Justin, she saw that he was just as moved. Eyeing one another, they smiled.

Chapter 26

Blythe opened the envelope from Khalil. This time the card read:

Ujima

> *The many of us who attain what we may and*
> *forget those who help us along the line—*
> *we've got to remember that there are so*
> *many others to pull along the way. The*
> *further they go, the further we all go.*
>
> Jackie Robinson

She ran her finger over the handmade card, savoring the feel of the glitter and the kente fabric glued to the paper. She was touched profoundly by the message in each of the cards she'd received so far.

She was actually looking forward to tonight's celebration at the Sanford home. She was like a sponge, absorbing everything she could about Kwanzaa. In its own way, Kwanzaa was drawing her family together. Even Justin seemed to be an eager student.

Nadine had come by earlier, announcing that she would be

attending tonight and every night thereafter. Harwood intended to be there as well.

Pushing back from her desk, Blythe stood to look out of her window. She was truly thankful. Khalil loved her and she had her mother. Now if only her mother and father could bring themselves back to each other . . .

"Hey, darling. You have a minute?" Harwood asked.

Turning around, Blythe smiled. "I didn't know—" she stopped. "Why are you dressed like that?" Harwood looked like a bum.

"Just a little experiment." He took off his ragged hat and sat down. "Wanted to see what was going on myself."

"What did you do?"

"Well, I got together with some friends of mine. I dressed like this. A couple of my black friends were dressed in decent clothes—nothing fancy, you know. Then I got a couple of my white friends together, too. We decided to do a little shopping."

She knew where this was leading. "What happened?"

"Well, it seems your young man was right. While all of the detectives watched me and the other two blacks, my white friends were able to steal the store blind."

Blythe's mouth dropped open.

"It seems I'm going to have a long talk with the security department. There may even be some positions opening up."

"Does Mother know?"

Harwood nodded. "She's in total agreement."

"Really?"

"She was furious."

Blythe had a hard time believing what Harwood had told her. "We're a black-owned store. I can't understand how . . ."

Harwood nodded. "I think we just looked the other way. Too many people were complaining and we never looked into it." He rose to his feet. "Well, I aim to change all that. I'll see you tonight. Right now, I need to change out of these clothes."

Blythe watched him leave. Khalil's words came back to her. He was right. Bloodstone's became a success thanks to the black community. Once they moved to Beverly Hills, things changed along with the new decor, new staff . . . It was time they gave back to the community. And not just by monetary means.

That evening, Khalil's mother lit a candle for Ujima. Blythe listened as Khalil talked about how important it is to help each other by working together.

". . . We must reach out to help others in need. I can't sit idly by and not be concerned about what happens in my community. My grandfather couldn't sit by and not be concerned with what happened in Birmingham when the Sixteenth Street church was bombed. My father couldn't stand by when people were murdered for trying to register blacks to vote . . ." Khalil's gaze roamed over her face lovingly. "I think Dr. Martin Luther King said it best. Whatever affects one directly, affects all indirectly."

Wilma moved to stand beside Khalil. "In the spirit of Ujima, I pledge to reach out and help others in need."

One by one, each person made a pledge. When it was only Blythe and Nadine left sitting, all eyes turned to them. Blythe turned to Khalil, silently pleading for help. He smiled and extended his hand to her.

Standing up, Blythe swallowed slowly. "Well . . . in the spirit of Ujima, I pledge to not only reach out to help others but . . ." She glanced over at her mother. "I'm going to reach out to my own family. I think it's important that I begin at home."

"You're absolutely right," Khalil's grandfather stated. "How can you help a total stranger and not be there for your own family?"

Nadine's turn came. She looked nervous. "I pledge to help others by organizing a clothing drive for the homeless and the less fortunate. I also pledge to reach out to my own children . . . As Mr. Sanford said, it's important that in working together, we are also keepers of our own families." She gave a tiny smile. "Listening to all of you, I realize that I wanted so much to avoid having my children grow up the way I did that I forgot to look at the bigger picture. I'm going to do my part to make sure it never happens again."

Iris reached over to hug Nadine. "That was beautiful."

Blythe smiled at the two women embracing. She felt Khalil's arms around her. Looking up at him, she said, "Thank you so much for allowing us to be a part of this wonderful celebration."

"I'm happy you wanted to be a part of it. It means a lot to me."

"Khalil, I would like to go home with you tonight. I really miss being with you."

"I don't just want your body, Blythe. I can get that from any woman. I want your heart as well."

"I'm prepared to give you all of me. Life is to be cherished, and I guess I've just realized how much of mine has passed me by. I have no one to blame but myself." Looking up at Khalil, she said, "I intend to change from now on." Her arms went around his middle. "I love you, Khalil."

"Where were you hiding that?" Khalil asked when Blythe strolled out of the bathroom.

"I was wearing it under my suit." She twirled around slowly, giving him a perfect view of the satin and lace teddy she was wearing.

"Wow!"

Blythe crawled into bed. "I've missed you so much. I hate sleeping alone."

Khalil pulled her close to him. "Move in with me?"

Propping up the pillows behind her, she sat up. "It's much too soon. I love you, but I did that once and it didn't work out. This time I'm not moving in with a man until I marry him."

Grinning, Khalil asked, "Sure you can wait that long?"

Inclining her head, she asked, "Just how long are we talking?"

"I don't know. Maybe five or six years . . ."

"I don't think so. You'd better make an honest woman of me before then. I'm not one for long courtships."

Pulling her down, Khalil threw back his head, laughing. He settled a kiss upon her temple, then traveled down to her mouth.

Blythe moaned in response and her sexily clad body arched in invitation. Khalil removed the teddy in a hurry. He could hardly wait. From the way Blythe was breathing, she couldn't either.

Khalil nudged his knee between hers and entered her, driving her to a quick and explosive climax.

They made love once more before surrendering to the peaceful balm of the lovers' sleep.

Chapter 27

"What's put such a big smile on your face this afternoon?" Adam asked.

Blythe leaned over and kissed him on the cheek. "Mother and I had a long talk yesterday."

"Is that so?"

She nodded. "She doesn't hate me."

He smiled. "I knew that. Your mother loves you very much. I hope she told you that. I think you two just didn't communicate with each other."

"That was certainly part of the problem, but it went deeper than that. But that's all over with. I have my mother and nothing could be better."

Just then, Nadine entered the kitchen. "Hello, everyone."

"Hi, Mother."

"Blythe was just sharing her good news about the two of you."

"And I have Khalil. A man who loves me as much as I love him."

Nadine embraced her. "I'm pretty happy myself. I have my daughter back."

Blythe reveled in her mother's embrace, but she had to go.

"If you two will excuse me, I need to go shower and change. I'm meeting Grandfather at the store."

Nodding, Nadine said, "I plan to stop in myself sometime this afternoon."

When Blythe left the kitchen, Adam turned to his wife and asked, "Honey, I'm so glad to hear you say that. How did all this come about?"

She told him about overhearing Parker and Blythe arguing. "And then I heard him tell her that he could understand why I hated her." Nadine shook her head sadly. "It nearly broke my heart."

"I could break his—"

"He's not worth the effort, Adam. Let's just move forward." She took a sip of coffee. "You know I've been wrong about so many things. I don't know if I'll ever be able to set things right."

"You're doing just fine, sweetness."

"So, you don't think it's too late for me and Blythe?"

"You saw her face. She's happier than I've ever seen her."

"And what about us, Adam? Is it too late for us?"

"Nadine, I've told you how much I love you. You're my wife and I want to keep it that way."

"I want very much to remain your wife. You're my best friend and these past few months have been terrible without you. I've been thinking . . ." She suddenly looked unsure of herself.

"Yes."

"I was thinking that maybe I should move into the bedroom downstairs. With you. That is if you don't mind."

"Of course I don't mind. I've missed lying next to you." Adam lowered his voice. "I've also missed making love to you."

She was too stunned to speak for a moment. "But you can't . . . can you?"

He laughed. "I still have feeling there."

"Oh. I didn't know."

They gazed into each other's eyes.

Nadine cleared her throat. "Where is Winston?"

"He's in his room. I told him I wanted some time alone with my wife. I'm going to have to depend on you . . ." he paused.

Nadine smiled. "I've been waiting to hear you say those words for a long time." She went and locked the door.

It was not surprising to Blythe when the messenger showed up at her door with an envelope from Khalil. She opened it quickly.

Ujamaa
> *We will either find a way or make a way.*
>> *Hannibal*

Alda rapped lightly on Blythe's open door, interrupting her musings. "Have you a free minute?"

Putting the card down on her desk, she said, "Sure, come in." Blythe waited for Alda to take a seat before asking, "What's up?"

"Well, something's been bothering me and I need to know something."

"Okay, what is it?"

"It's about you and Wilma."

Blythe's expression changed abruptly. "What about us?"

"There seems to be some tension with you two. I know she's been flirting with Khalil and I demanded that she put a stop to it."

Blythe was quiet.

"We're friends. You can talk to me about my sister. I know she's been flirting with Khalil."

"It's okay, Alda. Wilma and I have already discussed it. There's nothing she can do to me or Khalil. We love each other."

"She didn't mean anything by it, Blythe. She's in love with George."

"I know. She said they were going to get married as soon as she returned to France."

"I'm glad you're okay about this. I didn't want to be in the middle—"

"You're not," she interjected quickly. "This was strictly between Wilma and myself." Blythe decided to change the subject. "How are you and Justin? You two looked pretty cozy last night."

"Things are going quite well. In fact, Justin told me that he loved me. Actually, he told me that on our first date. He even proposed."

Blythe's mouth dropped open. "What? My brother, Justin?"

Alda laughed. "Your big brother."

She was genuinely happy for them both. "Well, what did you say? Are you and Justin engaged?"

Alda shook her head. "No. I told him to ask me again after we've had a chance to get to know one another."

Falling back into her chair, Blythe shook her head in disbelief. "Wow, I can't believe it. Justin . . . ready to settle down? It's incredible. I never thought he'd be ready to get married."

"He says he fell in love with me the first time he bumped into me."

Blythe smiled. "That's wonderful. You've been like a sister to me—I'm glad Justin loves you."

"I'm falling in love with him as well."

"That makes me even happier."

"Justin and I are going to Ghana in the spring. I want him to meet my family."

"Knock knock." Wilma stood in the doorway. "Am I interrupting?"

"No, you're not. Come on in."

"Your assistant told me you were up here, Alda. Are we still on for lunch?"

Standing up, Alda nodded. Turning to Blythe, she asked, "Would you like to join us?"

She shook her head. "No thanks. I've got a lot of work to do."

"Having lunch with that handsome Khalil Sanford?" Wilma asked.

Smiling, Blythe shook her head. "No, not today. I'll see him later tonight. Are you ready for the fashion show?"

Wilma nodded. "I am, but I'm nervous." Putting her arm around Alda, she said, "Come on, I'm starved."

Blythe waved at the two women and returned to her work. There were a few more things she needed to take care of before tonight's event.

An hour later, Blythe went downstairs. The decor of the store had been transformed to represent Africa. Flags, African art exhibits, food and specialty shops had been set up on each floor. She was pleased to see so many customers. People of all colors were stopping here and there, purchasing merchandise and sampling food or just looking.

Blythe toured each department before returning to her office. She planned to leave shortly in order to prepare for the event tonight. She prayed everything would go well.

Harwood's mouth gaped in amazement as they inspected the store together one last time. "Blythe, honey, the store looks wonderful. This was a good idea."

"Grandfather, I'm so glad you're pleased. I think it's fitting that the only black-owned department store in Beverly Hills join in the celebration of Kwanzaa." Blythe was proud of her hard work and the work of Khalil and Alda. Schools, libraries and special guests were slated to participate in the various programs to be presented throughout the evening.

On each floor, customers sampled various African dishes, met visiting dignitaries and learned about the seven principles of Kwanzaa.

One of the specialty shops, created solely for the event, was the Ujamaa Market. Customers could find everything from books to buttons, African fabric and jewelry. Grinning, Harwood held up a dashiki handmade in Ghana while someone snapped a photograph.

"We've gotten a lot of publicity," he was saying. "Good publicity. I'm very proud of you, Blythe. My father built this company for the black community. Somewhere along the way money became more important than our customers ..." He shook his head. "I don't want to make that mistake again."

Blythe hugged Harwood. "I love you, Grandfather."

"Where's that young man of yours? I thought he'd be here by now."

"He should arrive any moment. Khalil went to pick up his parents."

"He's a good man."

Smiling, Blythe murmured, "I think so, too."

Nadine approached them and both Blythe and Harwood did a double take. She looked stunning in a peplum suit featuring a bright metallic print that was perfect for the holidays. On her head, she wore a matching crown.

"Mother, you look beautiful."

"You look like an African queen," Harwood stated.

Nadine looked unsure of herself. "You really think so? Normally, I wouldn't think of wearing something like this, but when I saw this dress, I had to ... Does it really look okay?"

"You look wonderful, Mother."

"How do I look?" Adam asked as he was wheeled in by Winston.

"Father! I'm so glad you came." He was dressed in a long tunic with matching pants. The fabric was the same print as her mother's dress. "You look so handsome." Blythe couldn't believe that her father was here with them.

"Your mother has been telling me about Kwanzaa and its principles. She even let me read the book you gave her. I felt that we needed to put on a united front. This store belongs to all of us."

Blythe caught sight of Moira coming her way.

"The store looks incredible. You did a great job, Blythe." Moira embraced her. "For a minute there, I thought I was in the wrong store."

"Everything looks beautiful," Nadine agreed.

Blythe had never experienced such an overwhelming feeling of pride in anything she'd ever done. "I'm so glad all of you approve. I want this to be a night everyone will remember. I'm hoping to make this an annual event."

"That sounds like a wonderful idea." Nadine checked her watch. I think we should head upstairs. It's almost time."

"Tonight we remember our ancestors—the men, women and we must not forget the children—who gave their lives for our freedom. We remember their individual sacrifices, known and unknown. It is their sacrifices that summon us to continue their collective cause." James Sanford's voice carried across the room.

"Yesterday's movement succeeded—in part—because we became our own champions. When Mrs. Rosa Parks refused to stand up, and when Dr. King stood up to preach, we as a people came to the movement for civil rights. Most of those who made the movement weren't famous; they were the faceless. They were the nameless—like my father. He along with others marched with feet so tired he could no longer stand; he was one of the ones beaten back by billy clubs and fire hoses. Tonight we honor all of them.

"I was in Mississippi in 1964. I knew James Chaney. I grew up with him. I can still remember the day I heard that he was missing . . . " James Sanford's eyes became bright.

"I attended the funerals of Andrew Goodman, Michael Schwerner and James Chaney. I knew we could not give up. I went on to join Dr. King in 1966 when he led the march through Chicago's south side.

"You know, next to our ancestors and their sacrifices, we are called to give comparatively little. Our time, our energy, our caring. Our past is filled with painful and tragic memories. Well, I have to tell you that from where I'm standing, today is no different. We have forgotten what's important. And because of it, our children will continue to make sacrifices; they will suffer. Men, women, families and communities—we need to pull together for a common goal. Only then will we each realize our full potential."

Blythe whispered to Khalil, "Your father is a powerful speaker. He's seen so much . . ."

Khalil nodded. "Yes, he has, but he continues to have hope."

Sticking her hand in his, she said, "You're a lot like him."

"Yes, I guess I am. But if I had to be like anybody, I'd want it to be him and my grandfather. They are two of the best role models." Khalil glanced over to where her family sat. "I'm glad to see your entire family is present."

Following his gaze, Blythe agreed. "Me, too."

Alda motioned for Khalil to go to the dressing room.

"Well, sweetheart, I've got to go strut my stuff." He glanced back at her and winked.

Laughing, Blythe shook her head.

As Wilma commentated, models paraded back and forth down the runway that had been constructed earlier that day. Judging from the enthusiasm of the guests, they loved the new Heritage collection.

The grand finale was the bridal gown worn by Kuiana. When Alda came out, the crowd gave her a standing ovation. Harwood presented her with a dozen roses and so did Justin.

Refreshments were served after the fashion show. Blythe and her family were gathered at the front with Khalil's family. There were lines of people waiting to speak with Alda.

"I'm so glad you told us about Alda. I've never seen anyone that enthusiastic about David Garsone's designs," Nadine commented. "Look at those people. They all want to talk to Alda." Lowering her voice, she added, "And they are not all black customers."

Blythe smiled. "I guess we've all learned something this week." She spotted Khalil coming her way. "Would you excuse me, Mother?"

"Sure. I need to check on your father anyway." Nadine moved on.

Blythe met Khalil halfway. Standing beside him, she said, "You were wonderful out there, Khalil. You make a great model."

He shook his head. "No, baby. It's not for me." Khalil took her by the hand. "This event's a hit."

"I think so, too. It looks like everybody's having a good

time." She gestured toward Alda. "Look at all those people. They all love the Heritage collection."

Blythe and Khalil headed downstairs to watch a group of teens from his church perform African dances. They stood side by side as the youths moved to the sound of the drums.

Khalil was still with Blythe long after the store closed. When she stretched and yawned, he massaged her shoulders.

"You're tired. I want you to go home tonight and get a good night's sleep, okay?"

She glanced up at him. "You are so sweet and sensitive. I don't know what I would do without you."

"I intend to make sure you never have to find out," he whispered huskily. "I'm here to stay."

Chapter 28

Nia

> *None of us is responsible for our birth.*
> *Our responsibility is the use we make of life.*
> *Joshua Henry Jones*

Blythe smiled and placed the card with the others before leaving to meet her mother in the private dining room.

Setting her glass down, she asked, "What did you think of the celebration last night, Mother?"

"I have to admit I found it very interesting. However, I don't know if Khalil's father should have brought up such painful things. Some things I think are best left forgotten."

"Well, Kwanzaa is about recalling our past."

"But Blythe . . ."

"Mother, think about it. What he actually said made sense. Granted, we don't have to sit in the back of the bus or pick cotton, but the times are still turbulent. It's not just blacks and whites; it's blacks against blacks and families fighting with each other. He's saying that we should pull together instead."

Nadine was quiet.

"Mother?"

"Yes, dear."

"Are you okay? I hope I haven't upset you."

"No. I was simply thinking about what you were saying. I guess I didn't look at it that way."

"Mr. Sanford has seen a lot of painful things, Mother, but he's still out there. He's constantly speaking out about blacks coming together. He doesn't intend to just sit back and do nothing."

"That's very admirable. I suppose we all should follow his lead and not look the other way."

"I know I'm going to. We've got to find a way to make this a better world for future generations."

Nadine nodded. "You know we are always trying to give a better life to our children than we had—all they really need is love. Material things are nice, but . . . love . . . that's what's really important."

Blythe nodded in agreement.

Nadine leaned over and asked suddenly, "Do you know what my favorite memory is of you?"

"No, what is it?"

"Remember when you wanted to plant vegetables in the backyard at Harwood's old house?"

Blythe nodded and she continued. "You were so excited and very impatient. So much so, you couldn't wait for Rebecca."

"Grandmother was taking much too long." She laughed. "I took a packet of mustard seeds and scattered them everywhere."

"Harwood and Rebecca had mustard greens growing with the tomatoes, cabbages and watermelon."

"I combined some of the mustard seeds with the collards, too. Grandmother always cooked them together, so I thought I was making it easy for her."

Nadine doubled over in laughter. "I know."

Blythe covered her chuckles. "I'd forgotten all about that. Grandmother was upset but you stuck up for me."

"It's my favorite memory." Nadine pulled a thick packet from her briefcase. "I want to show you something."

"What's that?"

"You'll see."

Blythe's mouth dropped open. "You kept all of my drawings?"

She nodded. "I loved them. I have all of Justin's and Moira's too. What did you think happened to them?"

Nadine asked, "I thought that you threw them away."

"No, dear. I wouldn't do that. They're very precious to me."

"I have all of the gifts you've ever made for me too," Nadine stated almost shyly.

Blythe was moved to tears. She'd had no idea. "Why?"

"Well, because they were from you and I figured if I couldn't have you, I at least had a part of you."

Feeling ashamed, Blythe stated, "Mother, I'm so sorry I made you feel that way. I know how it feels. I'm so sorry."

"We have a new beginning. Let's make the most of it. The reason I pulled these out is because I have an idea and I'd like your opinion."

Blythe was filled with curiosity.

"I know you've always dreamed of painting and you're good at it. Well, I thought the store should have an art gallery. Not a big one, you understand. This first year will be a test. If it goes well, we can look into making it bigger."

"An art gallery? That sounds wonderful."

"We could feature the works of local artists and also some of your pieces."

"My work?" Blythe shook her head. "No, Mother. Not my paintings."

"Why not?"

"They're not good enough."

Nadine seemed shocked by her statement. "Blythe dear, I just don't believe you said that. You are an extraordinary painter. You have so much talent . . ." She smiled. "I'd hate to see you waste it working here at the store."

"I love the store, Mother."

"I know you do, but I also know your heart's not here. When your father and I suggested you go to college and major in something besides art, we didn't mean to infer that you give up your dream. We just wanted you to have something to fall back on. I always thought you would continue painting.''

"You've never said anything before."

"I know. There just never seemed to be a right time."

"You really think I'm good?" Blythe asked quietly. She had to know. Painting was what she wanted to do most.

"I love your work. I was so surprised when you stopped. I guess I just assumed that it had been a phase."

"No, it wasn't that. Anyway, it doesn't matter. I love the idea of the art gallery. Are you going to bring it up at the next meeting?"

Nadine nodded. "What do you think Harwood will say?"

"I think he's going to love the idea. I'm also going to propose a new specialty salon. I think we should have one that features ready-to-wear clothing from the homeland."

"Sounds like a good idea."

Blythe and Nadine continued to discuss new ideas for the store while they ate their lunch.

"I enjoyed listening to Kuiana speak. You all have inherited your father's talent for speaking."

Khalil laughed. "You call that talent?"

"It's not something everybody can do. Some people are born to be speakers." She accepted the plate he handed to her. "Thanks."

When Khalil sat down beside her, she said, "Oh, I have something to tell you."

"What is it?"

"My mother is thinking about putting an art gallery in the store. Each month we'll feature a new artist and this is the best part . . . she also wants to include some of my paintings." Blythe could hardly contain her joy.

"That's wonderful, baby." Khalil reached over and embraced her. "I'm happy for you."

"You know, listening to your sister . . . Until recently, I kind of just existed—I felt that I had no purpose. Now, I feel like

I've been reborn.'' She gave a small laugh. "I guess I sound kind of silly.''

"No, you make a lot of sense. When I first met you, you were so serious, Blythe. You never smiled—now I can't get you to quit and believe me, I'm not complaining. I never get tired of seeing that pretty smile of yours. It's like you were merely waiting to drop dead.''

"Was I that bad?''

"I think so. You are such a vibrant and talented woman. I think it's a shame that you've had to hide that fact for so long.''

"I realize it was my own fault though. Everybody tried to tell me that I was in charge of my own happiness, but I didn't want to listen.'' She reached for his hand. "I'm glad you didn't give up on me. And I am very happy—not just because of you, but because of me. I'm not going to punish myself any longer because of what others say or feel about me.''

"You are very special, Blythe. Don't let anybody tell you different. I love you and I want to spend the rest of my life with you.''

"That's a long time, Khalil.''

Shaking his head, he said, "It's not long enough.''

Khalil and Blythe entered his dimly lit house and headed straight to the bedroom. All night long, he'd wanted to pull her into his arms, kissing her until she pleaded for him to stop. Khalil helped her undress.

"Are you sure you don't want to move in with me?''

Blythe turned and looked up at him. "I'll move in the day you marry me.'' She removed her bra slowly.

"Then let's get married,'' he said, surprising them both.

"Excuse me?''

"You heard me. Let's get married.''

Blythe was speechless. "I . . . We . . . Khalil, we're moving much too fast, don't you think?''

Pulling her naked body to his, he wrapped his arms around her. "We don't have to get married tomorrow. We can get engaged.''

She pulled away and glanced up at him. "You're really serious, aren't you?"

"Blythe, will you marry me?" His eyes were filled with emotion. "I love you so much, sweetheart."

"I love you too, but I have to be honest with you. I've always rushed into relationships and I had hell to pay because of it. This time I want to take my time and get to know you."

"You won't ever really know me until you marry me," Khalil argued.

"I want to marry you, Khalil. I really do."

"Then say yes."

Blythe's bottom lip trembled.

"Trust me."

"Yes, I'll marry you." She closed her eyes to keep the tears of happiness from falling. One lone tear slipped down her cheek.

Khalil picked her up and carried her to the bed. Placing her gently down, he crawled in beside her. "We don't have to have a quick wedding. We'll take our time. I don't want to rush you if you're not ready. When you walk down that aisle, I want you to be completely at ease. Understand?"

"I love you." Blythe pulled him to her. "Make love to me, Khalil," she murmured huskily.

He did as he was told over and over again.

Kuumba
> *Potential powers of creativity are within us*
> *and we have the duty to work assiduously*
> *to discover these powers.*
>
> *Martin Luther King, Jr.*

Blythe placed this card carefully in the scrapbook along with the others. She labeled the book *My First Kwanzaa*, knowing instinctively that there would be many more.

She admired Khalil's long tunic of black and gold and the

matching kuffi he wore tonight. She had come to realize that it was his way of showing appreciation of his African heritage.

Khalil left the room for a moment and returned carrying a huge bouquet of kente cloth roses. He handed them to Blythe.

"Are these for me?" she asked. When he nodded, she said, "Khalil, the flowers are beautiful . . ." Blythe paused. "They're all individually wrapped. Is this the way they're supposed to be?"

Smiling, Khalil nodded.

Inclining her head, she asked, "You want to tell me why?"

Grinning, he replied, "I thought I'd be a little creative."

"I see. And what exactly am I supposed to do with a bouquet of individually wrapped flowers?"

"Oh, I think you can find a way to be creative."

Hearing footsteps behind them, Blythe turned around and saw her mother.

"Am I interrupting something?" Nadine asked.

"No, come on in, Mother."

"The flowers are beautiful," she murmured.

Eyeing Khalil, Blythe pulled one of the roses from the bouquet and handed it to Nadine.

"Thank you, dear." Nadine's eyes were tear bright. Inhaling the sweet fragrance of the flower, she closed her eyes.

Blythe felt the beginnings of joy seeing her mother's reaction. Reaching out, she took Khalil's hand, squeezing it. She was touched by his gesture.

When Khalil's mother entered, Blythe handed her a rose from her bouquet. She did the same for every woman present in the Sanford home.

Chapter 29

When Khalil's cousin descended the stairs playing an African instrument, the agogo, everyone gathered around the kinara. Tonight all of the candles would be lit. After Aunt Maida read several selections from the Bible, James began his libation statement.

"...We thank the elders and our ancestors for teaching us and for leading us. We honor them by living our lives according to their example." James poured a small portion of the fruit juice on the floor in four directions. East, south, north and west to honor the ancestors. He then passed the Unity cup to his father. After taking a sip, James Sr. passed the cup to the youngest member there.

"He represents the promise of a new generation," Khalil explained.

In the audience, each person had a paper cup. James Sr. gave the call to unity by shouting, "Harambee!" Seven times. "There is a proverb that says, 'As long as someone is here to speak your name, you exist ...' We call on the nameless, faceless children of the future. We ask a moment of silence for them because they have not been named, but we feel their presence."

Kuiana read a poem entitled *The Black Family Pledge* by Maya Angelou. Afterwards she talked about how the value of Kwanzaa has helped her.

Iris shared what she'd learned during the year, and when she was done, she invited others to do the same.

Surprising herself, Blythe stood up. "I learned that we shouldn't gather in recrimination, but rather in remembrance and renewed hope." Reaching for her mother's hand, Blythe continued, "I'm going to rededicate myself to strive for an understanding heart filled with love and compassion for others."

Nadine spoke next. "I'm going to rededicate myself to understanding that I am not the first to suffer, love or prosper, and that life, despite changes, is always a measure of the legacy our ancestors left. Good or bad."

Adam cleared his throat. "I'm going to rededicate myself to learn to accept the lessons and experiences of life, taking the best from all that has occurred."

Khalil spoke last. "May we enter the new year radiating peace, love and harmony. Let us strive to make our ancestors proud." He smiled at Blythe. "Lest we forget . . ."

After the children performed African dances and songs, it was time for the Karamu feast.

A long banquet table was laden with smoked turkey, baked ham, salmon croquettes, deviled crabmeat, mixed greens, red beans and rice, potato salad, banana nut bread, macaroni and cheese, fruitcake, peach cobbler and iced mint tea.

Blythe could just feel the pounds jumping on her. She sat next to her parents as they ate. Khalil was on the other side of her. "I think I'm going to burst if I eat any more."

Khalil murmured in agreement.

After everyone had eaten, Blythe and Khalil helped clean up. They were done in time to hear James say to his guests, "Travel in safety and security to meet again at the end of the new year to share in a harvest of unity."

Hugging her mother and her father, Blythe said, "Thank you both for coming. I hope you enjoyed yourselves."

"We did," Nadine stated.

They talked for a few minutes more before her parents left. Blythe joined Kuiana and Iris in the kitchen. "Can I help you with anything?"

Iris Sanford shook her head. "No thanks, we have everything under control."

Khalil came up behind her. "If you don't need us anymore, we're out of here." He crossed the room and kissed his mother's cheek. Khalil gave Kuiana a hug.

Blythe followed his lead and embraced both Iris and Kuiana.

"Happy New Year," she said softly to Kuiana.

"Same to you, Blythe." When Kuiana smiled, it was the first real smile that she'd seen toward her. The new year was indeed a new beginning for all of them.

When Blythe woke up, she found herself alone in Khalil's bed. She sat up quickly and glanced around once more. This time she spotted an envelope on the pillow. She knew instantly that it was another of Khalil's handmade cards. She opened it quickly.

Imani

> *We live by faith in others. But most of all we must*
> *live by faith in ourselves—faith to believe that we*
> *can develop into useful men and women.*
> > *Benjamin Mays*

Blythe looked up to find Khalil standing in the doorway watching her. In his hand, he carried a covered breakfast tray. "I thought you might be hungry," Khalil said as he strolled into the room.

She moved over to make room for him. "Is all of that for me?"

He nodded. "I thought you might need your strength."

Blythe gave in to laughter. When she removed the cover, all she found on the plate was a black velvet box. Her breath caught and she gazed into his eyes. "Is this what I think it is?"

"Open it and see."

Hands trembling, Blythe opened the box and saw a pear-shaped diamond solitaire. Tears rolled down her cheeks and she couldn't speak.

Khalil stroked her cheek and gently brushed away her tears. "Are you okay?"

She nodded. "I never thought I'd fall in love with someone like you, Khalil."

"I know. We are an odd pair. I think that's what makes it so intense and exciting. I'm glad you stormed into my office that day."

"I am, too."

Khalil leaned over and planted a kiss on her cheek. "You know, pretty soon we'll be celebrating Kwanzaa together . . . as man and wife. I love you Blythe Bloodstone, and I hope you don't make me wait too long. If I had my way, I'd marry you next week."

"When that time comes, I would be honored to be your wife, Khalil Sanford."

"I'm serious. I know we've only been together a short time, but I love you and I want to wake up beside you every morning for the rest of my life."

"I want that, too." She stroked his cheek. "This time I'm asking you to trust me."

one year later

". . . I introduce to you, Mr. and Mrs. Khalil Rhaheem Sanford," Minister Jordan announced to the overflowing guests in Calvary Baptist Church.

The audience exploded into applause for the newlyweds as they jumped over the broom before strolling down the aisle. Khalil glanced over at Blythe and winked. He smiled when she winked back. Together they walked to the front of the church.

"Happy, Mrs. Sanford?"

"I've never been more happy. I love you, Mr. Sanford."

278 Jacquelin Thomas

Blythe had never felt so blissfully happy in her whole life. She was married, her paintings were doing well in the gallery, and she finally had a relationship with her mother. It was not exactly the way she dreamed, but she knew Nadine was Nadine. Some things would never change, but Blythe was secure in her mother's love. Moving out of the house had helped. Her parents needed time alone to enjoy their marriage.

"You're a beautiful bride," Nadine whispered in her ear. "I'm so happy for you."

Blythe knew she and Khalil made an attractive couple. He was dressed in a long white tunic with a pointed neckline decorated with gold ornate embroidery that continued at the hem of his pants. On his head he wore a white kuffi with the gold trim.

She wore a white billowy top that featured a double-beaded collar in white and gold. The floor-length skirt had a side slit with beading around the hem. On her head, Blythe wore an elaborate, white-beaded head wrap. Someone tapped her on the shoulder. It was Alda.

"Congratulations, girl."

Blythe embraced her. "Justin told me that he's asked you to marry him. I'm so glad you said yes. He needs someone like you."

Alda, along with the other bridesmaids including Moira and Kuiana, was dressed in a gold and white patterned jewel-neck jacket with a detachable stole and ankle-length skirt. Blythe smiled. Alda had outdone herself not only with clothing the entire wedding party, but she'd also designed the gowns worn by Nadine and Iris. She turned around looking for Khalil, who'd wandered away as she talked to Alda.

Blythe found him with the groomsmen, laughing and chatting. The men looked splendid in the black tuxedos with bow ties and banners that matched the patterned gold and white bridesmaid gowns.

Nadine gestured for her to come inside. The photographer wanted more pictures. Khalil returned and they walked hand in hand back down the aisle.

After a grueling photo session, Khalil and Blythe were finally alone in the sleek black limo en route to the hotel where they were holding their reception. She was glad to finally be alone with her husband.

"I have something for you." Blythe pointed to the huge package on the seat across from them.

Khalil was like a little boy with a new toy, the way he ripped into the paper. It was a painting, she'd done just for him.

"I call it *Generations*. See, I started with your great grandfather and then your grandfather . . ."

"Here's my father and me—" Khalil looked over at her. "Who is this I'm holding?"

Smiling, Blythe said softly, "It's your son."

"My son?" He caressed her hand. "What if we only have daughters?"

She shook her head. "Our first child will be a boy."

He raised his eyebrows. "How can you be so sure?"

Blythe broke into laughter. "The wonders of modern medicine. I had to have an amniocentesis and when the results came back, the doctor told me."

Khalil's eyes lit up with excitement. "A boy. You're carrying my son. I'm going to have a son . . ." he kept murmuring over and over as he fingered the oil painting.

Watching his heart-rending gestures, Blythe's happiness sank deep to her soul. She reached out, placing her hand over his— together they looked toward the future but never forgetting the past.

GLOSSARY & PRONUNCIATION KEY

agogo (ah-GOH-goh): an African instrument made of two pieces of bell-shaped metal attached by a handle.

bendera (behn-DEH-rah): the red, black and green flag of African Americans, created by Marcus Garvey.

Harbari gani (hah-BAH-ree GAH-nee): Kwanzaa greeting in Swahili, meaning ''What's up?''

Harambee (hah-rahm-BEH): the call to unity and collective work. It is always said in sets of seven to honor and recall the seven principles of Kwanzaa.

Imani (ee-MAN-nee): faith, the seventh principle of Kwanzaa, meaning belief in self and our leaders and our teachers.

Karamu (kah-RAH-moo): the kuumba feast held on the sixth day of Kwanzaa, December 31st.

Kikombe cha umoja (kee-KOM-beh-chah oo-MOH-jah): the unity cup, one of the symbols of Kwanzaa.

Kinara (kee-NAH-rah): the candle holder, one of the symbols of Kwanzaa.

Kuffi (KOO-fee): hat worn by Africans or African Americans, usually made of patterned cloth or leather.

Kujichagulia (koo-ji-chah-goo-LEE-ah): self-determination, the second principle of Kwanzaa, meaning acting and speaking for oneself.

Kuumba (koo-OOM-bah): creativity, the sixth principle of Kwanzaa, meaning using one's talents and creativity to think of new ways to do things and solve problems.

Mazao (mah-ZAH-oh): the fruits of the harvest, one of the symbols of Kwanzaa.

Mishumaa saba (mee-shoo-MAH SAH-bah): the seven candles: 3 red, 1 black and 3 red. One of the symbols of Kwanzaa.

Mkeka (em-kay-KAH): a mat usually made of straw, one of the symbols of Kwanzaa.

Muhindi (moo-HIN-dee): the corn representing the children in the family, one of the symbols of Kwanzaa.

Nguzo Saba (nn-GOO-zoh SAH-bah): the Swahili term for the seven principles of Kwanzaa.

Nia (NEE-ah): purpose, the fifth principle of Kwanzaa, meaning having a purpose for doing what you do.

Tambiko (tam-BEE-koh): the libation performed at the beginning and end of the Karamu feast on the sixth day of Kwanzaa.

Ujamaa (oo-ja-MAH): businesses, the fourth principle of Kwanzaa, meaning that we should support each other in our business.

Ujima (oo-JEE-mah): working together, the third principle of Kwanzaa, meaning we work together to achieve our goals.

Umoja (oo-MO-ja): unity, the first principle of Kwanzaa, meaning that we stay together under all circumtances.

Zawadi (zah-WAH-dee): gifts, representing commitment or promises kept, one of the symbols of Kwanzaa.

Dear Readers,

I hope you have enjoyed *Someone Like You*. This story was a labor of love as well as a journey to knowledge. I had virtually no knowledge of Kwanzaa when I started this project, but I've learned so much since then.

It was interesting to find that the vision and values of Kwanzaa revolve around the practice of principles which celebrate and reinforce family, community and culture.

I learned that the celebration is a time of special reverence for the good in life and for life itself. It is a time of commemoration of the past. It is a time of recommitment to our highest ideals and living by the Kwanzaa values.

It is my fondest wish that each and every one of you will have the strength to reach your dreams and the courage to live by the Nguzo Saba or the seven principles.

I've included a copy of the Sanfords' personal Kwanzaa celebration program. Feel free to adapt this and make this part of your family's tradition.

Welcome
Opening Statement by eldest person present
Libation to the ancestors
Harambee—Call to unity
Statement of the principle and its meaning

Lighting of the Candles
Historical application of the principle
Relationship of ancestors and the principle
Group pledges for the new year

Cultural Expression
Poem or Music
Song or Dance
Stories of the ancestors
Historical incidents

Eating and Feasting
Libation to posterity
Farewell Statement

Feel free to write to me at: P.O. Box 7415, La Verne, CA
91750-7415
(please enclose a SASE)
or E-mail me: *jacquelinthomas@usa.net*

You can also visit my Web site for book signing dates and
other upcoming news:
http://www.geocities.com/SoHo/Gallery/6681/

Happy Kwanzaa!

Coming in January from Arabesque Books . . .